CW00406594

The Coffin Tree

MARION FANCEY

Copyright © 2019 Marion Fancey

All rights reserved.

ISBN-: 9781791976422

The Coffin Tree Published 2019

The right of Marion Fancey to be identified as the author of this work has been asserted. No part of this publication may be reproduced, stored in a retrieval system, or be transmitted in any form, or by any means, without the prior permission in writing of the copyright owner.

All characters in this book are fictitious and any resemblance to actual persons, living or dead, is purely coincidental.

Cover design by Imax. www.imaxweb.co.uk

The True Story - My Inspiration

My story of the Coffin Tree was inspired by a true story told to me some years ago, by a chateau owner. He and his wife live in a superbly preserved small chateau in Normandy, and he told me how, during the revolution, his ancestors had been taken away, as had all those perceived to be aristocratic or have aristocratic connections.

I was then very surprised to learn that the villagers, anticipating looting and damage by both soldiers and others, stripped the chateau and hid everything to keep it safe. The villagers then petitioned the ruling forces, in Paris, asking for the chateau owners to be released, explaining that they were good, decent people and fair employers.

The owners were subsequently set free and, upon their return, the villagers restored their belongings to them.

All other parts of 'The Coffin Tree' are pure fiction.

Happy reading. Marion Fancey

CHAPTER 1

My name is Ferelith Barker, Fay to all who know me, and I've just run away from my mother's funeral wake and am heading for France – I suppose escaping would best describe it. So, when Lynne and Dave Broome call to see me tomorrow I won't be here!

The day was already bad and I didn't think it could get any worse. Torrential rain had been followed by lightning, and then, typical of my mum - a clap of miserable thunder at the point of committal!

But it was when I overheard Lynne and Dave Broome discussing when they should tell me about my parentage that things turned really nasty, My what?!!!

Stunned, sick and dizzy with shock, I'd no idea what they could possibly mean, but one thing was for sure, I didn't want them to tell me, not today, possibly not ever, so there and then, in the middle of my mother's funeral wake, I fled.

Going straight home, well to my mother's home, although I do own part (complicated story) I opened her fanatically tidy desk. From the pigeon hole marked 'Certificates', I pulled out the envelope labelled "Fay" and, with shaking hands, sorted through the assortment of various school, swimming, cycling and other awards, until I found my Birth Certificate.

I'd seen it before of course, in fact my mother only had it because she was convinced I'd lose it, but those people had now made me wonder if there was a more sinister reason for my mother wanting to retain it, perhaps something on it I'd never noticed.

My mind was racing and my hands trembled, as I unfolded the pink document, and spread it on the table. Slowly, word by word, I studied it to the bottom of the page. There was nothing, absolutely nothing, that I didn't already know.

If I'd been adopted, I was sure there'd have been something on the certificate, because I had a couple of adopted friends, who I think had told me this, but there was nothing.

My father, "George William Henry Barker", my mother "Elizabeth Jane Barker", and me, "Ferelith", (an old family name) "Jane", (after my mother) "Margaret", (after my grandmother Barker, always known as Nana Molly to me, and whom I'd adored). I read through the rest, nothing unexpected at all. The mystery deepened.

Guessing that, when they realised I'd gone, The Broomes would come here to find me, I pushed the certificate into my laptop case, ran upstairs and threw some things into a couple of bags. I had to get far away, and as quickly as possible.

My stuff was only here because I'd stayed for the last few weeks of my mother's illness and, luckily, although goodness knows why, the things I'd brought included my passport.

I picked up the landline receiver, to ring the ferry company and ask about last minute availability, when I saw there was a message, so I clicked the 'play' button. It was Lynne and Dave, who, unaware of my eavesdropping, were coming to see me now! That was it! I was out of here!

Locking the front door, I threw my bags into the car and set off for the coast, hoping and praying there was room on the ferry when I got there. I had no Plan B.

Trying to concentrate on my driving, I fought back the tears, but eventually I pulled over and wept. It had all been too much, the funeral service, the eulogies, the sympathy, and then those people!

A short break, then calmer, and conscious of passing time, I set off again, filling up the tank as I approached the port, so I wouldn't have to look for fuel again for ages.

Driving onto the dock, I pulled up close to the ferry terminal, then, passport and purse in hand, I got out of my car, filled my lungs with the saline saturated air, and walked briskly to the window, where I asked if they had space on the next ferry to St Malo. The girl behind the glass, clearly surprised, but pleased, at my asking in French, smiled. I was just relieved she'd understood; it had been a while since I'd used the language.

She checked, but was doubtful as the overnight crossing, which was the

6

next one, seemed to be full. All of this was conveyed by a Gallic shrugging of shoulders, and shaking of her head, as she looked at a screen.

I entreated her, partly in English this time, explaining that I had to be in France - a funeral, I added. Well, it was sort of true, it was because of what I'd overheard at a funeral that I wanted to be in France. 'My mother's funeral,' I explained in English, adding "La funèbre de ma maman," to give extra weight.

At this she looked horrified. "Un moment mam'selle," and she slipped off her stool and spoke to a man at the back of the office. He looked in my direction, noted my black attire and nodded sympathetically; the girl returned and asked for my passport.

Formalities over, a boarding sticker on my windscreen and ticket in my hand proclaiming my victory over beaurocracy, I joined the appropriate lane. The ferry came in and docked, and I watched, impatiently tapping my fingers as the seemingly interminable line of cars, lorries, coaches and vans rolled down the gangway off the ship. At last we started boarding. Up the ramp I went and was guided into a parking place. I was aboard, I'd done it, I'd escaped! I gave a massive sigh of relief. They'd never follow me to France and, in the unlikely event that they did, they'd never find me, because even I had no idea where I was going!

Grabbing my overnight bag and laptop, I locked the car and clunked up the metal stairs to find my cabin.

Opening the door, I gasped; it was large and quite luxurious, for a ferry. Now I understood what the girl had been saying, "il y a une seulement, c'est tres chèr." There is only one and it's very expensive. Not fully understanding I'd replied "magnifique," and handed over my debit card, wondering why her eyes had widened to the size of tennis balls, and her eyebrows had disappeared into her scalp!

Thank goodness there'd been enough money in my account. I didn't dare look at the receipt, although I knew whatever it had cost, I'd have paid it gladly to be on this ship, but tomorrow I must transfer some funds.

I put my bag on the double bed and went into the large bathroom. "I deserve some luxury after what I've been through," I muttered to myself as I surveyed the wide range of 'complimentary' toiletries. I'd take the surplus with me, because wherever I stayed in France after this, it would have to be a pretty basic, an Etap hôtel, or a cheap logis.

Stripping off I stood under the hot shower, then, soaped and pampered, I wrapped myself in the gorgeous thick towelling robe, hanging on the back of the door, and pushed my feet into the fluffy mules. Unfortunately, brushing my wet hair caused me to look in the mirror, and the face I'd known all my life looked back at me, but, remembering Dave and Lynne's words, I now wondered 'who did this face belong to'? Who was I?

 Where did I get my almond shaped blue eyes from, and my small nose, which flared out at the bottom just a bit more than I'd have liked. My mouth was a bit wide too, I felt, but I had a nice heart shape to my face – one thing was for certain, I didn't look like anyone else I knew! Perhaps I'd always been aware of this, but assumed I took after a family member I'd never known? But now?

"Who are you?" I asked my reflection rhetorically.

Back in the bedroom, I opened the tiny fridge, took out a miniature bottle of gin and a little tin of tonic and, having poured them into a glass, I sat down in the comfy armchair, munching the crisps and biscuits I'd also found in the fridge. There'd be an extra cost, but it was worth it not to have to get dressed again and find the restaurant. A notice said anything consumed would automatically be taken on the same card as I'd paid on, unless I wanted to go to the desk and pay in cash. Well I didn't!

I looked out of the window. Just one or two last minute arrivals, followed by a lot of clanking, clunking and shouting, then my ferry blasted its horn and my tummy did a somersault. These were the sounds of setting sail, and they'd taken me right back to my childhood. The same excitement when the ship's thrusters began to push away from the dock side and we started to move forward. The magic was still there.

I finished my 'snack', lay down on top of the bed and considered the day. Everyone had told me the funeral would bring 'closure', and so it should've, but instead Lynne and Dave had opened up a whole new nightmare. I considered what they could mean – and how they might know whatever it was they wanted to tell me.

I knew Lynne had once been a very close friend of my mother's, but one day, without warning, my father had moved us more than a hundred and fifty miles away and, to my knowledge, we never saw either her or her husband, Dave, again. When I asked about them, and their three boys, two of whom, Tom and Jack, had been my friends all my life (I was eight by then), I was fobbed off with feeble reasons. Having no option but to accept this, I got on with my new life, in my new school, and made new friends, but for a while, I missed my old life terribly.

After a few weeks in a rented place, we moved into a rambling old house with a huge garden, chickens and a stream and this mini paradise became the adventure dad had promised, when we left our old home.

I'd begged for a dog ever since I was tiny, but always been told a town wasn't the right place, however, almost as soon as we arrived in this new home, I was given a beautiful brown, silky-haired, big-eyed mongrel puppy, and I called her Molly, after my nana, who'd sadly passed away not long before.

I think my parents thought the puppy would help me settle down, so I stopped asking, why we'd moved, and when we'd see Dave and Lynne and their boys again.

I suppose, I assumed they'd been planning our move for some time, but now I was looking back and considering that suddenly going far away, with no chance to even say goodbye, didn't seem planned after all. So, what had been the real reason and, was it linked to these people who now wanted to tell me about 'my parentage'? But if so, how?

I knew my parents had our holiday home in France before I was born, and also that they'd travelled extensively, then an awful thought occurred to me. Had I been stolen from somewhere, perhaps one of the countries they'd visited? My mother had been a nurse, so she could've easily walked into any maternity ward, with an air of authority and taken me!

I also knew she'd had problems conceiving, and she told me they'd have liked more children, but it never happened. What if it never happened with me either, and I was someone else's child? Perhaps my mother had confided this truth to Lynne, who'd then threatened to expose her, resulting in my father moving us away, and keeping our whereabouts secret?

O.M.G! There might be some poor people out there who'd lost a baby and had been looking for me for years. I shuddered.

I turned on my tablet and searched for 'missing babies, Europe, and my birth year, 1990'. There was nothing conclusive, but nothing exclusive either. Babies had gone missing, in various places, but there was no way of being sure, with one or two exceptions, whether or not they were ever found.

I sighed. Perhaps Lynne and Dave didn't really know anything. Perhaps there was nothing to know. Perhaps I was panicking for nothing?

I lay down on the bed, physically exhausted, but with my brain buzzing. I just knew I wouldn't sleep.

Extraordinarily, the next thing I knew it was 6 am and we were docking. Wow. I could hardly believe it; I hadn't even got into bed. I was still laying on the top, wrapped in the bath robe, in an itchy sea of crisp and biscuit crumbs and empty wrappers.

CHAPTER 2

I'd put jeans and t-shirt in my overnight bag, so I quickly dressed and brushed my hair, finishing just as the announcement, calling drivers back to their vehicles came over the cabin speaker.

I'd missed breakfast, but hey, this was France, and coffee and croissants would be available everywhere. My heart sang at the thought.

As I drove off the ferry, the sun shone brightly in the early morning sky, making the sea sparkle, as though it had been scattered with thousands of fragments from a shattered glitter ball. My escape into this sun filled haven suddenly became the beginning of a whole new life!

I laughed out loud, drove out of the port and turned south west.

I'd no idea where I was heading, and I didn't care. I briefly considered St Malo itself, because it's such a delightful fortified seaport, with lovely shops, cobbled streets and a beautiful cathedral, with a strangely crooked central aisle. If you stand at one end you can't see the other end, because of the slight bend in the middle. Bet someone got it in the neck for that mistake! Too much wine perhaps? "Trop de vin peut-être?" I translated to myself.

No, it was not a day for St Malo, perhaps on my way back. But perhaps I'd never go back. I could settle here in France and forget all about Lynne and Dave. I wish now I'd never contacted them about the funeral, but, strangely after all these years, my mother had asked me to.

I opened my car window and breathed in deeply, as I drove along the narrow winding country roads, past Brittany's famous cauliflower fields, which made them one of the world's largest producers. The smell was slightly cabbagey, but in a nice way.

I loved how each of France's regions had proud identities, Brittany's being cauliflowers, cider and Muscadet wine, which my dad had told me was perfect with seafood, although, being too young, I'd never got the chance to test it out. Perhaps on this visit I might?

I ought to spend some time in Brittany. We'd only ever used it on our way down to our holiday home, but I knew a bit about its past, how it only became fully part of France in 1491, when Richarde VIII of France married Anne, Duchess of and heiress to Brittany.

An uneasy alliance, my dad had called it, because as recently as 1932, Breton Separatists destroyed the monument depicting Charles and Anne's meeting. Even today Brittany has its own language, and fiercely protects its unique identity, with many buildings deliberately built so that they have their backs to the rest of France! Ooh la la!

I smiled and sighed contentedly. Oh, how I'd love to visit all the different départements Français, and check out the character of each. Normandy for Calvados apple brandy and Camembert cheese, The Loire Valley for large chateaux, wine and caves, many of which are still inhabited today, some even having double glazing and central heating! How cool is that?

"Only the French," I thought to myself. After that my knowledge gets a bit sketchy, but it really would be interesting to learn about and visit all the other French 'bits', especially the islands, like Corsica, although perhaps the far-flung islands, such as Martinique in the Caribbean, Tahiti in the Pacific, and Reunion, in the Indian Ocean, might not be practical, certainly not on this trip anyway, but in the future, why not?

I hummed to myself as I drove, and considered the layout and regions of France, which seemed exotic and romantic, and that brought me full circle to my teenage romance, and the 'boy next door', Christophe.

This was in the French region I know best, because it was where we'd had our holiday home, the Poitou Charente. Poitou from the area around the city of Poitiers, combined with the department of the Charente named like so many other areas, after its main river.

I drove on through delightful hamlets and villages amongst the rolling countryside, all bathed in the warm June sun, which deepened the red of the roofs and turned the stone a mellow, honey colour. Many of the homes I passed had bedding hanging out of the upstairs windows to air.

I noted the patches of wild flowers and wondered if they were still used by farmers, to mark the land they're leaving fallow. Government helicopters used to check on these from the air, to ensure the land really wasn't being farmed. All to do with EU subsidies of course!

Right, time for breakfast, so I parked outside a tiny building with tables and chairs set out in front, where several men sat, drinking coffee and smoking Gaulois cigarettes.

They stopped talking as I got out of my car and went towards them, "Bon jour messieurs," I called cheerfully.

"Bonjour mam'selle," they nodded, no smiles. None expected. At least they spoke!

Recklessly I added "Il fait chaud," which was a bit silly, as the weather was not hot, but I didn't know the French for warm. They clearly didn't think it was hot either, their shrugs conveyed this, and just to prove the point, they pulled their jackets tightly about themselves.

A man appeared from inside, pushing aside an oilcloth curtain, patterned with sunflowers, as he did so.

"Une café crème et deux croissants, s'il vous plais," I said, as I sat down at an empty table. Then I remembered how to say warm. It's simply 'less hot', or moins chaud, just as smaller is 'less big', and bigger is 'more big', or plus grand. This quirkiness is why I love France so much and chose it as my safe haven now.

Regarding the language, I remembered my father telling me that you have be specific in what you're saying, or they won't understand. He was a wonderful teacher.

Isn't it odd: it's my mother who's just died but it's my father I keep thinking about; then, with horror, I realised that he must also have been a party to this secret about me. I shivered at the thought. My dear parents, but were they my parents? Had it all been one long deceit?

For the last hour or so, I'd forgotten all about it and been happy again. Now the horror of my situation descended on me once more, like a grey mist, but soon my coffee and warm croissants were brought. The smell was wonderful and I was ravenous, so I enjoyed them in the sunshine, pushing everything else to the back of my mind.

The men had soon lost interest in staring at me and discussing 'l'étranger', loud enough

for me to hear, and resumed their chat. I couldn't follow much of it, and guessed they were probably using either a local patois, or perhaps their ancient Brittany language. Every so often I

heard the President's name mentioned and someone spat. It was a heated discussion, and obviously

political.

I paid the bill with the few euros I'd found with my passport and left.

I'd done this journey numerous times with my parents, but never driven over here myself, but strangely, I hadn't even thought about that when I decide to cut and run.

Then I realised that, without thinking, I was following our route of old, on the minor roads, down past Dinard, and then onto more main roads heading toward Nantes.

I stopped at a petrol station, bought a map and a coffee, topped up with fuel, and used their internet to access my bank accounts, and move some money. Not the best thing in public, but I was careful to hide what I was doing and felt a lot better, just knowing that my bank cards wouldn't be refused.

When I found somewhere to stay overnight I knew I'd have to send emails, to the people most likely to have been worried by my sudden departure.

I looked at the map and, with my finger, I traced the rest of the route we used to take. It was a big country and, although we'd toured a lot, there were loads of places still to see. Then I came to a decision, influenced I think by my earlier day- dreaming about Christophe, my teenage crush. I'd begin by driving down to where we'd had our holiday home, take a brief peek at the hamlet and the chateau, and relive some childhood memories, before putting together a plan.

I was sure nobody would know who I was, so I could have a good look round, then put the past behind me and move on. Maybe go down to somewhere near the Spanish border. Alternatively, I could drive over the amazing Millau Bridge and along the stunningly beautiful Tarn Gorge to the Med. and the   Côte d'Azure, where I knew the shore would be lined with palm trees, and the sea would be bright blue and sparkling like diamonds.

But first Poitou Charente; I sighed contentedly and set off again.

The journey passed quickly; the sun was out and the weather got warmer, as I drove South. The views everywhere were lovely and I was certain I'd done the right thing in coming to France.

Soon it was Rennes, then Nantes, and signs began appearing for Niort, and the fields now were full of sunflowers and young sweetcorn, and, surprisingly, in this day and age, tobacco. I reached Niort and drove right into the city and found a space in the central car park. I knew this place so well; my mother and I used to come here, for shopping and lunch, as a special treat. I smiled at the memories.

A "Tourist Information" sign caught my eye, so I followed the signs and went inside.

'Je voudrais un chambre, pour une personne, pour un nuit seulement', I said slowly and precisely.

Obviously not specific enough, as the tall, slim, elegant young receptionist, with perfectly polished nails (why did mine never look like that?) asked if the room, for one person, for one night only, which I'd requested, was for this night.

'Oui,' I replied, trying not to look exasperated.

Then she looked at me and frowned, as though I was mad to think there'd be such a room available in June. Oh well I'd just have to drive on.

Sensing I may be about to leave she said, 'Un moment,' made a telephone call, then announced, 'Il'y a une chambre prés d'ici, une village cinq kilometrès, "Le Logis Tour des Cloches".

She looked surprised when I said I'd take it, but since she'd only this one option, why would I say no? (I'd obviously learned nothing from my experience at the Brittany Ferries' Office!)

She drew a basic map, and wrote the address, on a piece of paper, explaining that it was surrounded by vineyards.

It sounded idyllic. Peace and quiet in the heart of the countryside. I thanked her and left, clutching the piece of paper she'd given me. Then, having got euros from a cashpoint, I returned to my car. and departed

Niort on the suggested road, turning off when I saw the sign for the village.

The route then took me down a narrow lane, almost a track, very common in France where there were sunflowers, in the fields either side of the lane. They'd soon be in flower, when they'd be a glorious sight, looking like hundreds of young girls, standing in lines and wearing yellow frilly bonnets. However, I'd have moved on by then, probably to a region where they didn't grow sunflowers. Perhaps I'd be amongst the lavender fields of Provence? I sighed happily.

When I reached the village, I was surprised by how busy it was. Women in shawls, stood in groups, arms folded, chatting, while their menfolk were seated on the steps of the houses, playing cards, and children ran around the narrow streets chasing each other, squealing and laughing.

I followed the signs for the "Tour des Cloches Logis," and pulled up outside. A big, bald man, with a paunch, came straight out and asked, in thick guttural French if I was Ma'moiselle Barker.

Oui,' I replied, and he put out his hand for the keys. I got out of the car while he explained, largely with gestures, that the street was very narrow, so he'd take my car, park it, and bring my luggage to me.

I nodded and went inside, where a crabby old bat, sorry but she really was, asked me, without a smile, for the money for the room. She pursed the tight lips in her miserable skinny face, expressing her disappointment with a frown, and a clicking of her tongue, that I offered a card and not cash. She took it in her thin bony fingers, scanned it, and gave me a key.

The man returned and I followed him up the steep narrow stairs. He stepped aside while I opened the door, with the key I'd been given, then he unceremoniously dumped my bags on the bed and, with a curt nod, he left.

The lane where the logis was situated, was so narrow that the heat of the day was caught between the two rows of tall stone buildings. Those the other side couldn't be more than 3 metrès away. The room also smelled musty, so I hurriedly opened the window for air, and closed the curtains for privacy.

Then I stripped off and went to cool myself down with a shower.

I pulled the curtain along and, as I turned on the tap, there was the most almighty 'boom'. My heart was racing with shock, especially as the noise continued. 'Boom', 'boom', 'boom'. I showered quickly, turned the water off and the noise stopped.

I giggled. I'd heard of noisy plumbing but that was unbelievable!

I lifted my case off the bed and onto a chest, opened it and took out a summer dress and sandals, but only a few minutes later, as I was brushing my hair, there was more 'booming' and then I realised the 'booms' were bells. We must be very close to the church – very close!

Then I also realised – 'La Tour des Cloches' meant the tower of the bells. The bells were actually in the same building as me, and they were going to make that noise every 15 minutes! I knew now why the girl at the Tourist Information office had looked surprised, when she told me the name of the logis, and I still said yes!

I thought I wouldn't sleep last night – fat chance tonight, I thought, and I went down the stairs and out into the street

I strolled along to the corner, and could see a small village square, not too far distant so I walked along to investigate, and discovered a bakery, a tiny flower shop, and a small restaurant, perfect for my evening meal. I certainly didn't want to eat in the logis, with its heat and noise, so I went in and was shown to a table.

I only had the local ham with melon slices, followed by fish with a herby sauce and creamed potatoes, but the little touches such as the pretty tablecloth, the mini basket of bread, the iced water with lemon slices, and the fresh flowers on my table, took it to another level. The French always manage to take a simple meal and make it something more.

I chuckled to myself, pleased to find the dessert menu was tarte tatin, crème brûlée, isle flottante, and a chocolate concoction; so the four of them were still the stock in trade puddings for these small restaurants. It had to be the isle flottante; I just love the soft meringue and creamy custard base and

the caramel sauce is divine.

I washed my meal down with an inclusive demi carafe of wine and, even with a coffee, the bill still only came to 14 euros. I could certainly live over here cheaply. Tomorrow I must give some thought to my economic situation.

I strolled back to the logis, and if I thought it was noisy before, the street was now being used as a race track by local youths on scooters. I dodged in and out between them as they roared past, turned and roared back again.

It was bedlam and the noise was unbelievable. It couldn't be further from the image I'd conjured up of a small logis set amongst vineyards; the village might be, the logis was not!

I couldn't possibly stay here, but then I realised I couldn't leave! Firstly, I'd no idea where my car was, and, secondly, I'd been drinking alcohol. I'd no choice but to stay.

I entered the logis and asked about my car. The crabby woman said it had been taken away and locked up, but gave no clue as to where this might be.

I nodded and went upstairs, just as the bells clanged again. I'd left my windows open, and now my room was full of scooter fumes as well!

Because I still had the curtains closed, I turned the light on, and a huge contraption which looked like propeller blades stolen from a helicopter, started up above my head.

I didn't know whether to laugh or cry. If I kept the light on, this fan would keep going and hopefully cool the room a bit, and the racket it made might partially shut out the noise of the scooters and the bells. Maybe that was the owners' plan?

I stuffed cotton wool in my ears and went to bed, I needed to get some sleep, but the noise reverberated through the very fabric of the building, especially through the pillows under my head!

At 9.45 pm, French time, I gave up and got out of bed. I might as well spend some time sending messages, one to my mother's solicitor and old family friend, John Harverson, and then to my two bessie mates, Rosie and Jules, who'd all been at the wake, and must be wondering where I was. At least the logis had Wi-fi. That was its first (and probably only) plus point.

My message to Rose and Jules was simply, "that I'd had to get away for a break and would be in touch, and that my 'phone had been switched off ever since I left home, and I intended to leave it like that. I just needed a bit of time to myself, but otherwise I was fine".

I said much the same to John Harverson, but then added 'This may seem a strange question, but how would I know if I was adopted?'

To my surprise, he replied at once. Even though it was an hour earlier in England it would still be getting on for 9pm, long after office hours. He reassured me that no, I wasn't adopted, but he wondered why I'd asked the question.

I replied that it was just something someone had said, that I'd obviously misunderstood. He offered no further comment.

Without mentioning Lynne and Dave, I'd asked all three of my email recipients not to give my email details to anyone, as I wanted to be left in peace, at least for the next few days.

Miraculously, at 10 o'clock, someone shouted at the youths, the noise stopped and I soon realised that the bells had ceased as well. The quarter hour came and went, and all was silent.

I got back into bed and went to sleep.

Tomorrow I'd begin my new life in earnest! Well, that was the plan.

CHAPTER 3

The following morning, sitting alone in the small dining room, I ate some of the allotted fruit, cheeses and cold meat, washing them down with the strong black coffee. Breakfast over, I collected my bag and my car appeared outside the door.

Applying like for like, I smilingly thanked the logis husband, then growled 'au revoir,' with a scowl, at the sour faced crabby one. I then left, and headed back to Niort, which I'd decided to re-visit for old times' sake, before heading south again.

This decision was based on my wanting to visit the Niort branch of Gallerie Lafayette, the upmarket department store which I used to love going to with my mum. Once there, I sauntered around its elegant displays and departments, attended by equally elegant staff.

Some of the clothes were fabulous, so chic, so elegant, so French, I sighed. Not only could I not have afforded them, I would've had nowhere to wear them either as I was unlikely to be attending any tasteful soirées, either here in France, or back home.

Eventually, giving way to temptation, I treated myself to a silk chiffon scarf, shaded, from one side to the other, in deepening shades of green and so sheer I could almost see straight through it. It was trés elegant!

Late morning, and I wandered slowly along the other shops in the street, happily holding my Gallerie Lafayette bag for all to see as I made my way back to my car, but at the patisserie I was tempted by the mouth-watering cakes, and smell of fresh coffee. A caramel iced, cream filled, choux bun should never be ignored, so I sat down with it, and a still water, and checked my emails.

There were replies from Rosie and Jules; both thought I'd done the right thing, by going away, but only if I kept in touch. (I'd known they wouldn't want to miss anything and it made me smile).

There was also a reply from John Harverson, who was not so happy, and said there were things we needed to discuss, regarding my mother's estate, and also that I was likely to need advice, now that I was a wealthy young woman.

I read this last bit again. Was it a joke? I'd never thought of John as having any sense of humour – he was a solicitor for goodness sake!

I suppose I must've have inherited the rest of my mother's house, but I'd hardly have called that being wealthy. He must be comparing it to my relatively recent penniless days as a student, and the tiny flat I now live in.

It seemed strange to think that I was here, wandering around France, currently sitting at a pavement café, and none of them knew! They probably think I'm holed up at a b&b in Brighton, and suddenly, what I was doing felt like a naughty adventure and this made me giggle!

Getting into my car, I set off again with only 40 kilometrès to go. Our holiday home had been just outside a village, in a small group of houses usually referred to by the village residents, as 'le hameau', or the hamlet. They were very old houses, renovated by their owners, to be holiday homes.

The really exciting thing, to me though, had always been the chateau. Only a small one, but a chateau nevertheless, and, as I grew up, the even more exciting thing to me became Christophe, who lived in the chateau!

The owners had 3 sons and I used to play with 2 of them; Stèphane, the same age and myself, and Christophe, who was 3 years older, but often joined in our games. The third of the boys, Romain, was older by another 5 years, and so I hardly ever saw him.

My parents were friendly with the owners, Monsieur and Madame Richarde, and we sometimes barbecued together, either in our garden or in their grounds, but we had the real magnet, probably the main reason Christophe wanted to be included – we had a heated swimming pool!

I laughed to myself as I thought about those happy, carefree days.

No doubt all the holiday homes would've changed hands in the intervening 11 years or so, and I knew the chateau definitely would, as Monsieur Richarde had said many times that, as soon as the boys were grown up, he intended to sell the chateau and they'd all live in Paris.

That probably happened long ago. Strangely, we'd never kept in touch.

Anyway, I'd still have a peek at the chateau and the village. After that I'd decide where I was going next and, should I decide to settle in France, I was sure there were lots of places I could get work. Waitrèsses were always in demand, and gardeners and cleaners were needed by holiday home owners. I wasn't too proud to do any of this, and French Estate Agents often needed Anglo-French speakers, for English speaking clients, plus I had experience in pool maintenance. Pretty good employment prospects really, I convinced myself.

I thought about 'the old days', as I drove and realised it was yet another part of my life that my father had brought to an abrupt end, when he announced one day that he'd sold our holiday home, so we wouldn't be going to France any more.

He said that, since I'd be going to university, (his decision) I had to spend all my time, including holidays, studying. He wouldn't discuss it any further, so I knew it was pointless arguing, but I was devastated. What would I do without Christophe to dream about? But, as before, when I lost my friends and a home of sorts, I coped.

I was now approaching the delightful small town of Melle, with the most amazing church, which my mother and I often used to sketch, because it made a fascinating study from every angle. This felt so like coming home, it was just a shame that no-one I'd known would still be around.

I turned off the main road and cut through the countryside and, half an hour later – deep intake of breath - I saw the chateau. My stomach did a somersault. It looked exactly the same, well so it should, why wouldn't it? Daft thought.

I stopped the car and sat staring. It was delightful, with turrets and towers and limestone walls and I wondered who lived in it now. It still seemed beautiful, and mysterious, and romantic, oh so romantic. I sighed, as I pondered where my teenage idol might be these days.

In my early teens, when I'd had my terrible crush on Christophe, who'd shown no interest whatsoever, besotted as I was, I'd imagined marrying him and living in the chateau. Silly really if their father was going to sell it.

I sat quietly, wondering if Christophe was still as amazingly good looking as he'd been aged 18, when he'd seemed like perfection to me.

Tall, slim, blonde-ish, broad shouldered, athletic, brilliant at everything he did, sports-wise and academically.

The sound of a small tractor snapped me out of my thoughts and it soon came into view, in the chateau grounds, towing a mowing attachment. The man driving it saw me looking and waved as he turned and went back the other way. I expect he was used to tourists stopping to look at the chateau, as it really was delightful.

I started my engine and drove around the perimeter of the chateau grounds, and into our 'holiday home lane'. Getting out, I put on my sunglasses and sun hat, and went to look at our old house.

As I did so, I thought how odd it was that so many things could look pretty much exactly the same, when everything else in my life had changed hugely. The house was all closed up, in fact all the houses in the little close were shuttered, so I guessed the owners hadn't yet arrived for their holidays.

As a child, I used to think the shutters looked like eyelids, and the that the houses must be asleep when they had their shutters closed. I smiled at the childish thought. Happy days.

Then I turned and wandered back up the short lane to gaze at the chateau, and emotion welled up in me. Oh I loved it just as much. Would I have still loved Christophe as much, I wondered, with a sigh?

The workman, in blue overalls, on the tractor, was going back up the other way again, so I walked right up to the gate for one long last look, before I left – for good. The tractor turned and began making its way back down again, and I started back to my car. Upon reaching the bottom of the slope, the tractor engine stopped.

 By then I was nearly back at my car. 'Un moment,' a voice shouted and, surprised, I stopped at the command and turned around, soon wishing I hadn't.

The workman, who had a thick beard, jumped of the tractor, vaulted the chateau wall, which was quite low at that point, and strode over to where I was standing. He began speaking very fast in French. He must be the gardener, or handyman, employed by whoever the Richardes had sold the chateau to.

I waved my hands about, to show that I didn't understand.

'Huh, Eenglish?' he said and I nodded.

'Why you go down there?' he gestured to where the holiday houses were. He must've been able to see me from his elevated position on the tractor seat, at the top of the sloping lawns.

I didn't know why he was asking, or why I should deign to answer him, so I turned to go and began walking again.

He came round in front of me, stopping, so that I had to do the same. 'I ask why you go down there? I'll take note of your car number and, if there are problems, I give it to the gendarmes,' and he took a piece of paper and a pencil out of one of the many pockets in his overalls, walked to my car and, very officiously, jotted down my car registration details.

'This is private property,' he gestured around him, 'you 'ave no rights'.

'Don't be ridiculous. Do I look like a thief?'

He shrugged. 'What does a thief look like? So, what were you doing?'

'If you must know I was reminiscing. Going back in time', I explained when he clearly didn't understand. 'We used to have a holiday home here, a long time ago.'

He frowned, 'I don't think so. Which one?'

'That one,' I said angrily, pointing to ours.

'Huh,' he said conveying disbelief. Suddenly his expression changed, he studied what he could see of my face and then pulled off my hat and sunglasses. 'Fay?' he exclaimed in astonishment.

I had my hand on my car door, about to open it and get in. He was not the only astonished one. Who was he and how did he know my name?

'Yes, but who are you? I demanded.

He threw back his head and laughed, and that laugh was very familiar. 'Even my mother also says she does not recognise me with my beard, I'm Stèphane Richarde.'

'Stèphane!' I exclaimed, as he picked me up and twirled me around. Then he put me down and studied me more closely, just to be sure. As I looked back at him, those warm, twinkling, chestnut coloured eyes, that

I'd known so well, looked into my blue ones. What with the hat and beard, his eyes were the only bit I could identify.

'But I thought your father was going to sell the chateau. I never expected you'd be here, any of you.'

'There's only me. My family are in Paris. You must 'ave coffee,' he looked at his watch, adding, 'I'll make you an omelette. We must talk'.

Goodness it was nearly 1 o'clock. He told me to bring my car, then strode off, getting on the tractor, going back up the lawns and disappearing around the back of the chateau.

Feeling more than a little dazed, I did as I was bid and took my car up the imposing drive, my stomach churning with excitement. I'd never expected this, even in my wildest dreams, I was so sure that the chateau would've been sold long since.

 I parked on the gravel area at the rear. I could hear barking, so they still kept dogs.

The back door was open and I went in, through the boot room, following the sounds which were coming from the kitchen. It was like stepping back in time, as I was greeted by two very hairy, exceedingly boisterous, dogs.

Stèphane snapped a command and they sat down. He introduced them to me, Trixie and Germaine – known as Gemmy. Mother and daughter, bearded collies. I patted them both and they put up their paws to 'shake hands'. They were adorable.

'My mother's' Stèphane explained, 'She'd like the dogs to live 'ere always, but my father does not want to leave Paris, and I find it difficult to look after them all the time, and still work on my passion.'

I frowned, 'working on his passion' sounded a bit 'iffy' but I let it pass, for now.

As he talked he threw a salad together and gestured for me to sit at the table, which I did. The chateau kitchen filled with the smell of fresh coffee, and the omelettes Stèphane was cooking, talking all the while. This gave me a chance to study him, and now that he'd removed the hat, I could see the dark curly hair, which was collar length at the back and tumbled over his forehead at the front. Yes, it was definitely Stèphane.

'Romain is now married with 3 children. My mother says the Richardes who do produce children always 'ave 3. She 'as documents to prove it – the histoire of the chateau and all its residents, back to before Napoleon Bonaparte. Christophe is very clever, and very busy. He's now a famous architect, in great demand. Mes parents are 'olidaying on 'Réunion, – one of our dépendances in the Indian Ocean. They take many 'olidays since papa stopped working.'

'Retired?' I said.

'Oui, en retrait,' he agreed

Then, with a flourish he put the omelettes, a jug of coffee and two glasses of iced water on the worktop with a bowl of salad, crusty bread and a carafe of spiced oil. I stood up and went over.

'I don't offer you wine, because you – conduire?'

'Because I'm driving?' I supplied.

'Exactement!' and he put the all the food on a huge tray and offered me a large pepper mill, but I shook my head, having seen him season the omelettes, as he was cooking them.

Stèphane carried the tray outside, where we sat under a tree to shade us from the sun. We used to sit here, under this same tree, long ago and my mother hated it. She always said that 'things' dropped off its branches, onto her food. I told Stèphane this, and we both laughed. Sharing this joke somehow made the intervening years fall away. But then I related the story of the 'Tour des cloches' from last night, which I now thought was hilarious.

Big mistake. I could hardly tell him for laughing, but he couldn't see anything funny at all. His look said 'what did you expect with the name 'Le Tour des Cloches,' and I remembered my father (my father again!) telling me that the French never understood English jokes, and vice versa, so never try.

We ate in comparative silence, and I began, stupidly, to wish I could just stay here forever. Forget about Lynne, Dave, my parents, who I am, or might be. It was still heavenly. I sighed.

Stèphane poured more coffee, and then he produced a bowl of fruit and some yogurt. I studied him as he did so. He was taller and broader than he had been at 15, when I last saw him, but not as tall or as broad as I remembered Christophe being. His lovely thick dark curly hair still fell forward in an unruly looking heap, but his beard, although as dark as his hair, wasn't at all curly. There was no way of telling how good looking, or otherwise, he might be now, for all the fur.

'You've told me about the others, but you've said nothing about yourself', I said enquiringly.

'Nothing much to say. I theenk I am what you call 'an 'opeless case'.'

I laughed, and he continued. 'I went to college, passed exams, attended university, passed exams. I could 'ave a job, but the 'ouse needs constant maintenance, so I offered to come here and stay, in return for not being nagged to get a job. It was reluctantly agreed. The 'ouse is safe and attended (by this I assume he did all the odd jobs, such as mowing, cleaning and so on) and I 'ave time to develop my passion.'

There it was again, his passion? Was he referring to a woman, or a hobby, or something else? Best not to ask. But, when he saw me trying to understand he said, 'Finish your coffee, then we'll 'ave our quiet time. After that I'll show you my passion.'

I could hardly keep a straight face, when I thought of the possibilities that statement conjured up, but I wasn't going to risk trying to turn this into another joke, and instead reflected that French habits hadn't changed, and the French, like the Spanish, still had a siesta time after lunch, when they sat quietly, or had a nap.

We closed our eyes and sat back in our chairs. I must've dozed off and was awoken by the dogs nudging me.

I glanced at my watch, half past two. 'More water, you must drink,' Stèphane put a glass in my hand, the weather was hot, although cooler under these trees, but my mouth still felt parched.

'Now I show you my passion,' he said when I'd finished, and I hesitantly followed him to one of the outbuildings. He opened the door and we went in, shutting the dogs outside.

'Their tails, they knock things down,' he explained.

We were in a large area of a single storey stone building, which had been dry lined and converted into a – well, a showroom, I suppose.

'Oh, you collect beautiful objects,' I said as I looked around at superbly elegant pieces, simply displayed on the various shelves.

'I **make** beautiful objets,' Stèphane corrected me.

'You made this jewellery, painted those pictures and carved these wonderful wooden pieces?' I gasped questioningly, surely I'd got it wrong?

'Not the carvings, they are by someone else, but yes, every other piece,' Stèphane agreed. 'You like them?'

'Like them, I love them.' He looked pleased, and then he took me through to where there were two other doors. 'My clean workroom, and my dirty workroom,' he announced as he opened the doors with a flourish.

One had a large window, an easel and a huge range of paints, brushes and other artistic paraphernalia, plus a load of unframed paintings stacked against one wall. My mother would've loved it.

The other room had a workbench, where the jewellery must be made, as it had a row of tools and part finished pieces and on the wall above were large scale designs, presumably for some of his work.

'Wow!' was all I could say. So this was his passion.

Both rooms were both surprisingly neat and I remarked on this. 'I didn't think artistic people were known for being so clean and tidy,' I laughed.

'Oh that's not me, that's Francoise from the village. She keeps trying to retire, she's seventy-six, but I need her, so I keep persuading her to carry on.

If she didn't come I wouldn't be able to work, because I'd never tidy or clean, that's not what creativity is all about, but at the same time, I work better in a clean and tidy studio.' He shrugged at the paradox.

'So, what do you do with it all?' I asked stupidly, and he looked at me, confused 'Do with it?' he repeated.

'Well you can't just keep making things, so you can look at them in your showroom. You must sell them to someone surely?' I explained.

'Ah, that's the problem. I keep making things, everyone say they love them, but 'ow to sell? I try inviting people to visit, but no-one comes.'

He didn't look too bothered, which is probably what annoyed his mother. He must've read the look on my face.

'I mow the grass, it's a big job,' he said defensively,' and I'm expected to organise or do any repairs. I also sweep all outside paved areas and maintain the piscine. It all takes time, and I need as much time as possible for my passion.' He'd made his argument sound perfectly acceptable.

'You have a pool now?' was all I could think of saying, adding 'piscine', when he didn't understand.

He nodded, 'Off the salon, there is now a large terrace and piscine, I show you.'

The living room, or salon, had always seemed family friendly to me, compared to some of the more formal rooms in the chateau, and I followed Stèphane, as he took me through to see the terrace and pool.

On the way I noticed that, although the salon had been redecorated and refurnished, the large picture which I remembered clearly, still hung in the same place on the wall. It was of a woman sitting side-saddle on a horse, with a child on her lap. I thought I remembered she was an ancestor, but I couldn't be sure. Then I saw the pool!

'Oh, that's wonderful. What a great addition!' I exclaimed, at which he suggested we swim. I explained I had no costume with me and then, typically French, he couldn't see the problem. 'Les Anglaise', he laughed as though we were a lost cause.

He then suggested I was wearing underclothes, surely that would do? I declined and got the Gallic shrug.

'You Eenglish are such prunes,' he shook his head.

'Prudes' I corrected him 'and no we're not, well only a bit. I don't want to swim because I must think about going.'

'But you've told me nothing about you,' he said.' My mother will be un'appy if I say you've been and I 'ave no news for her.'

With recent events still so raw, I carefully chose what to say and kept it brief.

I told him that both my father and my mother had died, in fact it had been my mother's funeral only the day before.'

My eyes filled with tears, and he leaned forward, put his arms around me, and stroked my hair.

'Poor Fifi,' he said softly.

I'd forgotten his childhood name for me, although I was remembering that he'd held me in much the same way, when we received news that my darling dog Molly, left with friends in England, had died, whilst we were holidaying here.

'Is that why you come to France?' he asked 'You look for comfort of past, 'appy times peut-être?'

I nodded and said no more. I certainly was not about to tell him that I wasn't sure who my parents were, that I might have been abducted, or bought from someone, or perhaps be a Romanian orphan, who my parents had taken to the UK saying I was their natural child, or a myriad of other possibilities.

'So where are you going?'

'I don't know. I just got into my car, after the funeral was over, and drove onto a ferry. I hadn't planned anything.'

'Do you intend to stay en France, or is it an 'oliday?'

'I don't know that either.'

'Then I think you should stay here, at least tonight. There are many rooms, you can choose. We make bed for you now I think, after we get your luggage,' and he strode out to my car, with the dogs bouncing along behind. 'Is this all?' he said, when he saw just the two bags.

I nodded. I think he probably guessed I'd left in a hurry, but he asked nothing.

As for me, I felt I should protest and say I couldn't possibly impose, but it would be such a relief to stay the night, especially when I had no idea where I was headed. Anyway, how could I say no when he'd already brought my bags in? and it was so much easier to go along with it, and sleep overnight in the chateau I'd always wanted to stay in!

Stèphane fed the dogs, and afterwards took me to an upstairs room and we made up the bed together, then he went off to swim and I had a shower. My room had no en-suite, so I took a change of clothes, a summer dress and sandals, along with me to the bathroom, which Stèphane had pointed out, and luxuriated in the hot massaging shower jets, before switching to the overhead spray and washing my hair.

I dried and dressed, tidied the bathroom, which was devoid of any personal items, so I guessed Stèphane either had an en-suite to his own room, or perhaps there was another bathroom, along the corridor.

I looked out of the bathroom window; Stèphane was swimming strongly up and down the large pool, bigger than ours had been. If only I'd had a costume with me.

He emerged and disappeared in through the door below the bathroom window. It was a few minutes before I heard him come up the stairs, and his footsteps recede into the distance.

I towelled my hair dry, this time without giving my reflection a second thought, then I went downstairs.

In the kitchen I saw the dirty stuff from lunch and washed it up, finishing just as Stèphane appeared.

He nodded in thanks, when he saw I'd cleared up.

'Francoise would've done it in the morning, but thank you.'

"Oh, he really was a spoilt little boy", I thought, but of course he was no longer a little boy, he must be 26, the same as me.

'Can I help with supper?' I asked.

'We eat out tonight, it's a celebration,' Stèphane replied. 'I take you le Moulin Blanc, I've already booked the table', he added when he saw me about to protest, 'Mais first an aperitif,' and he poured two small glasses of Pineau, the local aperitif, cold from the fridge and carried them through to the salon.

It was as sweet as a sweet sherry, and not what I'd have chosen, but I thanked him politely and we both sat down. I was facing the picture and commented on it.

'Ah' he sighed wistfully, 'she was painted around 1820 we believe, and is the ancestor who returned first here to the chateau, after the all the troubles.'

I didn't get a chance to ask any more, as the bell clanged at the front door, Stèphane, jumped to his feet, locked the back door, and we walked along the corridor to the front.

The man at the door seemed to be a taxi driver; we followed him to his car, and Stèphane opened the door for me.

To my surprise, he then got in the front with the driver, and the two of them talked very fast and continuously, for the whole journey. I couldn't follow the conversation, but hearing words like équipe, and balle, and imbecile, I guessed the heated discussion was about football.

We stopped and got out, then Stèphane put his hand under my elbow and guided me into the Restaurant, where the proprietor, Pierre, was waiting to greet us.

Stèphane and he exchanged a few words, and then I was introduced to Pierre, who hoped I'd enjoy my stay in France.

I replied in French that I was sure I would, and was looking forward to our meal.

He assured me, in that unassuming way the French have, that it would be perfect!

In England the phrase would be 'hope you enjoy your meal', in France they are sure you will, they expect no less – of you or themselves. Annoyingly – or reassuringly – they're almost always right!

Needless to say, Pierre was right, it was a fabulous meal, eaten over the customary 3 hours. Everything was made on the premises, he told me proudly, they even smoked the salmon themselves. All the other fish was fresh from the Loire, the meat from the Limousin, and the vegetables, were local, the soup and bread home-made that morning.

We were given a basket of tiny cheesey pastries, to nibble whilst we studied the menu, and a champagne cocktail, 'courtesy of the house' to welcome me. I felt very special.

The first of the 5 courses, a fishy and herby appetiser, was served with a tiny jug of aromatic sauce and a basket of fresh bread. We drank iced water with this.

Then, for my starter I chose the trio of salmon, and was told in which order eat them, which made me smile. Stèphane, having seen my smile, explained that the order was important, going from the mildest taste to the strongest, in order to appreciate the subtle flavours of each. I felt suitably chastised!

For the main course I had chosen 'sandre', a fish from the Loire, which I was told was a cross between Pike and Perch. This meant nothing to me, but I nodded knowledgeably.

 Stèphane must have chosen the wines as they appeared without anything being said, a different one with each course.

We chatted all the while, remembering back to those glorious holidays of old. I then told him I'd had a crush on Christophe and he stuck his bottom lip out, 'Always Christophe, it's always Christophe, every femme falls for Christophe. Why didn't you have a 'croosh' on me?'

I decided to do the French thing and shrugged, and we both laughed.

A huge covered trolley appeared, Pierre rolled back the lid with a flourish and began to point to each cheese, brebis (sheep's cheese) from Limousin, a black coated cheese from the Pyrenees, Roquefort, then a goat's cheese or, chevre de Charente, very local, on and on, I thought it would never end, but it did with a fromage du nord. I knew this meant "of the north", and so I asked where exactly, and he gesticulated to describe where the north was, prés de Pas de Calais he added.

'Ah presque d'Angleterre,' I exclaimed, but at the suggestion that his words might be interpreted as 'nearly England,' he threw up his hands in horror and, reminiscent of Charles de Gaulle, said 'Non!'

We all laughed, clearly a joke that did cross the language gap, then I chose Normandy Camembert, the local Charentaise goat cheese, and then, adventurously, I added one from the Basque area, which was covered in red 'bits', asking for just a 'petit morceau' of each.

Unfortunately, the 'red bits' turned out to be chilli flakes, and nearly took the roof of my mouth out, before I realised what they were. I'd forgotten the Basque country was famous for growing hot peppers.

Dessert was a creamy panacotta, with a fabulous lavender flavoured coulis, and I felt well and truly replete, but, because the meal had been over some three hours, I didn't feel over full and throughout the whole meal Stèphane and I had happily reminisced.

Coffee followed, served with tiny chocolate and nut delicacies, again made on the premises, I was told, but I waved away the decanter of Brandy which appeared.

'But it's 'locale', 'Cognac de Charente', Pierre protested.

I insisted that the answer was still no, although Stèphane was happy to partake. I now knew why he'd ordered a taxi, as French driving laws are strict, one glass of wine and you're up to the limit.

As we left, Pierre was waiting by the door, to say goodnight, and he offered his condolences on the loss of my parents, saying they'd sometimes dined at the restaurant, when we had our French property, so he'd known them.

It was thoughtful of him to wait until we were leaving, to say this, rather than risk casting a shadow of sadness over our meal.

I thanked him, shook his hand and told him the meal had been merveilleux, he smiled, nodded and replied 'Merci', 'modestly' adding, "mais bien sur" – but of course!

The car was waiting and we drove back to the chateau in happy silence.

It was very late, so, when Stèphane tried to persuade me to have a brandy I declined. He then kissed me on each cheek, and said 'dormis bien Fifi, sleep well,' and I went up to bed.

CHAPTER 4

I awoke next morning wishing I could just forget everything else and stay here forever, then, hearing the telephone ring, I silently willed it to be Christophe.

Stèphane would of course tell him I'd turned up, and he'd come rushing down from Paris, to declare his undying love for me. Probably unlikely. Who was I kidding? 100 per cent unlikely. If he really is successful architect, now he most likely wouldn't even remember I ever existed.

I looked around at the lovely room Stèphane had put me in. It was to the left, at the top of the main staircase. I say main because, if I remembered rightly, there were other staircases, two of which led to the turrets.

The views from up there must be amazing, in fact, they ought to be pretty special from this room, so I got out of bed and went over to the window. I could see the road I'd driven along to get here, and the drive coming up through the grounds. I supposed our old holiday home was over to the right, but there was a group of trees obscuring my view.

Then I looked about me, at the china blue painted walls and the luxurious heavy brocade curtains, which were in the same colour, but woven with a gold fleur de lys pattern. They also had ornately pleated tops and hung from a gold coloured pole.

There was a huge ornate gold-framed mirror to the right of the door and a large ivory coloured armoire, or wardrobe, looking lost against the vast expanse of wall. A blue brocade chaise longue at the foot of my bed and a couple of pictures on the walls completed the décor.

I dare say there was bedding to match the colours of the room, and certainly the bedspread was in the same brocade as the curtains, but to make up the bed last night, Stèphane had just pulled a couple of sheets and some pillowcases, plus a few towels, from the linen cupboard, further along the corridor.

It was a very comfortable bed, and I'd slept well, but my heart was heavy at the thought of leaving.

Reluctantly I went along the corridor, washed and dressed then went downstairs to the kitchen, having put my bags together in the hall, ready for my departure.

I was greeted by Gemmy and Trixie, but there was no sign of Stèphane.

Fruit, yogurt and cheese, plus a fresh crunchy baguette and preserves, were laid out on the counter top, and coffee was in the jug on a hotplate, so I helped myself.

Considering how much I'd eaten the night before, I still devoured three chunks of bread, with strawberry preserve, thickly spread. Just as I was finishing, the exterior door opened, and Stèphane came in, wiping his brow.

'It'll be very 'ot later,' he said, and then, through the open door, he spied my bags in the hallway. 'Not a day for you to drive,' he observed.

I didn't know what to say. How could I not drive?

He poured himself a coffee and sat down.

'Do you 'ave any plans at all Fifi?' he asked. 'No', I replied, then my heart skipped when he said, 'I 'ave a thought, a request peut-être.'

Holding my breath, I waited expectantly.

'Since you 'ave no plans, would you perhaps like to stay a little longer. If you were 'ere to feed the dogs, I could go away for a short trip. Take some of my work, to show to people who 'ave contacted me through my website, but don't want to come here. I so rarely get any responses, I don't want to miss the chances.'

Well, put like that, what could I say?

'Of course, if it helps, it's the least I can do, to thank you for putting me up. Why not,' I grinned broadly, and Stèphane immediately took my bags back to my room, returning in seconds.

'I'll make contact, put some pieces together and leave at once. They're in the Auvergne region, 4 hours' drive. If I know I don't must drive straight back, I could perhaps call at other places, to show my work?'

'Don't need to, not "don't must", I corrected him automatically, 'and yes, I'd be only too happy to help.' I smiled – "only too happy" – who was I kidding? I was flippin' ecstatic!!!

Over dinner last night, Stèphane told me that the chateau still had to be sold, because the debts kept mounting. "It must be a huge burden', I'd agreed sadly. Your father always talked about selling it, when you'd all grown up, that's why I didn't expect to find any of you here."

'Everyone still wishes the 'lost treasures' could be found, then the problem would be solved', Stèphane sighed.

'Oh yes,"the "lost treasures",' I laughed, remembering the talk from my childhood. 'Do you still believe they really exist?'

'Of course. We surely know they did exist, because we 'ave documents to prove this. My mother 'as watched every sale of antiques and pictures for years, and nothing on our list 'as ever appeared, so we believe they must still be concealed somewhere.'

'Weren't they hidden by the villagers or something?' I was trying to recall the story.

'Yes, you 'ave a good memory. It 'appened in places all over France, during the Revolution of the late 1700's. Many so-called dignitaries were carried off to Paris. A lot were guillotined, but in villages, where chateaux owners had been good and kind, the villagers emptied the houses and hid the treasures, before Napoleon's forces stole or burned them. Then the villagers petitioned the new Regime, asking for clemency for their employers.'

'Wow. Still sounds like a fairy story. What sort of treasures are we talking about?

'Silver, glass and fine porcelain, not furniture, because that was removed and hidden by the villagers and brought back when our ancestors were pardoned, although even then they were still kept under house arrest in Paris, eventually managing to escape to England where they stayed for some years. The missing paintings are the main thing as they could be worth a great deal of money, which could be used to save the chateau.

When our ancestors returned, about 1820, things were still not very settled here in France, and so the recovery of the treasure was postponed. Sadly the lady on the horse, in the painting you were looking at last night, was the only person to have been told the location, and, shortly after, she died of typhoid, taking her secret to the grave.'

'But someone else must have known? 'I protested

'Well there is a story about an old lady in the village, 'Eloise Chevron, who was supposed to have chanted, "the treasure", "the coffin tree", and "thirty metrès," in French obviously, but they decided she was senile, and didn't know what she was saying'.

'Ah yes, the Coffin Tree', I'd forgotten about that and the old lady. The very description 'Coffin Tree', still made me shiver.

'Even she lived long ago,' Stèphane continued, 'and we're now in the 21st century?' He shrugged, resignedly, adding, 'Looking for it was why we spent so much time here, but, like many of our ancestors, we've searched and searched and found nothing.

Maman 'as many papers, but they've been no 'elp.' He sighed, and I guessed that he was sad that there was no money to repair the chateau.

As a child, and then a teenager, I'd always hoped that a handsome prince, (who co-incidentally looked exactly like Christophe) would come along and discover the treasure, and he, and the beautiful daughter of the chateau (who looked remarkably like me,) would marry and live happily ever after. Sadly, it seemed it was never to be.

Stèphane loaded up his car, kissed me on both cheeks, hugged me, thanked me again for agreeing to look after things, and drove away.

As I watched the car disappear from view, I marvelled at the events of the past 24 hours, none of which I could ever have imagined would happen, then, wondering what to do with my time, I thought I might as well try my hand at locating the treasure. Apart from anything else, it would give me a valid excuse to have a good look around this beautiful building.

'Well doggies, where do you think it is?', I asked them, and they did that doggy thing of putting their heads on one side and then the other, as though they understood. I patted them and laughed and they wagged their tails.

I finished my coffee, locked the outside doors and went upstairs, then began my search in my own room, tapping all the walls and examining the floor for evidence of removable floorboards, but since they were about 300 mm wide; I doubted I'd have the strength to lift them anyway.

Drawing a blank. I went along to the next room, which was full of very beautiful ornate gilded, but empty, picture frames. I gasped. The pictures must have been removed from them by the villagers. I suppose it was sensible, because rolled up canvasses would have been easier to hide.

I carefully moved each frame, checking the walls and floors under and behind them, but again nothing. As I did so I wondered about 'the coffin tree' and what it could mean. I looked out of the window, but even if it was important, where could it be? There must be hundreds of trees on the estate, but maybe there was one with markings carved on it, but why would it be called 'The Coffin Tree'? Was this term really important, or were people right that the old lady had been 'barking'?

The next room was the same, minus the picture frames, and I'd just opened the door to what appeared to be a study, when I spotted the seventy-six year old Francoise, from the village, coming up the drive.

I quickly closed the door and went downstairs, hoping Stèphane had warned her I'd be here, or the shock might kill her! Pas bon!

I reached the kitchen, just as she unlocked the back door.

'Mamselle Fay, ca va. C'est bonne de vous voire.' Not a hint of a smile.

'I'm well thank you, and it's good to see you too.' I replied in French, but I smiled. She still didn't. No change there then, since I couldn't recall ever having seen her smile.

She nodded, put down her basket, took off her coat and rolled up her sleeves. It was boiling hot outside, how could she wear a coat? She saw my look and shook herself as though she'd been shivering, reminiscent of the men where I'd had breakfast the day before yesterday.

Suddenly I had an idea, if she was here, with the dogs, perhaps I could go pop out and buy a swimming costume.

'Combien de temps êtes vous ici, cet matin?' I asked, and she replied that she'd be here for 3 hours'.

'Bon,' I replied, trying to think how to say shopping, instead I decided to risk asking if there was a market nearby today. 'Es'que un marché prés?' I asked hopefully.

'Oui,' she nodded, and named a place only 10 miles away, so I'd have ample time to get there, shop and get back.

'J'ai besoin de' I began, so I'd got as far as 'I have need of', but swimming costume defeated me totally.

I pointed at the pool, then ran my hands down my torso and made swimming movements. She stared back at me. It was easier to say 'I go to the market for 2 hours,' so I did. She shrugged picked up a broom and began sweeping the ancient stone floor of the kitchen.

I grabbed my handbag, sunhat and sunglasses, said "au revoir, a plus tard" and left.

It wasn't until I was well on my journey that I realised I hadn't brought a key to get back in, so I'd better be back in plenty of time, otherwise I could be stuffed.

I adore French markets, the sights, the smells, the hustle and bustle of the busy stalls and I wandered happily from one to another, among the groups of neighbours and friends, who were using it as an excuse to socialise.

There were small tractors for sale, next to a stall of garlic, expertly arranged, then carrots, next to a stall stacked with cupboards, many painted with beautiful flowers, and these were beside the electrical goods stall! It was great fun.

 I bought some cheese, including one that looked like the peppered cheese from the Moulin Blanc, and couldn't resist indulging in a bag of nougat, very different from the stuff we get back home.

After this I came across a stall with t-shirts and shorts. Dad always said, if you don't know the French word think about the English word, because if that sounds as though it could be a French word, it probably is. It presumably was, because, when I said 'piscine', mimed swimming strokes and added 'costume', the woman pulled out a box, weighed up my size and produced several suitable swimming items.

I chose one costume and one bikini, paying for them with the last of the money I'd got from the cashpoint, then she stuffed them, unceremoniously, into the flimsiest bag I'd ever seen and gave them to me, with my change.

Then, just to complete the truly French scene, an oompah band came marching past. I'd have loved to stay longer, but I'd already been gone more than two hours, so I found another cashpoint then headed back to the chateau, where, just like when I was younger, I went up the drive pretending I lived there, only this time I sort of did, temporarily. How exciting was that?

I parked round the back, and the dogs came bounding out to greet me. I could see Francoise through the window of Stèphane's workroom, and I waved to her.

I mimed "would she like a drink?" and she nodded curtly and carried on working.

I went inside, opened the cupboard and got out the jug Stèphane had used yesterday. The kitchen was now so clean and tidy, I hardly dared use it, but I poured half a carton of orange juice into the jug, filled it up with water and ice, added a sprig of mint, from a pot on the windowsill, then I took it out to the garden with 2 glasses.

Francoise came over, so I poured some into a glass and beckoned to her to sit down, "assayez vous", I suggested, but, looking horrified, as if she couldn't possibly stop working to sit drinking, she snatched the glass up and took it back with her. I laughed to myself.

Eventually she finished and left, and I stood in the salon, looking at the picture of the lady on a horse, willing her to somehow convey to me where the treasures were hidden.

Not surprisingly, I learned nothing, so went back upstairs to continue my search. The room I'd been about to start on, when Francoise arrived, was indeed a study, Monsieur Richarde's, judging by the ledgers and files. I had a good look round, but again nothing suggested 'hidey hole', so I quickly left.

The rooms at the rear were bedrooms, and, like my own, sparsely furnished and easy to check over. There was another room near the far end of the chateau, which I was sure this must be Stèphane's, as I thought I'd seen him going into it, so, deciding that searching it would be too intrusive by far, I checked the other rooms along the front of the chateau, but there wasn't a hint of anything.

I even tried to imagine where I would hide treasures. What about the turrets, there was one at either end of the building? I made for the furthest and found the staircase leading to it was leaning to one side, like a drunken sailor, as it wound upwards, and it felt most unsafe. With difficulty, I pushed open the door at the top, and jumped as I was met with a flapping of wings and scuttling of feet, and the smell was gross.

I quickly shut the door again, feeling quite sick, and went back down to the main landing, then fearing the same thing, I went up the other turret staircase. Thankfully this was upright and, the door at the top opened easily. There were no creatures, but I could see there were no obvious signs of trapdoors, false panels or anything else either, so I didn't even go in.

Disappointed, but not surprised, I admitted defeat for now, went downstairs to the kitchen, and put on my new swimming costume. Opening the French doors from the salon, (whilst wondering whether the French called them French doors), I padded along the terrace to the ladder and slowly lowered myself into the water. It was lovely once I was in, but I guessed it wasn't heated as ours had been.

Stèphane had shown me a downstairs shower room, so, I used it when I'd finished swimming. Then, towelled dry and wrapped in a lovely thick robe I'd found on the back of the door (and which I pretended to myself might be Christophe's) I got myself some bread, cheese and salad, and sat on the terrace to eat it. I sighed, this was the life, and I intended to make the most of it while I could.

It was now early evening, but still wonderfully warm and, feeling relaxed and happy, I fell asleep, to be woken by the sound of a telephone ringing. Trying not to trip over the dogs, who thought it was a game, I rushed inside, eventually locating it in a room, off the hall, which I judged to be another study; but it had stopped ringing.

It couldn't be anyone for me, so I just hoped it wasn't anyone important with a message for Stèphane. What if it had been Christophe? The thought struck me with horror. I might've just missed speaking to Christophe!

I waited to see if the caller rang again, but then went into to the kitchen to clear up from my supper. Typically, I'd just got there when it rang again.

This time I reached it in seconds 'allo' I said 'le residence des Richardes', laughter at the other end signalled the call was from Stèphane. 'Bon soir mam'selle', he chortled, 'Ca Va?'.

'I'm well thank you. Did you call a few minutes ago?' he agreed that he had. 'I couldn't find the 'phone' I said, and he laughed again.

'Have you arrived safely? Have you seen anyone yet, and what did they say?' I asked.

'Oui, all is well. Madame 'as insisted I stay with them and Monsieur 'as commissioned me to make a special piece for her. They 'ave also bought two of the pieces I brought to show them. Tomorrow I go to see some friends of theirs; I should be back late tomorrow evening. Is that ok?'

'Of course. I'm fine here with the dogs, so why not take another day?' I suggested and it was agreed. This meant I now had the whole of tomorrow and at least part of the day after, to continue my search for the lost treasures – and to pretend I lived here!

'Do you have a mobile number?' Stèphane asked.

Realising it would sound silly to say no I replied, 'Yes, but it's not working. We'll talk about it when you get back.'

'O.K. Sleep well Fifi,' he said softly, and rang off.

I don't know why but, weirdly, I suddenly felt like I really did belong here. I didn't want to go home – ever, so I'd either have to find the treasures – unlikely – or a way to make myself indispensable, so that Stèphane would want me to stay longer.

I went upstairs, got my tablet and checked for emails. Thankfully, no-one had given Dave and Lynne my e-mail address, but I just knew there'd be messages from them on my phone, so, without turning it on, I shoved it right down to the bottom of my large bag.

I took my tablet downstairs with me and had a look at Stèphane's website, to see if I could tell why he got so little response from it. When I found it, I knew the answer immediately - it was dull and uninspired.

Tomorrow I'd alternate my time between playing with a few website suggestions for him, searching for the treasure, and fitting in more swimming along the way.

I sighed happily, then suddenly realised that the dogs had not been fed (helped by nudges from the furry ones). I'd not thought to ask Stèphane about their food, what they ate, or even where I might find it, or perhaps

I was supposed to have cooked something for them?

I went into the kitchen and opened cupboards and, finding nothing, I went out to the boot room. Trixie and Gemmy followed and stood panting expectantly by a particular cupboard. I opened its door and there was a large bag of dried dog food.

'Clever doggies,' I said and they wagged their tails. I was able to translate enough of the French instructions to dish up some grub for them, and it was soon gone, followed by the water in their bowls, which I refilled.

'Good girlies', I patted them both, then tidied up the kitchen and let them out for one last wee before bedtime. They were soon back and I checked that all the windows were shut and the doors locked. then, feeling slightly nervous, now that night was here, I took the dogs upstairs with me.

Locking my room door, with the large ornamental key, I just hoped the dogs wouldn't ask to go out during the night, as I didn't fancy opening any outside doors for them. The chateau suddenly felt isolated – which of course it was, especially with all the nearby holiday homes being deserted.

I hadn't even thought about being alone in the chateau in the dark, but now I found it daunting and I'd already encouraged Stèphane to stay away for longer!

CHAPTER 5

I couldn't get to sleep, so lay thinking about the 'hidden treasures' story, shivering when I thought about the Richarde family members who'd been taken from this house Then an awful thought occurred to me, they must have included the lady on the horse. Stèphane had said she was the first to 'come back' to the chateau. She may even have been taken from this very room!

Having frightened the life out of myself, I now jumped at every creak and groan, eventually dropping off to sleep through sheer exhaustion, but waking again at 6.a.m. The dogs were snuggled up together on my bed, and I had a feeling Stèphane wouldn't approve, but they looked so cute, like little furry angels, so I left them and was soon asleep again.

At 8 a.m. I wakened with a start, from a nightmare. The coffin tree had wound its branches around me and was wiping its wet leaves back and forth across my face, but when I opened my eyes I found that the 'wet leaves', were actually the doggies licking my face, nudging me to get up. I sighed with relief, put on the towelling gown, went downstairs and let them out. I'd survived the first night!

When they came back in, they barked and looked expectantly at their bowls. No doubt if I gave them food they'd eat it, but should I? Oh, they were hardly going to put on weight by being overfed for one or two days, so I measured the scoops into the bowls and it was gone in no time.

'No more,' I said firmly, when they looked at me expectantly again. 'Pas plus. Finis. C'est suffis!'

Then I decided to implement the same routine we'd used every morning at our holiday home, swim, shower, then breakfast outside while the sun dried us, but first I couldn't resist another look at the painting, on my way to the pool.

Who was this lovely lady sitting side saddle on the horse, in her elegant dark green, riding clothes? On close scrutiny she was older than I'd always thought, perhaps in her early fifties, so who was the child she was holding? Unlikely to be hers, since he looked to be only about four years old.

There was a surprising amount of scenery, from a large tree to her left, to a small tombstone at the far right of the picture, and I wondered why the artist hadn't painted her closer up, with less background. Then I mused that perhaps the tombstone was for a beloved pet, or even a lost child, so she'd insisted on it being included?

I got into the pool, and, as I was swimming back and forth, I realised that this was exactly how I wanted my future to be, and I believe I'd just hit on the perfect way of achieving it. Shivering with pleasure at these thoughts, I put any chance of the chateau being sold to the back of my mind.

Getting out of the pool, I lay on a sun bed, eating fruit and yoghurt and letting the sun drying me, while I thought through my plan in more detail. Stèphane's website is rubbish, and I'm a web designer by profession, so 'all' I have to do is persuade him he needs a new one (which he does), to be created by me, of course. It was the perfect solution - and the first time that I'd ever been glad that my father had insisted I study graphic design at uni!

I say 'my father' because I'd now decided that 'my parents' were really my parents after all, and that whatever Lynne and Dave thought they knew, it was probably imagined.

Anyway, excited that I'd hopefully found the answer, I got dressed and began to implement my plan, because I must have a preliminary design prepared, in order to persuade Stèphane when he returns tomorrow.

Naturally, I'd have to stay several weeks to complete it and, by then, surely I'd have found a way to make my stay permanent?

My plans involved photography, so taking the key to the workshop and studio, which I'd seen Francoise hang up in a cupboard, I went over and let myself in. shutting the door behind me, to keep the dogs out. I then looked through the jewellery and chose pieces which I was thought should photograph well.

The right lighting was going to be essential so, by using a couple of anglepoise lamps I found under a bench, I reflected their light back off the ceiling. This, together with the large mirror from my bedroom, which I carried carefully downstairs, achieved exactly the soft diffused effect I was after.

Now all I was short of were the right materials for the background. I wished I'd thought of all of this when went to the market yesterday, but there was bound to be another one, not far away today.

The Mairie in the village should have this information and so, reasoning that it was ok to leave the dogs alone for a while, as Stèphane must do so when he was working, I wrote a shopping list, got my purse and drove into the village. Luckily the Mairie was open.

'Bon jour. Avez vous une liste des marchés locale?', I asked the neat, fair haired woman behind the desk (who I thought was wearing a bit too much make up).

'Oui,' came the crisp reply, from the scarlet lips. A list of markets was produced, a copy was made and handed over.

I thanked her and left, but not before curiosity got the better of her, and she asked if I was staying locally.

I replied with immense pleasure, 'Oui, au Chateau Richarde,' and quickly closed the door behind me.

Today's market was in the village of the Moulin Blanc, where Stèphane had taken me for our meal, and my route took me over a bridge across the river Charente, where I stopped briefly and watched the water rolling gently over a shallow weir.

It was a charming scene, with a stone water mill, picturesque even though it was dilapidated, and a heron standing, fishing on the weir, completed the picture. I'd have loved to stay longer, but I knew I mustn't waste precious time, so I drove on again, located the market, which was smaller than yesterday's, and quickly found the material stalls.

I was looking for silks and satins, in rich colours, to show off the jewellery to best effect, but the first stall was patterned cottons, perfect for summer dresses, and the second stocked thick, heavy, upholstery fabrics. Just when I was losing heart, I found a third stall and this one had a great range of reasonably priced softly draping silks and satins, so I bought a metre of each of the colours on my list.

The stallholder would only take cash, so it cleaned me out of funds again! I'd just enough left for two of the local Charentaise melons. I'd been taught long ago, here in France, that when melons are ripe and ready to eat you can smell it, and these smelled mouth-wateringly good.

Next stop, cashpoint – again!

Back home in the Chateau – I knew it was dangerous to start thinking of it as 'home', but I'd decided to allow myself to fantasise, at least until Stèphane came back, The dogs came sleepily to meet me and I guessed my bedroom door wasn't shut and they'd probably spent the morning on my bed. Whoops.

Lunchtime, so I had goats' cheese, with biscuits and grapes, and a huge slice of melon, by the pool of course; after which I spent the next couple of hours scouring the downstairs of the Chateau for signs of the 'lost treasures' or "les trésors perdus", as I supposed they must be called in French.

Searching these rooms was tricky as their walls were draped in heavy brocades and tapestries, and there were heavy rugs on the floors, so, reasoning that they'd probably been searched long ago anyway, I turned my attention to the outhouses, discounting Stèphane's workshops and gallery, as they'd recently been dry lined.

The other stone buildings were very dark and damp, and the small torch which I'd got from my car, barely lit the walls well enough to check them properly. This only left the large outdoor bread oven which, long ago, would've been used daily by the whole village.

In the summer, when we were here, it was used once a year for a Fête du Pain, a bread fête, and I wondered if this still happened, or whether, with the family now in Paris, it had been abandoned, which would be rather sad.

I opened the door. All the ancient tools were laid inside, ready for use, and there was clearly nowhere to hide anything.

Well, I knew it had been silly to imagine I'd find something no-one else had been able to locate, in all the years that had passed, so I went back into the house, and got my material pieces.

I was setting up displays, ready to photograph, when the telephone rang, making me jump. I hadn't realised there was an extension out here. It was Stèphane, enquiring if I was still ok; if not, he could drive home tonight?

'No, no,' I protested, 'pas necessaire', then I asked how his day had gone.

'Quite well, I've sold two more pieces, so with yesterday it 'as been a very worthwhile trip'.

Stèphane then asked what I'd been doing, so I replied that I'd bought a swimming costume, from the market, plus nougat and some cheese similar to the chilli cheese from the Basque country, which we'd had at the Moulin Blanc.

As I put the phone down I laughed, sure that Stèphane had only asked out of politeness, replying 'bon, bon, ca c'est bon', to everything, before ending the call.

I got straight back to my photo shoot and, by late afternoon I was pretty pleased with the portfolio I'd amassed. I'd even spotted an old potter's turntable on wheels and trundled it into place, then, gently working the turntable with the foot treadle, I'd been able to photograph and video moving displays, which looked good.

My back was aching, and I was really hungry, so I replaced everything, took my camera and material pieces and left, locking the door behind me.

After I'd eaten, I saved the pictures from my camera and my tablet to my laptop, then I opened my design program. By now my brain was nearly bursting with all my ideas, so I began experimenting.

The chateau must feature prominently; tomorrow I'd take some pictures of that, but for now I played around with different shapes and ideas.

I was thrilled with the effect of the turntable, gently rotating and showing off the jewellery, I faded it in as it began to turn, and then faded it out when it completed a rotation. The result was impressive. Then I added some still pictures, zooming in, to show each piece from different angles.

Stèphane must be really impressed by what he saw, in order for him to want me to stay on and complete a new website for him. It was very late, but my mind was still active, so I poured myself a glass of chilled white wine and sat on the terrace. It was warm, the air was still and, with no light pollution, the thousands of visible stars were breath-taking.

Eventually, giving in to fatigue, I called the dogs and went up to bed. No listening to noises tonight, I went straight to sleep, and awoke in the morning to wet noses being pushed into my face once more.

I went down and opened the back door, then swam and had breakfast, although I had to toast the bread, which was now like a brick.

I'd just got dressed when Francoise arrived. She had a basket over her arm, from which she took out a fresh baguette and presented it to me like a trophy.

Not wanting to offend her by saying I'd already eaten, I tore of a lump off, then I spread it with butter (to her disgust) and jam.

'Je prefer le pain avec le beurre,' I explained, but she just shook her head as though she couldn't understand why anyone would spoil fresh bread with butter.

She muttered 'Les Anglaise', it might as well have been 'Les Philistines', if they use such a word, for the disgust it conveyed, then she picked up some cleaning tools and went off elsewhere in the house.

I chuckled to myself and reflected that William the Conq. had probably felt much the same as Francoise.

Breakfast done, I got straight on with photographing the outside of the chateau from all angles, and by lunchtime, I was feeling pleased with the results.

As soon as Francoise left, I went for another swim. Eyes closed, I was enjoying the water when there was a splash and I opened my eyes, expecting to see one of the dogs in the pool, but to my surprise it was Stèphane.

'Hello, I didn't expect to see you until this evening,' I smiled.

'I made excellent time. You swim good' – 'well' I corrected him.' Nice costume, the ugly duck is grown to a swan,' he laughed and began thrashing up and down the pool.

Hurt, I got out of the water. When was I an ugly duck, and it was duckling anyway?

I went inside, showered, took the robe, now hoping it was Stèphane's and it would annoy him, then I went upstairs and got dried and dressed. But while I was doing this, I was thinking back and wondering if 'the ugly duck' had been a secret joke to the boys and they'd been laughing at me behind my back all the while.

In a fit of pique and, despite all my hard work, I felt like deleting Stèphane's new website, which was now in an advanced state. I looked at it and slammed the laptop lid down. Ugly duck, how could he!

Needing to be away from him temporarily, I got in my car and drove to the local plan d'eau and parked close to the lake. I love these simple park-like areas provided for family picnicking.

Ugly duck, so now I knew why Christophe had never shown any interest, but why did I care what Stèphane thought? It couldn't just be because I was desperate to stay at the chateau. Confused, I started the car and drove back.

Stèphane was sitting under the trees with a large jug of iced lemonade and two glasses. He wore shorts and a t-shirt and looked very fanciable. He motioned for me to join him, said nothing about my going off in the car, but instead asked if everything had been alright while he'd been away.

'Yes, everything was fine. I wasn't sure how much or how often to feed the dogs, but they survived. Francoise was disgusted that I put butter on my bread. Otherwise pretty uneventful.'

'Yes, sorry, I should have left you some notes' There was a silence then he added 'Why did you drive away just now?'

'I didn't like being called an ugly duck, and it's duckling anyway, and I'm not.'

He looked astonished. 'I didn't say you were ugly, I called you a swan.'

'You said I was an ugly duckling'.

'I meant in your young years you weren't beautiful, like you are now. That's all!'

I mellowed. So, he thinks I'm beautiful. Wow!

I sat down and drank some lemonade. 'So, you have a commission, and have sold four pieces, is that good?'

It was his turn to be miffed. 'Of course it's good! I 'ave gone months without selling anything,' he said crossly.

'Do you expect to sell from your website?' I tried to sound casual.

'Obviously or I wouldn't 'ave spent time and money on it.'

This was my chance - 'You mean you paid someone to put up that dreary boring site for you?' I asked with my eyebrows raised as high as they'd go.

He looked at me in astonished anger. 'You come here, I let you stay and you attack me, and criticise my web site!'

I thought it was probably his turn now to drive to the plan d'eau to calm down, but resisted saying so.

He glared at me and I thought I'd blown it until he asked, 'You 'ave looked at the site?'

'Of course, and I feel I have the right to criticise, because I am a trained web designer.'

His jaw dropped.

'I think you need a new site Stèphane – one of a standard high enough to compliment the jewellery you create.' (I don't know how I hit on that angle, but it sounded good, even to me). 'I've been putting together a few ideas if you're interested.'

His tone instantly mellowed. 'You really think my work is that good?'

'Yes, you're very talented. Do you want to see what I've been doing? Of course, It's nowhere near finished,' I added, seizing on what could be my only chance to sow of the seeds of my plan to stay longer.

'I'd be very interested,' he replied. Phew!

I got my laptop, and he came and sat right next to me, so he could view the screen. I was very conscious of his close proximity, the warmth of his body and his heart beating and I had to concentrate very hard to stay focussed.

I opened up the screen, to show the pieces slowly revolving on the turntable, which was concealed by the satin and silk drapings. As one colour led into the next, the picture blurred and faded and the next piece of jewellery, on its individually coloured background faded in. I told him that this was specially planned to get the viewer wanting to see what was appearing next, from the right, as soon as the piece on the screen moved to the left and began to fade.

I also explained that my next plan was for the site to open with the Chateau, which would look as though it were turning, due to the way I'd videoed it. After that the screen would zoom in to his workshop.

'That's as far as I've got' I finished.

Stèphane was silent.

'You don't like it?' I asked him in French. 'Tu ne l'aime pas?'

'C'est magnifique,' he answered in awed tones. 'I didn't know you are so talented,' he added in English.

'Well of course It needs speech and links, and of course more pictures, to create the romance of the chateau. It must convey the message that these pieces are all made in the artisan's workshop, at this beautiful place, a setting befitting works of such high quality. A building that has been the family home for hundreds of years.

We'll have to sort out the wording. Perhaps I could do the English voiceover and you could do the French, then we'll have to decide on the what other languages to cover.'

He'd gone very quiet, and was looking at me in amazement.

I continued, 'You also need to adjust your prices, they're far too low. How many pieces to you make of each design?'

'I don't set a figure. I show the designs and make them to order.'

'Well, my advice is that each design should be limited and carry your mark and a number and a certificate of authentication.

It's amazing how much people want something when it's rare.'

'Oh, I love that idea,' he exclaimed! 'As it is, I do new designs, but I can't really make any more pieces, because I haven't sold what I've already made.'

'So you have designs you've never used?'

'Yes lots, and many more in my head, but this website sounds like a lot of work, which sounds trés cher?'

I couldn't believe it! The opportunity I'd been hoping for. I grabbed my chance – 'Yes, very expensive indeed,' I agreed, 'my fee would be to stay here for at least another month'.

He looked astonished. 'You're saying if you can stay 'ere another month, you'll not want paying for your design work?'

I nodded. He grabbed me, kissed me on both cheeks and then on the lips.

I think we were both a bit taken back at the latter.

'Are you 'appy with your room?' He asked. 'You can change to another if you prefer.' Adding 'Mine has a bathroom, it's the only one.'

'Are you inviting me to share your room Stèphane?' I teased him, forgetting again the differing French sense of humour.

He looked confused, clearly wondering how I'd misunderstood.

So I laughed, to break the tension, and said I was happy where I was. He looked relieved. I would analyse the reason for this later, for now I was just delighted that I was settled for a while.

Tomorrow I must speak to my mother's solicitor as I'd had several more emails, pressing me to contact him. I'd also been neglecting Jules and Rosie, who'd been brilliant friends over the years, so I must reply to them all, but, I still wasn't ready to share my location with anyone else.

However, tonight a bigger problem was Stèphane, and I lay in bed wondering why he'd looked so relieved when, after my attempted joke about sharing, I'd said I was happy to stay where I was.

He seemed to have lots of friends, male and female, many of whom popped in from time to time, and the 'phone rang often and, since I'd learned that it was not with orders for his work, these calls must be personal. However, he never divulged anything, and had never mentioned girlfriends, although, in fairness I'd not talked about either of my ex's either. But I was concerned that Stèphane was hiding something, I'd no idea what, just a feeling that it was so.

CHAPTER 6

The next couple of weeks passed really quickly. Still no sign of Christophe, either on the telephone or in person.

Stèphane and I photographed jewellery pieces which I'd not included originally, plus some of his detailed design drawings, an art form in their own right.

At the same time, I continued with his website, whilst he worked on some new items, because I was certain his site would quickly attract a following and we must have new designs ready.

I even made a short film of Stèphane working through, from design, to creation and completion. Once edited, this would become part of his website, establishing a further 'contact' with his customers, encouraging them to purchase the pieces.

Filming Stèphane also gave me the opportunity to analyse how long it took him to make each piece, and from this Stèphane and I agreed that he could make ten of each piece (to order) and bring out three new designs each month.

By having new designs ready, in advance of the launch of his website, he'd be ahead of the game and this hopefully would avoid any potential strèss. Also, to this end, I drew up a proposal for a weekly timetable, with three days allowed for making the pieces, a further day for creating new designs and then a day each week for miscellaneous things, such as ordering materials, catching up, if he'd got a bit behind. There should also be a little time allowed for meeting customers, but this would be kept to a minimum, and be strictly by prior appointment only.

Stèphane loved the 'relaxed' timetable, but the item still to be discussed was pricing, and I knew this was going to be a bit of a battle. Stèphane thought I wanted to ask too much, but I insisted that asking less would lower the 'perceived value' of the pieces. In the end it was agreed we'd begin with my prices, adjusting these later if sales were slow. Any future designs would be priced accordingly.

I told him he must have more faith in his own talent, but I actually wanted him to have more faith in my suggestions!

In the end his he only reservation was potential visitors, so I explained that this personal touch was solely necessary for the very small number of customers who'd want to meet, in person, the artisan who produced such objéts d'art'.

'Oh "objéts d'art," he mimicked, your Français is improving! I threw a cushion at him.

I could feel the process of making myself a permanent fixture was going well!

Over the next few days Stèphane, who spoke German and Spanish, as well as French, found people among his old college friends who covered Italian, Greek, Dutch, most of the Scandinavian languages and others we deemed necessary.

Together we devised the wording, and supervised each speech recording over the internet. Visitors to the site would use a drop-down menu to select a language.

I felt worryingly at the mercy of the people who did the voice recordings. They must get them right, since there was no way we could tell whether they had or not. Hopefully there were no practical jokers among them either, who'd record something totally different for a laugh.

It was the sort of thing Rosie and Jules would do and think it hysterical. I smiled to myself. Rosie and Jules! I'd been so busy I'd been neglecting them again. I looked in my 'sent' box, it was only a few days, but it felt like weeks.

All commentaries 'in the bag', Stèphane and I chose classical background music. I say 'Stèphane and I', but it was Stèphane, obviously. I couldn't even tell you who wrote 'the Wedding March'. When I said this to Stèphane, I swear he thought I was joking.

'You know it was Mendelssohn really, don't you?' but my blank expression told him I was serious. The French as a nation are much more into classical stuff.

'But you must go to concerts?'

How could I say 'Yeah right, Glastonbury, Readin', Isle of Wight, Bestival. It would've probably been his turn to look blank! So I said nothing.

The website and ancillary stuff sorted, Stèphane and I planned the release of new designs, with me suggesting we allow for a 'Collection Majestique,' in a year's time – a few very special pieces, possibly one-offs?

Stèphane loved this idea, and didn't even question my staying for another year, in fact I think he was coming to rely on it. Perfect!

It was now July, and Stèphane took me to the Moulin Blanc, both for my birthday and to celebrate the progress of his website, which was now almost ready to go live. The young man I'd thought of as lazy, when I arrived, had worked 14-hour days for the last few weeks, because he was doing something he loved.

With the imminent launch of the website, Stèphane began to worry about coping "if he got orders". I insisted it was 'when', and reminded him the website had been designed to stop accepting orders when the allocated number had been sold.

He looked at me, full of admiration, and I complimented myself on having made him more and more dependent on me. This was the part of my plan I didn't share with him, nor my intention to stay here forever, although I did begin introducing the subject of such a complicated website needing much on-going maintenance and updating, then, as soon as he looked concerned, I reassured him that I'd be here.

My French had improved greatly, as had Stèphane's English, although I still couldn't get him to pronounce 'h'. We spent a whole hour trying words beginning with 'h'. I said hedgehog, he said 'edge'og, I said happy to hope for a hedgehog, he said ''appy to 'ope for a 'edge'og. I said h h h h hedgehog – how could that fail. He said h h h h 'edge'og. I gave up!

I'd also now given up waiting for Christophe to come rushing down to see me and claim me for his own. He must know I was here, but hadn't bothered to make contact, so although I was sure I'd never love Stèphane the way I'd loved Christophe, I was making Stèphane my future, well Stèphane and the chateau! The question I was avoiding was, "Would I want a life with Stèphane, without the chateau?"

I knew the chateau was the real focal point of my future, and the reason I'd made it so prominent on the website. "Fabulous jewellery made in a fabulous setting."

My long-term plan was to make Stèphane so successful he could maintain the chateau financially, and I also wanted us to be married before this came about, so he didn't get any ideas of independence.

It seemed to be working out well, as everywhere we went, Stèphane either put a proprietorial arm around my waist, or linked my arm in his but, although he kissed me on both cheeks regularly, disappointingly, he'd not kissed me on the lips again. Even so, I was still planning towards permanence here at the chateau, deliberately not facing up to this problem.

I still couldn't stop myself thinking about Christophe, bringing him into the conversation from time to time and, when Stèphane asked once again, now that I was staying longer, if I'd like to move to another room, my first thought had been to wonder which had been Christophe's room? I'd love to move into that.

I just couldn't help thinking of him. Perhaps I never would be able to.

Since my crush on Christophe, when I was 15, I'd had boyfriends, well two really, who I thought might become my future, but there'd never been the right depth of feeling, to make 'forever partners'.

Anyway, enough of that, back to the website, everything is nearly ready to go live on line and I was about to suggest a day and time for the upload, when Stèphane suddenly said. 'What will you do now your work is almost finished?' It was so unexpected that I was lost for words.

'I don't know' I stuttered. I'd become so used to thinking I was in control of the situation, that it was a shock. It sounded like he was suggesting I'd be moving on.

It must have shown on my face, because he hastily added 'Don't look like that Fifi, I don't ask you to go. 'Actually,' he hesitated 'I'd like it if you'd stay here permanently?'

Wow! I'd just gone from being asked to leave, to being asked to stay permanently, in one sentence. I had to stop myself from punching the air with a loud 'Yes!'

Then Stèphane then said, 'We talk in the morning,' and with that he kissed me on both cheeks, and then gently on the lips, looked deep into my eyes, then he went up to bed.

Result!

However, things were very different next day, and I guessed Stèphane had asked me on impulse.

'We must get something clear Fifi, I can't guarantee staying 'ere at the chateau,' he explained. 'It will almost certainly be sold, because of the costs of the keeping-up'.

'Upkeep,' I corrected him absent-mindedly, more concerned because it felt as though he could read my mind. 'Is it that bad, really, and what happens if it's sold and the new owner finds the 'lost treasures'?

Stèphane shrugged, 'I think that's the only reason we still have the chateau, the belief that the 'lost treasures' are hidden somewhere. However, I must go and talk to someone. I have a bag,' and he produced a holdall and held it up. 'I return late tomorrow, and we talk some more. OK?'

I nodded, he bent down and kissed the top of my head, then he tipped my face up and said 'Dear sweet Fifi,' and left!

I didn't know what to make of any of it. Why did he suddenly ask me to agree to stay 'permanently', but not make any real commitment himself? Why did he never kiss me properly? And why was he being so secretive about where he was going, when he'd gone into detail about his previous trip?

One thing was for certain, his statement about the chateau had thrown the 'hidden treasures' into sharp focus. How could he, or any of them, ever deny me the right to live here if I found them and thereby single-handedly saved the chateau? The lost treasures were my insurance, and I was now determined to find them!

Francoise arrived and I sat on the terrace with my coffee, considering the chateau. No doubt the leaning turret was the big problem and no doubt the biggest expense, and probably the main reason for selling. So once again I climbed the leaning stairs, this time prepared for the awful smell, in the room at the top. Still unsure of the state of the rotten looking floor, I thrust the door fully open, but stayed in the doorway. Things squawked, and squealed, and scampered, at my invasion of their space, but this time I stood my ground, surveying the room thoroughly.

It smelt wet and musty, and of animal wee and poo, and the window slits were open to the elements – and the flies! Ugh!

I had to admit it would probably be a huge job to put it right, so I reached for the handle and pulled the door shut, before going back down the stairs, which seemed to be leaning more than ever.

On the landing below, I stood by the huge window, looking along the wide corridor, to an identical window at the far end, picturing how it might have once looked. I imagined huge paintings adorning the walls and chaises longues and inlaid semi-circular tables and ottomans, covered in rich brocades, placed along its length.

I sighed, thinking of the Richarde ladies of long ago, who'd almost certainly promenaded along this corridor for exercise in inclement weather. Like me, they too would've looked out of these windows and a little shiver ran down my spine, knowing that, If I found the missing pictures, some of them would be portraits of these very women. I shivered again then I walked along to the other staircase, and went into the room at the top.

I thought it would make a wonderful poet's garret, then I realised this turret had a perfect view of our old holiday home, including the rear garden and swimming pool, which all looked incredibly unchanged.

I went back downstairs, just as Francoise was about to leave.

I picked up my French dictionary, 'Un moment Francoise, s'il vous plaît', she waited while I looked up 'turret', but then she began tapping her foot, so 'le tour' would have to do. She'd understand what I mean by 'the tower' surely?

'Le tour?' I asked, leaning as I did so, 'Qu'est que le problème?' She looked blank, so I added 'les escaliers, for the stairs, and this time she understood that the stairs were leaning.

'Trés, trés dangereux' she shook her head vehemently, and wagged her finger at me, conveying that I must not use them.

'Oui, mais qu'est que le problème?'. Thankfully, this time, she understood that I was asking why the turret and stairs were leaning. She opened the back door, gesturing for to me to follow her, as she marched off along the outside of the chateau to the base of the turret in question. I followed, wishing I was wearing sturdier shoes.

Once there, she pointed to the ground, which looked soft and wet

'Une petite rivière, sous le terre,' she explained, copying the leaning gesture I'd used.

I interpreted slowly, Oh, "A little river under the ground," was causing the turret to subside, that was the problem. Wow!

'Merci, je comprends,' I thanked her. She grunted, marched back to the kitchen, got her basket and left, giving me a brief wave as she did so.

I stood there, surveying the scene, wondering how much of the chateau was being undermined by this 'petite rivière'.

My father had been very practical and he might've had a suggestion for tackling the problem. He'd certainly solved the problem of heating our holiday home, when we thought it would be exciting to spend Christmas in France. We hadn't realised how cold it got in a Poitou Charente winter, nor did we understand how it would affect our limestone house.

We'd arrived with the car loaded down with all manner of food, presents for the Richardes, a fake tree and decorations and, thank goodness, we'd taken the bedding home with us at the end of the summer, so that was in the car and dry, ready to use.

Then we'd opened the front door to see the walls glistening wet, with moisture which had leached through from the other side, due to the cold.

My father immediately lit the log burning stove in the kitchen, then he and my mother carried the mattrèsses downstairs, and we kept rotating them until they were warm, dry, and safe to sleep on.

The Richardes said we could stay with them, but my father went over to view the accommodation, and came back to say that the chateau was not heated either, and he thought it was even colder than our house. I was disappointed, because at seven years of age I thought it would be magical to spend Christmas in a castle.

Next day my father was gone until evening, and the following day everything needed to put in a central heating system arrived. So, the whole holiday was spent with mum and I huddled in front of the log burner, and dad installing central heating. Occasionally we went to the shops, not because we wanted to buy anything, but to thaw out, but mostly we were too cold and miserable to move. What a Christmas that was!

CHAPTER 7

We never came to France for Christmas again, but, once we had heating we were able to spend more time here each year. However, the best thing of all was that my dad used the same boiler to heat our swimming pool! Bliss.

Anyway, back to the present, having seen how bad the problem affecting the tower was, I walked despondently back to the kitchen and made myself a cup of coffee, making a mental note to get some instant from the supermarket. It would probably horrify Stéphane, but it was easier when I was on my own.

I prepared some lunch, which I ate sitting under the trees. I loved it here so much that it hurt and couldn't bear the thought of it being sold, which could happen at any time. As I sat, considering the situation, the only conclusion I could come to was that finding the 'lost treasures' was the only solution. No matter that no-one else had found it in more than 200 years, it was imperative that I succeeded, and as quickly as possible!

However, first, I must see if I could trace the water source, which was being so destructive to the chateau so, I went back to the base of the turret and began following the wet land. It disappeared into rough grass then through some undergrowth, where the ground began to rise gently, then more steeply up a slope. At this point I suddenly realised I must be close to the disused silver mine which I'd forgotten all about. The family used to say that all the missing silverware, which was part of the 'hidden treasures', had been made, long ago, from silver mined in the chateau grounds.

We'd been told in no uncertain terms, as children, that we mustn't go into the mine, because we may never be found, in the miles and miles of tunnels, well, I expect they said kilomètres.

'Never be found,' echoed in my brain – just like the 'lost treasures' had never been found? Could it possibly be they'd not been found because they were in the disused silver mine? It sounded like it ought to be the perfect place for exactly that reason, but where would the 'coffin tree' come into it. There could be no trees in a mine. Perhaps it was painted on a wall of the mine? Maybe even marking the spot?

Excited by this thought, I located the entrance and stood peering in through the metal grid, while the dogs, who were clearly unhappy, whimpered and cowered and barked, in turn. I patted them to calm them, then I turned to go back.

As I began to walk down the slope, I looked up at the chateau and could see the window in the 'safe turret', where I'd stood earlier, and which overlooked our old garden. I wondered when that turret room had last been used. My guess was that, being smaller it had been a guest room and, originally, probably occupied by servants.

It was mid-afternoon, so I had a swim, then spent the rest of the day, and evening, checking over Stèphane's web site, to see if I should make any last-minute changes, as I was planning for it to go 'live' when he returned. I did a couple of test uploads and it all seemed to be working perfectly, although this didn't mean there'd be no problems once it was up and running. It was never possible to cover all the bases.

The following morning, I swam, then breakfasted by the pool, checked my emails then got dressed. But today, while I was still upstairs, I decided to check out Stèphane's room, prior to my eventually moving into it with him, which I was now determined I would do eventually. I just had to be patient, but I might as well know what it was like, in advance, although the fact that it had an en-suite bathroom made it favourite.

Feeling just a little uneasy at my intrusion, I pushed the door open. It was relatively tidy and I guessed Francoise probably cleaned it as part of her duties.

It was larger than the room I currently occupied, and had a huge double bed, which looked very comfortable. I tried it out. Yes, it would do nicely. I lay down on it and stretched out, then I checked out the bathroom. It was large and surprisingly luxurious, with a huge bath and separate walk-in shower.

The only thing left to check out was the storage, so I opened the doors of the enormous armoire, to ascertain what space might be free, for my clothes. It wasn't a lot, but what rivetted me to the spot, and shook me to the core, was the number of women's clothes hanging on the rail, and high heeled shoes on the rack below!

I felt sick with shock. So this was Stèphane's secret and why he'd been reluctant to take our relationship any further. It also explained his reaction to my asking if I was moving in with him.

I sank onto the bed. Suddenly I had a raft of new problems and questions, not least of which was, "Could I marry a man who was at very least a cross dresser, in order to live in this beautiful chateau?" I wasn't sure I could, and this then led me to wonder if I'd loved Stèphane in the same way I'd loved Christophe, would I have felt differently?

Still trembling from the shock, I shut the armoire and went quickly out onto the landing, firmly closing the door behind me.

Lunchtime came, but I had no appetite. I felt as though all my hopes and plans had evaporated when I'd entered Stèphane's room and opened that wardrobe.

At first restless, then angry and bitterly disappointed, I went into the grounds and walked about, not knowing what to do or to think. I needed something to occupy me, something to stop me thinking about it. Then I remembered the silver mine, although, just at the moment, I wasn't sure I even cared about the hidden treasures any more, but it gave me a focus.

I returned to the chateau and found a large battery powered lantern, and found a warm a jumper, guessing it would be cooler in the mine. I put on my walking shoes, and a jacket as well, then tucked a notebook and pencil into my jacket pocket, intending to note each twist and turn, so I didn't get lost, and would be able to re-trace my steps.

The doggies, fed and watered, scampered along at my heels, but became less happy as I neared the mouth of the silver mine, although Gemmy looked less scared and more curious than Trixie.

I didn't care whether they followed me in or not. It was only intended to be a quick recky to get an idea as to whether it could be a hiding place for the treasure. I wouldn't be long.

Carefully removing the pieces of metal and wood barring the entrance, I went in, gingerly picking my way and holding the lantern ahead of me.

After the first few tentative steps, Gemmie decided this was a new game and went bounding off in front of me, while Trixie hugged my ankles and rubbed against me.

'You don't have to come', I smiled and bent down to pat her. She nuzzled my leg for reassurance.

Gemmie came bounding back, shaking herself, ah so there was water. I must be careful.

Seeing Gemmie return seemed to give Trixie more courage, and the two of them headed off into the depths of the mine, with me following slowly. The roof height was pretty good at this stage, but I soon came to a fork in the passage and the roof became lower in both directions.

I stood for several seconds trying to decide which route to take and opted for 'le gauche'. I could just make out that the passageway was descending, and soon it turned, and there were others leading off the one I'd chosen. I took what I considered the main one, until I came to another fork, where they both seemed of equal importance. Then I decided that, if I stuck with 'le gauche', on the way back I'd only have to remember to reverse it by turning right.

Because I was being careful and also checking the walls for drawings, or other possible signs, it was slow going. It was also much colder than I'd anticipated, and soon I wasn't able to move my hands easily, so I had to keep changing the lamp from one to the other, to keep them both working. Gloves would've been good, and a hat. Perhaps I should go back and try again another day.

But I couldn't be sure of Stèphane's movements, he might not go away again for ages and I didn't want to wait. I wasn't expecting to find the treasure at this stage, just to decide whether or not it could've been stowed somewhere in this mine long ago, and remained hidden.

I'd no idea how long I'd been in the mine, and I didn't want to uncover my wrist to look at my watch. My teeth were chattering, and I'd lost count of how many times I'd turned left, and I was aware that at least once, or was it twice, I'd been forced to turn right.

Common sense told me to it was time to stop, decide on the possibilities of a hiding place, based on what I'd seen so far, and return to the chateau.

The floor had become slippery and I could hear water dripping, so, one last look around and I'd head back, but as I turned, my foot slipped from under me. The paper and pencil flew out of my hand and I felt my small torch slip out of my pocket, then there was a splash as it fell into water.

I fell to the ground with a crash, as did the lantern. It remained alight but was out of my reach, and I was terrified where the water might be, and how deep. I was too frightened to move, and then I realised, to my horror, that I couldn't move. The pain from my leg was excruciating and the last thing I remember was sinking down onto my back. The light from the overturned lamp was playing on the ceiling and, as I lay there, I became convinced that there was a crack in the tunnel roof, and I could see something shining, then I passed out.

'Imbécile!' was the word that awoke me. Stèphane had returned and he was angry. 'It's as well I came back early. Get up!'

There was no sympathy, no kindness, no tenderness, no concern.

'I can't', I replied, close to tears. 'My leg,' and I passed out again.

Next time I came round it was to voices and lights, and uniformed men kneeling by me and trying to assess my injuries.

'êtes-vous anglaise?'

'Oui.' I replied in a whisper.

'Vous avez le douleur?'

'Oui',and I pointed to my leg to show where the pain was.

A huge lamp appeared and lit up the area and I yelped as the man felt my leg, to assess the damage, then I passed out again.

Next thing I knew, but I don't know how much later, I was fastened to a padded stretcher and being carried through the tunnels to the outside, where I was transferred to an ambulance and taken to hospital.

All the while, Stèphane was berating me for my stupidity, until one of the men told him to shut up. I also heard the same man ask Stèphane if I was his wife, to which he'd replied vehemently 'Certainement pas!' From the tone, I guessed that vehement 'certainly not' meant 'not now, not ever!' So much for thinking it was my choice!

At the hospital they ascertained that I'd banged my head and must have a brain scan, to make sure there'd been no bleeding.

I began to cry but Stèphane still showed no sympathy. I must've been mad to ever consider marrying him. (Like I'd been asked!)

Having had X rays on my leg, and scans on my skull, I returned from the X Ray department with my leg in a big padded boot.

The physical pain had ceased, however, the pain of feeling sorry for myself remained. I'd lost my chance of saving the chateau, or even staying at the chateau, plus any chance of marrying Stèphane. I'd lost my future!

I knew I'd been a fool in more ways than one, not least because I'd been prepared to settle for Stèphane, mainly because I couldn't have Christophe. At this point, he came into my room.

'Why are you being so horrible to me?' I asked, expecting him to soften and apologise.

'I'm not being 'orrible to you. To be 'orrible to someone one has to care, but you're nothing to me, just a girl I used to know who turned up again.'

'B-b-but you asked me to live with you - permanently,' I persisted.

'That was a mistake.'

I thought I'd reached rock bottom until that point.

'Well at least I'm normal, not like you, wearing women's clothes,' I hit back.

'Stupid Anglaise', Stéphane spat at me.

'Suffi!' a voice commanded, and Stèphane stopped at once and stepped aside.

O. M .G. It was Christophe! He was drop dead gorgeous, even better looking and more wonderful than I remembered. I was sure my heart had stopped beating momentarily and I could hardly breathe.

'Allez!' Christophe commanded and Stèphane, looking sheepish, immediately left the room.

Christophe brought a chair and came over to my bed. He smiled, gently stroked my face and, bending down, kissed me on both cheeks. Had I died? Was I in heaven?

'All ma petite Fay, how are you feeling?' he asked in almost perfect English.

'Very stupid,' I replied, unable to take my eyes off him.

'I mean the injuries, your head and your leg?'

'They've given me an injection and I can't feel any pain now.

'That's good. I've spoken with the doctors. Your leg is 'sprayed' I think is the English word.'

'Sprained' I corrected him, still hardly able to believe that he was actually here, with me.

'Sprained' he repeated. 'Your head has a bump, which will soon heal and there has been no blood from the brain, but you must stay here tonight, then, if all is well you can leave tomorrow.'

"Great!" I thought, "how bloody wonderful! Where the hell would I go?"

As if he could read my thoughts, Christophe took my hand in both of his and said 'You'll return to Chateau Richarde, until you are well, then we'll talk.'

I thanked him in a whisper, and he continued, 'It's wonderful to see you after all this time, but I'm so sorry to hear about your mother and', he hesitated, then added, 'and your father.'

I must have looked as though I was going to cry, because he held me close again, and I leaned my head against his chest. I wanted to stay like this forever.

Suddenly, but gently, he moved me away from him.

'Fay, we must talk. I was going to save it for the chateau, but I think now might be better.'

I frowned, he looked very serious. Then, as though he was telling a story, which in a way I suppose he was, he began.

'When I was a teenager, I loved you very much'. I gasped. 'I used to watch you from my bedroom window in the tower. I could see your garden and your swimming pool, and I day-dreamed about a future together.'

I couldn't believe what I was hearing.

'I dreamed about a future with you too,' I said breathlessly 'but you never seemed interested. When I came back here I only agreed to stay with Stèphane, because you must've known I was there, but you didn't bother to get in touch. Stupidly, I thought if I couldn't have you, I'd settle for Stèphane, even though I wasn't in love with him. I think I was in love with the chateau, but I was still in love with you, if I'm honest.'

'Sh,' he said gently and placed a finger on my lips to stop me talking.

'You were only 15 and I was 18, so I knew I must wait, but one day my mother was in the chateau grounds, near the old mine, and she saw me at my window. Apparently, she waved, but I didn't see her, so she crept very quietly up the stairs to my room, opened the door and saw me watching you.'

So the turret room with the perfect view of our back garden had been Christophe's!

'It was then that she told me that I must not look at you in that way, because you are my sister. I cried for days.

I understand she also told your father, about your mother's affair with my father, and that was why your maison-secondaire was sold, and you no longer came to France.'

Horrified didn't come close to describing how I felt. Just when I thought things were turning out wonderfully, it was like a punch to the solar plexus.

'No, no, no!' I was almost shouting, not wanting to believe him.

'I think that's why Stèphane was horrible to you just now, and also in the mine. Thank God he came to see both myself and Justine.'

'Justine?' I questioned.

'Yes, he came to Paris to tell me that you were back and he wanted to marry you, and to tell Justine that his 6-year romance with her was over. Until then, I didn't even know you were at the chateau.'

'Because you'd agreed to living permanently with him, when he'd always thought you wanted me, he believed he'd scored a victory, until I told him the truth. Then he was horrified at what might have happened between you. Sadly, he then, wrongly, blamed you. This brought the anger.'

'And Justine?' I asked

He'd not said anything to her. Perhaps now, at last, he'll ask her to marry him.

'So they'll live in the chateau?' I asked enviously. It certainly explained the women's clothes in the armoire.

'We'll see, probably not. I think Justine won't want to leave Paris. She's never even been to the chateau'.

I frowned, so they weren't her clothes then.

As though he could read my mind Christophe said, 'Now tell me about Stèphane wearing women's clothes. When did you see this?'

'I haven't actually seen him wearing them, but, because I thought that I'd be moving in with him, I went to "recce" 'the room and the wardrobe space. Check it out', I explained at his frown. I was really shocked to find numerous women's dresses and shoes in the armoire.'

'Which room was this?' he asked with a twinkle in his eye.

'The one with the salle de bain'.

'I thought so' he laughed. 'I think you'll find his clothes are next door, which is meant to be his room. The other one is our parents' chamber, but when they're not at the chateau, he sleeps in there because it has a bathroom. The women's clothes are my mother's. They frequently visit and she finds it easier to leave some stuff there.'

'Oh no, now I feel more stupid than ever,' I sighed.

'You have nothing to feel stupid about Fay, in fact, having seen the superb website you've designed for Stèphane I feel very proud to have you for my sister.'

I know he meant well but his words still made me feel sick. Sick that all my dreams, all those years of daydreams since I was 15, had been for nothing. I looked at him, but I couldn't think of him as my brother.

A nurse came in and asked if I'd like something to eat, 'Crepes Suzette peut-etre?' Christophe raised an eye-brow at me and grinned mischievously.

'You remembered,' I laughed. His father had cooked crepes on the barbecue, poured orange sauce and brandy over and set fire to them, then he'd then given one to me, and my mother had been really cross.

The nurse ignored his 'silly' suggestion and held out a list. Christophe took it from her and decided I should have a croque monsieur and then yogurt.

'But it won't be cheddar,' I wailed.

'No, it will be Emmenthal. Most people in hospital in France send out for pizza', he told me laughing. The nurse got the gist of what he was saying and told him off, before leaving with the order.

'We make cheddar now, here in France, you know,' Christophe told me, quite proudly.

'No you don't' I protested, 'you make something you call cheddar, but it's not. I bought some in the market and it was disgusting.' We both laughed. It seemed liked a turning point. Perhaps in time it could work, 3 brothers I didn't know I had.

While we were waiting for my food, Christophe asked why I'd come to France, so I told him what I'd overheard at my mother's funeral.

'Now that you've told me the truth Christophe, I can only suppose that my mother had confided in Lynne, although it was all a bit strange. My mother and Lynne were really good friends, we lived near them and I played with their sons, then one day, when I was eight, we just moved, about a hundred and fifty miles away, and I never saw them again.

I only asked them to her funeral because she'd said she wanted them to be there. I was surprised, but I was even more surprised when they said yes.'

'So, if you'd waited and they'd told you the truth, would you have still come to France ?' Christophe asked, studying me carefully.

'No, probably not' I replied. 'I'd have assumed you didn't know, and it was better left like that. But why Lynne and Dave thought they had the right to tell me, when my own parents hadn't, I don't know.

'I'm glad you didn't let them tell you, because it's much better this way, that I tell you.'

I wasn't sure I agreed.

The nurse, who seemed rather taken with Christophe – and who wouldn't be – brought a croque and yogurt for him too, and juice for us both.

We ate in silence, then the nurse returned, saying it was time for Christophe to leave.

'Will I see you again?' I asked afraid he was going straight back to Paris.

'I'll telephone the hospital tomorrow morning, and, if all is well, I'll take you back to the chateau.'

'And then?' I had to know, was I to be left at the mercy of Stèphane.

'I'll stay for a few days, then I have to go overseas, but first I must see Stèphane's website go live. It's very exciting. Another talent in the family.'

I knew he was trying hard to make things work, and I was grateful. He kissed me on both cheeks, wished me 'bon soir' and left.

I supposed I'd try and enjoy the chateau for the next few days, what option did I have, but then what?

I fell asleep thinking about the chateau, and how the turret room I'd stood in, with the view of our pool and garden, had been Christophe's, and I hadn't known.

Next morning, with a polythene bag fastened around my boot, I showered, then got dressed, ready to leave.

The doctors came, gave me a check over, then Christophe arrived to take me back to the chateau. He looked amazing, in a white top, jeans and trainers, with a sweater tied loosely about his shoulders, the archetypal handsome hunk, (although I shouldn't be thinking like that).

He asked how I was feeling.

'Embarrassed at falling over and causing all this fuss,' I told him, as he sat down on the edge of the bed – I was occupying the only chair.

'Pas de problem' he replied, with a dismissive wave of his hand, then an office worker brought me a bill for my treatment, so I showed my blue European Health card, but she waved it away.

'You must pay now, but I believe you can claim much back,' she said, standing firmly in the doorway, making it clear she wouldn't leave until the bill was settled – and nor presumably would I!

 It was 800 euros. I was shocked. I had nothing like that in my bank account, so I'd have to transfer some funds, however, when I got my phone out, she pointed to the notice forbidding use of mobile phones within the hospital.

'Mon Dieu!' Christophe exclaimed, I should've realised. I've not brought my wallet with me.

'What can I do? I could pay by card, but there's not enough money I the account,' I wailed. I need to move some from another account.

Christophe thought for a moment and then an idea obviously occurred to him, but equally obviously he dismissed it.

'What?' I asked, 'Have you thought of a way?'

'Well, I could take your 'phone outside and transfer the money for you, if you give me the details?' he offered.

I hesitated, fully aware of all the dire warnings I'd been given over the years about passwords and secrecy.

Christophe recognised my dilemma. 'No, this is not the solution' he said 'you shouldn't give this information to anyone.'

But he wasn't just anyone, he was Christophe.

'I'll write the details on a piece of paper, I know I can trust you,' I whispered and he smiled back at me, that devastatingly charming smile, convincing me, if I needed convincing, that I was doing the right thing.

A few minutes later he returned triumphant. It had all worked perfectly. I gave my card to the office worker, and Christophe gave me back the piece of paper on which I'd written my details.

I breathed a sigh of relief.

'I hope your email access is not the same code', Christophe said, but I had to admit that I used the same code for almost everything. 'It's easier to remember just one code", I explained.

He nodded in agreement and admitted he did much the same himself.

CHAPTER 8

Christophe and I sat in silence, awaiting my receipt.

'You don't have to stay,' I blurted out, 'you must have far more important things to do.'

'I'm sorry, I was thinking about my trip overseas, which I'm not looking forward to, but it's necessary,' he replied apologetically.

Before I could ask about this trip, a senior nurse arrived and I instantly sensed her attraction to him. Perhaps it was as well he was my brother after all, because I don't think I could've constantly competed with other women for his attention, although how our relationship would pan out from now on I couldn't begin to imagine. As for Stèphane, well, I was still considering punching him for the way he spoke to me yesterday! The jury was out on that one.

I glanced at Christophe, just as well he didn't know what I was thinking.

After explaining that I must have both rest and exercise, the nurse gave Christophe 'that look' again, professional, but with a hint of something more, and left, just as an older woman, with a clipboard, came into the room and addressed Christophe.

'Mam'selle Barker has been visited this morning by Doctor Mishau, for the head, and Doctor Arnau for the leg. They're pleased with her and she can go home to,' she looked at her paperwork 'le Chateau Richarde?' she looked questioningly at Christophe, who confirmed the address.

'And you are Monsieur Christophe Richarde?' she asked, as though trying to establish our relationship, but Christophe just nodded.

She handed me my receipt and a print out of the exercises I must do each day, then a junior nurse brought a wheelchair, and I was taken out to the car, where Christophe opened the door, then scooped me up in his arms. Oh, how I'd dreamed about such a scene, Christophe picking me up and carrying me off – but not like this – never as my brother! I smiled weakly as he put me into the front seat.

Wondering if he was inwardly cursing me for messing up his routine, I suddenly realised that the only shock for him had been learning that I was in France and had had an accident! He'd had 11 years of knowing that I'm his sister, yet he'd never told Stèphane! What is all the needle between these two?

When we reached the chateau Stèphane appeared at once, wanting to help me, which was a bit of a surprise, since we'd hardly parted on good terms. Christophe gave him the hospital crutches and then carried me in himself.

A downstairs room had been turned into a bedroom for me, and it was there that I was taken. 'It would be handy for the downstairs shower room,' Stèphane explained.

My bags were on the small table beside the bed, so they must've cleared my bedroom.

Stèphane followed my glance and said quickly, 'Francoise packed your things,' as though he didn't want to be accused of anything to do with women's clothes again. I couldn't help laughing and he laughed too. The ice was broken.

'I'd love to sit outside,' I said, 'please pass me my crutches'.

Christophe hesitated, but Stèphane handed them over and I pulled myself upright. I wasn't going to tell them, but my plan was to get fully mobile as quickly as I could – and far away as soon as possible!

I started off along the corridor, but it was an enormous physical effort.

Stèphane followed and began chanting "go Fifi go", and it was like years ago, when we were kids. We began giggling so much that I had to stop and lean against the wall.

Christophe wasn't laughing, and, if I didn't know now that he was my brother, I'd have said that he was jealous of Stèphane. He caught me frowning at him and tried to make light of it.

Once in the garden, it was even harder going on crutches, and I had to admit defeat. Christophe carried me to the seats under the trees, and Stèphane went to make some lunch.

'I used to hate it when we were kids and you and Stèphane did that,' Christophe suddenly said crossly.

'Did what?' I asked perplexed.

'Shared private jokes and shut me out.'

I looked at Christophe in disbelief, explaining that we just liked the same things, and laughed at the same things, and did daft things together.

'And shut me out,' he said again.

I changed the subject.

'Why have you never married?' I asked, since he was now close to 30.

'For a long time, I was very mixed up over finding out you are my sister, but since then I've had one or two fairly serious relationships, but each time there was something missing. How about you?'

'Similar really. I compared everyone to you and found them wanting, but of course, my mother didn't help. She criticised everyone. Boyfriends, school-friends, work friends. She encouraged me to take them home, so she could meet them, and then discouraged me from having any more to do with them.

'Sounds like she was frightened of being left on her own. When did your father die?'

'Six years ago. He was due to retire and went to Holland on one last business trip. The car he was in was in an accident on the way to the airport, to catch his plane home.'

He held my hand gently. 'I'm so sorry. You're very young to have lost both of them'.

'Yes, but of course I haven't lost my father, have I?' I replied bitterly.

Christophe sighed and let go my hand. 'No,' was all he said.

"Well what else was there to say?" I thought angrily, as Stèphane, followed by the dogs, appeared, carrying a laden tray.

'Oh hello girlies, I wondered where you were,' I leaned down and stroked them both.

'I shut them in, so they don't knock you off your sticks,' Stèphane indicated my crutches.

'Oh, you are so good,' I patted them and rubbed their backs and ears, and under their chins.

'They're better than you know,' Stèphane said. 'If it hadn't been for them you would probably be dead.

I looked up in surprise.

'When I came home and couldn't find you, they barked and yapped and jumped about until I followed them to the mine. I felt sick, not knowing what I would find, and when I did . . .' he tailed off.

I looked down at the two little bundles of fur, who'd saved my life.

'Why did you go into the mine?' Christophe asked quietly.

'Stèphane and I had been talking about the famous 'hidden treasures' and I was stupid enough to think that perhaps no-one had considered them being stowed away somewhere in the mine,' I explained.

'I'm afraid that possibility was exhausted long ago. It even resulted in a detailed plan being made of the interior of the mine,' Christophe explained.

I sighed, yet more disappointment.'

'You were delirious when I found you, talking about the 'Coffin Tree', and shiny things in the ceiling' Stèphane said 'but I think the bump on your head made you see things that were not there.'

I suddenly remembered what he meant. 'Yes, I saw something metallic, where the beam shone, when I dropped the lamp' I replied, but that didn't explain why I'd been saying 'The Coffin Tree'. These words, which the old woman had reportedly used, intrigued me, in a creepy sort of way.

'Almost certainly a vein of silver,' Christophe said firmly, 'there are still some unworked'.

'Is that what you use, for your jewellery?' I asked, but Stèphane, shook his head.

'Oh but you should! It would add enormously to the value, "Jewellery made from the chateau's own silver mine!"

'It's not safe to work it any more', Christophe explained. 'That's why the entrance was closed off,' he looked pointedly at me.

Conversation wasn't easy, so, before long, I went to my room and to bed and was soon asleep. However, I awoke several times in the night, once with pain in my leg, and at least twice with dark thoughts about the last few weeks, and trees and coffins.

Next morning I sat on the edge of the bed, exercising my leg, as recommended at the hospital. I longed to get in the pool, but decided to leave it for now.

However, my big achievement of the day was launching Stèphane's website, then ironing out the glitches which surfaced. By the end of the day he was getting a reasonable amount of interest and, over the next two days this grew and the 'sold out' sign went up on one of the pieces. Stèphane was ecstatic, and we drank champagne to celebrate.

I was now getting around easily and could sense the improvement, as the pain had subsided and much of the swelling had gone down.

The following day a group of villagers came to prepare for the Fête du pain, which would take place at the chateau that weekend.

I was delighted to learn that it still continued and went to see the preparations being made. Stèphane brought me a chair, so I could sit and watch as the villagers cleaned out the huge stone bread oven. Then, to dry it out, they lit fires with bundles of dried twigs, which they called 'fagots'.

In the afternoon Stèphane and Christophe went off together to buy the supplies for the barbeque which, apparently, they always operated together. This surprised me as they rarely seemed to be in accord on anything.

I waited until the car was out of sight then 'crutch walked' to my room, put on my swimming costume, unwound my bandaging, went to the pool and slid into the water. What bliss.

However, getting out was more difficult, pulling myself up by the heavy metal poolside table, then, using the towel I'd brought to dry off, so that I didn't drip my way through the house to my room, where I got dressed.

I sat on my bed until I got my breath back, then picked up my crutches and hobbled round to where the boys had left me sitting. I'd just made it back when they returned, with the barbeque stuff.

It was quite nice being looked after, but I soon got restless, so, the following morning Christophe, sensing this, settled me on the terrace, put up a huge parasol and brought me some paperwork.

Oh God he wasn't going to 'bang on' about the 'our' father business again! I'd accepted, mostly, that he was my brother and didn't want to talk about it anymore, so I was surprised when I saw that what he'd brought me was about the chateau.

'Because of your interest in the "hidden treasures," I thought you'd like to see this stuff. It should stop you getting bored for a few hours, then, if you want another swim, Stèphane or I will help you into and out of the pool. He tossed this last bit at me as he walked away. I threw a towel after him. How did he know?

I asked Stèphane later and he told me, with a grin, 'It was the trail of right foot only, wet footprints, from the pool along the terrace!'

So much for thinking I'd got away with it.

I spent the rest of the day looking through the chateau paperwork, and I learned that the lady in the painting in the salon was the Countess Emilie Mathilde Richarde. She'd kept a journal of sorts and it mentioned their return to the chateau. She wrote that both she and her husband had thought it wise to drop their titles, also agreeing not to reinstate the hidden treasures in the chateau, until things were more settled.

So, this was the proof that the treasures existed and were hidden. Much of the rest of the paperwork was lists of the items concerned and general family paperwork.

Disappointingly, I could find no hint as to where the treasures might be, not even in Emilie's journal, although it was interesting to read about the painting of the picture which hung in the salon. She described the artist as 'intense, but a treasure' and told how she'd had to sit still on the horse until she could sit still no more. This was repeated on several days, it seemed, but she was very excited by the finished painting. "It is exactly as I wanted it to be, my picture is a treasure", she had written.

Next day the villagers returned, raked out the oven and lit more fagots, and by late afternoon announced that it was ready for use. Curiously other villagers, by the dozen it seemed, appeared with pizzas and pies to cook, later taking them home sizzling hot for the evening's supper.

People had come and gone all day. Marquees went up, on the chateau's lawns and benches and chairs by the dozen were set up inside them. Trucks, tractors, vans and even small lorries, came and went, bringing games, slides and small roundabouts for the children, boules for the adults, plus other ball throwing and target games, and many weird and wonderful things that I could only guess at.

A table was set up by the gate. There'd be a small fee to come into the grounds, and a charge for the warm crusty bread, which would be baked in the oven. A band would play all afternoon, games and competitions would be held, and the barbequed meal would be cooked and served.

In the evening, everyone, would repair to the Mairie Salle du Fêtes, where dancing and drinking would last until the small hours.

All money raised would go into the village coffers, to provide 'extras' for the following year. It was a very old tradition and I was really chuffed to find it all still carried on. However, I'd been dreading Monsieur and Madame Richarde returning for the fête, but thankfully they didn't. I'm afraid he'd always be just 'Monsieur Richarde' to me, regardless of what he might have been to my mother.

The Fête du Pain was an enormous success, with two or three hundred people, from around the commune, visiting the chateau, buying bread and enjoying the barbeque. The atmosphere was wonderful, and I was sorry when the day came to an end, because it also meant that it was almost time for me to leave.

Not surprisingly I opted out of the gig at the Mairie, and turned in early, although, even from a quarter of a mile away, I could hear the thumping beat of the music, but I'd had such a good day, and was so tired, that I didn't care.

The following day while everyone was occupied with clearing up, I had two things planned; one was to photocopy the chateau paperwork Christophe had lent me, then I was going to see if it was possible for me to drive my car. Theoretically it should be, since it was an automatic and it was my left leg I'd injured and couldn't use. Of course, had it been a French car it would've been a different matter.

No-one saw me get into the driving seat and start the engine. I drove a few yards, then reversed back into the same position. It'd been easier than I'd dared hope. I turned off the engine and hobbled back indoors.

Christophe was going abroad next day, and I'd be glad when he left. In fact I didn't want to see any of them ever again, especially not the parents! I shuddered at the thought.

So, professing exhaustion, I again went to bed early. I don't think Stèphane totally believed me and Christophe was concerned. 'Just a couple of long days,' I said, 'I'm fine. Goodnight, I hope you have a good flight tomorrow,' and I left.

Once in my room I locked the door, then put all my stuff together, except for what I'd need in the morning.

The house was silent when I awoke. It was quite late, so I knew Christophe would be gone. I went along and had a quick wash, cleaned my teeth, got dressed in the shower room, then I had breakfast, putting everything away afterwards. I thought longingly of the pool, and a lovely morning swim, but resisted the temptation

The window was open in Stèphane's workshop which must mean he was busy out there – perfect.

So, back to my room, where I opened the window and dropped my two bags, plus extra stuff I'd bought here in France, onto the grass, less than a metre below.

I'd already written notes, one for Stèphane and one for Christophe. Stèphane's said goodbye and wished him well. It also said I'd let him decide when he told Christophe that I'd gone, and gave him the other note.

Christophe's message was more difficult. I decided to be honest and told him I just couldn't think of him as my brother, so I couldn't see him again. I asked that neither he, nor any member of his family tried to find me.

One last check round, to make sure I'd left nothing, then I crept along the corridor to the front door.

'Bye, bye doggies,' I whispered as I gave them one last pat and hug, then shut the door so they couldn't follow me, and reached my car as quickly as I could.

Luggage stowed, I started the engine and left - this time forever - forcing myself not to watch the chateau, my beloved chateau, receding in my rear-view mirror.

CHAPTER 9

Despite my being injured, this escape didn't seem nearly as dramatic as my last one, perhaps because I'd had time to book my ferry. Now all I had to do was get to St Malo in time!

As I drove, I reflected that, only a few short weeks ago, I might've thought this trait of making sudden departures was inherited from my father, you know, in my genes. However, now that I knew he wasn't even related to me the man I'd called 'dad' all my life, figured nowhere in the genes stakes!

The sunflowers were now gloriously at their best, fully open and turning their lovely faces to the sun. They looked so happy, I momentarily wished I could be a sunflower, until I recalled the fate in store for them. Left in the fields until they turned black and dried up, they'd be harvested and crushed for their seeds. I shuddered.

Anticipating I'd need to take it easy, I'd allowed all day for the normal five-hour drive, which soon proved sensible as, with only 40 miles covered, I was forced to stop because my injured leg was aching. I pulled into one of the areas off just the road in France, where motorists can stop and have a break. This one even had loos, although they were the 'hole in the ground' type - ugh!

After a rest, and a short 'crutch-walk', for exercise, I got back in my car. I daren't take painkillers, because I was driving, but it was a worry that my ankle was bothering me so early in the journey.

Thankfully, due presumably to the rest and exercise, my leg stopped hurting, but I wasn't going to take any chances.

I drove another 60 miles, then I stopped for lunch at a Routier, a sort of café/restaurant for people travelling. I knew this would have proper toilet facilities, and it did sort of. The fact that they were unisex stopped them being ideal! I hate having to walk past guys stood peeing, in order to get to a cubicle! No doubt Stèphane would once again think I was an English 'prune'.

After lunch I tried walking using only one crutch, which worked well and gave me a hand free for opening doors. My leg wasn't good, but it wasn't bothering me too much to continue.

It was now 2.p.m. with 150 miles still to go, but, as much of this would be over more minor roads, my progress would be slower, although I should still be in plenty of time. However, with only another 50 miles done, my leg was throbbing and I was forced to stop for a complete rest.

With difficulty, I put the passenger seat down flat, got into the back seat, and stretched my leg out, level with my bum. The relief was instant, so I locked all the doors and fell asleep.

It was 5pm when I awoke. I gingerly moved my leg, no pain, so I slid out of the car and went back to the driving seat. A slug of water, and I was ready to go.

Check-in time was from 8.30 pm and by 7pm I was close to the port, so, to avoid having to walk about a moving ship with crutches, I stopped again for a meal break, arriving at the port and checking in at 8.45pm. Boarding was from 9.30.

Because I'd explained about my injured leg, when booking, I learned I'd been allocated priority boarding, so, when instructed, I drove onto the ferry, and someone appeared with a wheelchair and took me to my room.

It was a smaller cabin this time, but well equipped for disabled passengers. I supposed that was me at the moment!

Sitting down on the edge of the bed, I wept with relief, sadness and disappointment. I don't think I'll ever recall ferries again without remembering tears.

Eating before boarding turned out to be an even better decision idea than I'd anticipated, because it was a pretty stormy crossing. I woke several times in the night and was finally wide awake at 5 a.m. – an hour before we were due to dock. I didn't want to oversleep, so I got up and dressed. I couldn't shower, because I didn't want to unbandage my leg, which was wonderfully pain free this morning.

Having made a cup of coffee I put everything together, ready to leave the ship. Then I sat thinking about the mine, my foray into it, what I thought I saw and Christophe's subsequent comment, regarding 'something shining in the roof crack' being a vein of silver ore

I glanced through my copies of Madame Richarde's paperwork, but it was the mention of 'The Coffin Tree' that grabbed and held my attention yet again. What could it possibly mean? If the treasure really was still hidden somewhere, I felt certain this was the clue that would lead to it, despite other people dismissing the ramblings of the old crone.

Then it struck me - I'd never know, because I was never going back. I sighed despondently.

Continental breakfast, ordered the night before, arrived, then someone took me down to my car, and, 30 minutes later I was on dry land again, and back to reality.

Firstly, I must catch up with Rosie and Jules, although I wasn't sure yet what I was going to tell them, and I really had to see, dear old John Harverson, Mum's solicitor. His emails had become quite insistent, and it was only fair to let him tie up the loose ends. It was also the only way I was going to stop him pestering me!

I must also contact Dave and Lynne, although I guessed they'd probably still want to meet up, even when I told them that I now knew the truth about Monsieur Richarde being my father.

I drove straight to my flat, mum's house would be for another day. I'd have to sort through it, and get rid of stuff, but I still felt sore at being having been deceived by her, all my life. She didn't even come clean after dad was killed. How could she deny me the facts about my own father?

I suppose if I were honest, I knew the answer to that, Christophe had supplied it when he said she was probably frightened of being left alone, and I had to admit he was right. I could well have just walked out.

I parked my car near the rear entrance to my block of flats as I could, took my bags to the lift one by one, then went up. Once in my flat I shut the door quietly behind me, hoping no-one would guess I was back. I needed this day to myself.

Over the weeks, in my contact with Jules and Rosie, I'd never even hinted as to where I was, and my latest email, sent a few hours ago, had simply said that I'd be "home tomorrow". I'd also suggested they might like to come round, then and perhaps we could go out for lunch.

Next, I organised Lynne and Dave for Sunday, and solicitor John for

Monday. As I did all of this, I realised the freedom I'd had by running away. For weeks now, no-one had expected anything of me, nor questioned me, other than superficially. No-one had intruded on my space in any way, but now I was back it would all be very different.

Jules and Rosie would try and drag every last detail from me, seeing it as their right – no secrets between 'bessie mates', but if I was right, about mum having told Lynne that Monsieur Richarde was my father, then it should be a short meeting.

However, I'd no idea why John Harverson, was pressing me so hard to go and see him. Did he too know the truth about my "real father"? I certainly felt he'd been evasive when I'd asked him if I was adopted.

I spread out the chateau paperwork on my small table, to look at one last time. There was no pointing keeping it and, in such a small flat I'd learnt to throw things away on a daily basis, or it was impossible to keep tidy. However, when I reached towards the shredder, tucked under my tiny desk, I couldn't do it. I just wasn't ready. Perhaps in a week or so. I shoved the papers into a folder, which I pushed onto the top of a cupboard.

Then I drove to the local shops and got some fresh bread, sadly not crusty like the baguette Francoise had brought every other day! A bottle of wine and a few essentials, then I added – naughtily – a small chocolate selection. Proper chocolate, not like the French stuff, which I hated, one of the few things I didn't love about the place!

When I got back, I opened all the windows to air my flat, which smelt musty from having been shut up for so long. The girls had replied to my emails, saying yes to lunch, but they'd bring something for us to eat, so we could sit on my terrace and dine al fresco.

This sounded grander than it was. My 'terrace' was a balcony, just big enough for a tiny table and 3 small chairs, but I was glad we weren't going anywhere public, in case I burst into tears, or anything else equally stupid, when I recounted my story, although possibly not all of it.

The weather was lovely, so I took a book and sat on said balcony. The sun was hot. I closed my eyes and pretended I was back in France, about to go in the pool, and that Christophe was not my brother. Now that I'd never see him again it didn't matter what I pretended. Sadly, there wasn't room for a parasol, so I soon had to go back indoors, to escape the intense heat of the sun.

I was restless, and my leg was itching with the boot, the bandaging, and the heat so I unpeeled it, stripped off and stood under a lukewarm shower, then towelled myself dry and put on a loose robe.

I began to wonder if my mother's house was any cooler. She certainly had a garden umbrella. Perhaps I should go there, but the thought of re-bandaging, and using my crutches again, in this heat, was too much.

All too soon it was evening, so, although this brought the relief of the temperature dropping, it also meant it was nearer to Jules and Rosie coming for lunch, probably staying all day. Might even be overnight, depending on how much we drank. I was dreading it, but this only made me feel guilty.

I reflected that if there was one thing I'd noticed about the French, there seemed to be very little over indulging. They were brought up with wine from an early age, albeit watered down, and it was taken with meals only. As for the meals themselves, they were eaten over a longer period, so generally, they ate less too. Even those wonderful meals at the Moulin Blanche, with Stèphane, although they'd been 5 courses, each course had been quite small. I sighed, it all seemed so long ago.

I wondered what Christophe would say about the amount Jules, Rosie and I drank when we got together. I was both sad and glad that he'd never know.

The following morning I flicked a duster around, then sat down with a cup of coffee to think about how much I was going to tell the girls, but I'd not come to any firm conclusion before they arrived.

'Wow look at you,' Rosie almost shrieked! 'You're like golden bronze'.

I smiled, and wondered if there was such I colour?

'So where've you been babe? And what've you done to your leg, looks as if you've like mangled it? Did you prang your wheels?'

They'd both had the sense to bring large floppy hats. Jules's plain straw, perched on her short blonde bob, and Rosie's looked like something she might've worn to a wedding, with its bright blue colour, matching ribbon and flower trim. It was very flattering, framing her dark curls. Their hats made me wonder why I'd not worn mine yesterday. Then I knew, it was because that was how it all began, when Stèphane took off my hat and sunglasses and recognised me, and I'd not wanted to be reminded, but now it would be silly not to wear it, so I did.

The food they'd brought was dumped, some on the kitchen worktop, some shoved in the fridge, and the first bottle opened. Not even 11a.m. Christophe and Stèphane would be horrified.

Stop it! Stop it! Stop it! I must stop thinking like this. I filled my glass to the brim, the girls grinned in approval.

'I had to get away after mum's funeral', I began and they nodded sympathetically. 'I was like spaced', Oh God I'd not spoken in this rubbish way since I went away. "Like" being every like other word. Why start again now?

So, making a conscious effort, I told them, calmly, that I'd been to France for a break.

'But why the secrecy babe, you like disappeared and we didn't know if you'd been like kidnapped.'

'From a funeral?' I asked and the humour of that situation started us giggling; well that and the wine.

End of the first bottle and onto the second, time to get food, I decided. All I'd told them so far was that I'd got in my car, crossed on a ferry and driven until the evening, then I stayed overnight at the 'Tour des cloches'.

They laughed hysterically as I told them about me being in the shower and thinking it was noisy plumbing. Jules brayed like a donkey, I'd never noticed that about her laugh before.

'Gross,' was all Rosie could say, but then Jules said with a frown, 'Didn't you realise that there'd be like bells? I mean 'cloches' and all that? Doesn't 'cloches' mean like bells?'

Suddenly I was in the chateau with Stèphane, who'd asked much the same question. I just wanted them to go, to be on my own. I could feel my eyes watering.

'Why're you cryin' babe? Was it that bad' Rosie asked?

'I'm crying with laughter,' I pretended, 'and yes it was awful'. Then I recounted the details of the hatchet-faced hotelier's wife, my 'missing' car and the scooter riders.' It sort of lifted my spirits.

'So what did you do? Like, deck the old bat and scarper?' Rosie said eagerly.

'I couldn't, because they'd taken my car away.'

'Wow.' Jules said earnestly, 'Poor you. Sounds like a horror film. Like trapped in the bell tower, no-one can hear her screams for the scooters roaring past. Unable to escape because they've like hidden her car, they drag her to cellar and she's like never seen again,' and with this she tipped her head back and drank straight from the bottle of wine – it was the third!.

I sat looking at them. Were these two females really my best friends. Their way of life suddenly seemed so stupid, as I suppose mine had become, before my mother died, and I'd overheard Dave and Lynne.

I'd been hoping to confide in them about Christophe, and how I felt, but now, not a chance. A couple bottles of wine and they'd probably blab to anyone who'd listen.

'So what happened next then 'babe?' Rosie jolted me out of my thoughts.

'Oh, not a lot' I replied carefully. 'I didn't have a plan, so I just drove down to where we had our holiday home.'

'Oh ya, I remember when you used disappear off, for like months, with your parents. We always hoped we might be like asked along, didn't we Jules?'

Jules agreed that they 'like'did.

'Oh, there wouldn't have been like room in the car, so we couldn't,' I replied, as though it had ever been considered a possibility - I don't think so!

My dad didn't like either of them. He didn't say much, but I once overheard him telling my mother that he thought they were 'flighty', which I'd assumed wasn't good.

'So did you like find your old gaff?' Jules asked.

'Yes, but all the houses were closed up, and there was no-one about.' Mostly true.

'So what did you do then? I mean you were like gone months!' Jules persisted.

So I told them I'd been lucky enough to get a temporary job, designing a new web site for a man I got talking to. Accommodation was part of my pay, well most of it I suppose.' Again mostly true.

Suddenly I just wanted them to go. My flat was now a tip, and, despite me making them go onto the terrace to smoke the ciggies they'd rolled, they'd left the door open and now the place smelt awful. I was sure my hair stank of it, my clothes too.

I must've had well over a bottle of wine, downed far too quickly and I felt sick. Christophe and Stèphane would be horrified if they could see me now.

I called a cab for the girls, saying that I wasn't feeling well, and showed them out, as soon as the buzzer went to say the taxi had arrived. Then, closing the door quickly behind them, I leaned against it and sobbed.

I wanted everything to be alright, but it never could be. I'd lost my father, my mother and the man I loved, and I'd found that my whole life had been built around deceit, by both my parents. It wasn't fair. I slid to the ground sobbing, crawled to the loo and threw up, then I crawled into bed.

I felt awful when I awoke next morning. My breath stank and my flat was still a tip. Thank goodness I was meeting Dave and Lynne at my mother's house, rather than them invading my personal space here.

After some muesli and toast, I felt a bit better, then I resolved that, after tomorrow's meeting with John Harverson, I'd move on from the dismal place in my life that I am now at.

I set to and cleared up my flat, took the bottles down to the bin and had some lunch. Just a bit of cheese and a boiled egg and soldiers, funny Sunday lunch, but it would do.

Then I got ready and went to my mother's house, arriving far too early and wishing this pointless meeting was over!

Her house smelt even more musty than my flat had done, so I opened lots of windows and found some perfumed air spray. I'd taken some milk with me, knowing, because I'd been staying there, that everything else would be to hand, then I sat waiting.

I idly opened a drawer and took out the photo frame which was upside down near the top of the drawer. It was a picture of my parents, in happier times I'd say.

I thought back to when we moved here. My mum had seemed more subdued than previously, and older somehow. I couldn't fully describe it to myself, but she wasn't the same.

We still went to France, and there she was more like her old self, as she happily drove us to places, while my dad pottered about. We were lucky enough to know someone who would look after my dog and the chickens, back here.

I sat looking at the picture and wondered how long ago it had been taken, and why it was upside down in the drawer. After my dad died, my mum had removed all photographs, except ones of me – on my own, or with her. She wouldn't talk about my father, except to say that he wasn't the man I thought he was. Well, no, if he wasn't actually my father then that was clearly an understatement!

I'm sure they been happy before we moved to this house. I was only eight then, but I remembered laughter and fun at our previous home, not something I could associate with this place at all. Stuck out in the country, miles from nowhere, with no transport, my mum must've felt pretty isolated at times. I certainly did.

Then, after they sold the French house things got worse. My dad was away a lot, mostly in Holland, with work, and my mum became really depressed. I couldn't wait to get away; but even going to 'Uni' and what I studied, was decided for me by my dad - which he wasn't!

'You can do anything you want after that,' he'd said 'but there'll always work for graphic designers, so you'll never be short of a job opportunities.'

He'd been right, but I still wondered sometimes what it would have been like to go to a proper art college. I always carry a tiny box of water colours and a little sketch pad with me, but having seen Stèphane's wonderful pictures, in his studio at the chateau, any sketching and painting I did I kept secret.

Thankfully I found graphic artistry also fascinated me, and the advances have been exciting and, after I'd completed my degree, I'd followed it up with a one-year photography and interior design course.

I looked around me at this drab uninviting room, feeling guilty that I hadn't been more sympathetic towards my mum.

I glanced at my watch, they'd be here soon, so I put the kettle on. Hopefully, I could give them a drink and get rid of them quickly. Biscuits on a plate, cups on a tray. I sat down again.

While I waited, I thought about Dave and Lynne. They may seem like strangers now, but once upon a time I knew them well. Lynne taught me to knit and sew and I used to pop round to use her sewing machine.

They also had 3 sons, of similar ages to the Richardes, Tom who was my age, almost exactly my age, I was one day older than him. I used this age advantage to boss him about. Then there was Jack, a couple of years older and Paul, who was the oldest. I wondered where they were now.

When we were small, Dave would crawl around, on the floor and Tom and I would ride on his back, then he'd play board games with us. I smiled at the memories. My own father hated board games, and never crawled round on the floor.

I remember my mum and Lynne used to have coffee together, and would baby sit for each other, and sometimes they'd go shopping. We were always in France for the summer weather, but we always had some time with them over Christmas.

As I thought of these happier times, I mellowed towards Dave and Lynne; after all, I had no reason to dislike or distrust them, they were just old friends my parents lost touch with, so whatever they had to tell me, it really wasn't their fault, I mistakenly persuaded myself

The doorbell rang. I jumped, and glanced out of the window, then I opened the door and invited them in.

Having briefly explained my bandaged leg and crutch, being from a tumble, I made tea for us all, (they'd declined coffee) and Lynne carried the tray into the sitting room for me.

I sat down expectantly. This shouldn't take long.

They asked how I'd been keeping, what I'd been doing with myself, career-wise, then, eventually, thinking they'd never get to the point, I said 'I'm afraid I've got rather a lot to do, you know sorting this house and everything, so . . .. '

'Of course,' Dave spoke quietly. 'We were most surprised when you said you knew why we wanted to see you Fay. I guess your mother must've decided to tell you everything?'

'No, actually she didn't, I found out recently, while I was in France, not surprisingly.'

But, strangely, they both looked very surprised, so I added, 'That Monsieur Richarde, of the Chateau Richarde, is my father. I turned to Lynne, 'I can only assume my mother confided this to you?'

They frowned at one another, with a mixture of confusion and astonishment. It was clearly not how they'd expected the conversation to go. Now I was confused too.

There was complete silence, then Dave said, 'I don't know why you were told that Fay, because I'm your father'.

I looked at Lynne in amazement, 'and you don't mind him claiming this rubbish?'

'It was a long time ago, well of course 26 years,' Lynne said calmly.

'A brief fling, very brief. Lynne forgave me, thank God, and we put it behind us, but, not unnaturally, I've wondered about you many times, over the years.'

'So why did you choose to tell me now?' I was angry. 'In fact, why did you have to tell me at all, and why then does Monsieur Richarde claim that I am his? In fact my father could be just who I always thought he was.' I was so close to tears. I just wanted them to say they'd made a mistake and go.

Clearly this conversation hadn't gone how any of us had thought it would.

'Why don't you go for a walk dear, and give Fay and I a chance to talk,' Lynne said and, reluctantly, Dave left.

Lynne came over and sat beside me. 'I can't begin to imagine how you must be feeling', she said, but why don't you tell me about the

Richardes, and see if we can make some sense of it. Perhaps, you know, with the language thing there's been some misunderstanding?'.

'What misunderstanding can there be, when the man you're in love with tells you he's your brother?' I sobbed and Lynne cradled me in her arms, while I wept buckets.

'Start from the funeral,' Lynne persuaded gently.

'I overheard you and Dave saying that it was time I was told about my parentage. I was really shocked at your words, and so stressed over my mother's death and everything, that I couldn't face, or even begin to imagine what you were going to tell me' I began.

'Oh Fay I'm so sorry, that's dreadful. We should've been more careful, so what then?'

'I went to my mother's house, where I'd been living, with her, for the last few weeks and checked out my birth certificate, but it told me nothing I didn't know, so I just grabbed a few things, got in my car and drove to France.' I didn't bother saying this was to avoid seeing her and Dave.

I didn't know where to go, so I headed for the area I knew, and went to look at our old holiday home. Oh, I'd loved it there so much, but, just like when we left where we lived near you, my father suddenly sold it and we never went back. I was devastated, because, even at the age of 15, I knew I was in love with Christophe and wanted to spend the rest of my life with him. He lived at the chateau.' I added.

'What did your mother say about any of this?' Lynne asked

'We never talked about anything personal really although, when I was younger we drew and painted together, and went shopping occasionally, but she was often distant. I don't think she was like that when I was small, but I can't be sure.'

Lynne nodded 'No, she wasn't, she was a happy, very loving mother, and a very good friend.'

'Anyway' I continued, 'I was surprised to find that the Richardes still owned the chateau where I'd played as a child. They have 3 sons too. Stèphane, my age saw me looking at our old home and demanded to know who I was. He had a big beard and I didn't recognise him.

Anyway, when he recognised me, he took me over to the chateau for something to eat, then, realising I had nowhere to go, he said I could stay for a few days, if I looked after the dogs while he went away.'

'Where was the one you'd been in love with?'

'Christophe, oh he was in Paris. I'd never really got over him, but I assumed that Stèphane had told him I was there, and, since he made no effort to come and see me, I had to accept that he wasn't interested.'

'So you never saw him?'

'Yes I did, eventually', and I recounted my disastrous venture into the silver mine, my accident and Christophe's visit to the hospital, where he told me how he'd loved me in his teens, but then his mother had told him I was his sister.

'I felt sick', I sobbed.

She hugged me close and stroked my hair 'I'm sure you did. How is your leg now?'

What? My world had been blown apart - and she wanted to know how my leg was!

'Much better' I replied politely, wishing she'd just go.

'So then what?' she prompted.

'Christophe took me back to the chateau, but I couldn't bear it. I'm still in love with him, and I just couldn't see or feel about him as a brother, so I came home.'

'When did you get back?'

'A couple of days ago.'

'And have you heard from him since?'

'He has no way of contacting me. He had to go abroad and so, while he was gone, I left him a note, explaining how I still felt, and asking him not to try and find me.'

It was such a relief to say it all out loud,

Lynne sat looking thoughtful, assessing the situation, then we heard footsteps on the path.

'That'll be Dave, you stay there and rest your leg, I'll let him in,' Lynne said, and she went to the front door, pulling the sitting room door almost closed behind her.

'How is everything?' I heard Dave ask.

'Confused,' Lynne replied. Then Dave said something more, and I heard another voice

They came into the room and Dave smiled at me, 'I found this young man wandering along the road, trying to find this address. He swears he knows you.'

Christophe appeared in the doorway.

'OMG no!' I exclaimed. 'I asked you not to try and find me.' I turned to Dave and Lynne 'this is the young man whose father is . . . .

'Not your father,' Christophe finished.

'What did you say?' I almost shrieked.

He pulled me to my feet. "I'm not your brother". I felt faint, as he wrapped his strong arms around me, holding me tight, making me feel safe, but dizzy with confusion. I closed my eyes, wishing I could stay like this forever.

After a minute or two, I realised that Dave and Lynne were waiting patiently.

I explained to Christophe who they were, as in the couple who'd been at my mother's funeral and had said they had something to tell me about my parentage, then I turned to Lynne and said 'This is Christophe'.

'Ah Fay,' she smiled, 'I can see why you would fall in love with him. I think I'd find it very easy too'.

Dave looked at her in surprise and we all laughed, and I suddenly remembered that Lynne had always been brilliant at defusing any situation.

'Perhaps the young man, Christophe, could explain his statement?' Dave said and we all sat down.

'Of course,' Christophe replied. 'I've been to see my parents, and it seems my mother jumped to a wrong conclusion, all those years ago. My father is furious with her and she has apologised, although it's not enough.'

'You've been to Réunion?' I asked incredulously, 'You mean that was the overseas trip you had to make?'

'Oui.'

'Christophe's parents have a holiday home, on the French dependency of Réunion' I explained, adding 'It's an island in the Indian Ocean'.

'How lovely,' Lynne smiled. 'Well,' she said as she took Dave's arm, 'I think we should go now and leave these two to talk, but I'm sure you'll understand Christophe, that we'd like to hear the full story, and we need to talk more with Fay, so could we pick you tomorrow morning and take you both out for lunch?

She was right, we did still need to talk, and there was no point in delaying it.

'Thank you, yes,' Christophe replied, putting a reassuring hand on my shoulder. I felt safe, having him here, making my decisions for me.

They all went into the hall, then closing the front door behind them, Christophe came back and sat down, beside me, and held me close.

'Are you sure we're not related?' I begged for reassurance.

'Of course I'm sure, and I'll now tell you what happened. 'I went to reunion because I needed my mother to confirm what she'd said, eleven years ago, about you being my sister.

At the time she asked me to tell no-one else, and I didn't, until Stèphane came to Paris, to inform me you'd come back and he was going to marry you, so of course I was forced to tell him the truth.

Then, when you fell and went to hospital, I could see the way you felt when you saw me, so I had to tell you also. This then made it necessary for me to see my mother, to make her aware that I'd had to tell both you and Stèphane everything. I needed it to be face-to-face as I wanted to say all of this in front of my father, because it was time he confirmed it also.

However, he was shocked and denied it, demanding to know why she'd thought such a thing. She then explained that she'd seen him and your mother together in the barn, with their arms around each other, and the following summer, when your parents returned, they had a baby with them - you.'

My father was really angry to learn she'd then told me you were my sister, but he was even more cross to hear that she'd also told your father this.

'It seems my father was comforting your mother, because he'd found her in tears. She'd then confessed to him that she'd had a liaison, with someone in England, and thought she might be pregnant by this other man.

Your mother couldn't decide whether to tell your father or not, and my father said he'd advised her to say nothing.

Anyway Fay, I believe we now know the reason for your holiday home being sold years later, as it followed my mother telling your father what she believed to be the truth,'

My parents are now not speaking. Papa because, with no proof, my mother believed he'd cheated on her, and maman is silent because she knows she's done wrong.

I left them to sort it out, but I told my mother that, assuming you'd agree to marry me, I didn't want her at our wedding.'

Then he kissed me like I'd never been kissed in my life before.

When we came up for air, he said 'It's been a long journey from Reunion, do you think I can I have a cup of coffee? '

'Of course,' I laughed, but Just before I went to make it, I quickly brought him up to date on what Dave and Lynne had said.

'So, he must have been your mother's mystery lover?' Christophe said sleepily.

Floating on air, I made the coffee and prepared a sandwich for him, but, when I took it into the living room, the fatigue from the journey had caught up with him and Christophe was fast asleep on the sofa.

I looked at him, unable to believe all that had happened in the last couple of hours. Was he really mine? Had he really said he wanted to marry me? Then I sat gazing at him for ages, until I too got sleepy and I went upstairs to my room.

CHAPTER 10

It was late in the morning when I awoke, and I wondered if I'd dreamt yesterday's events. I opened my bedroom door - total silence greeted me so, was Christophe really in the sitting room, or would I find it empty.

I sighed, went into the bathroom, washed and dressed and went downstairs then I stood in the hall for a moment or two, before I plucked up courage to open the sitting room door, but there he was, really here and still asleep! I quietly put the coffee maker on.

Since I'd not been expecting to be here, there was no food, other than biscuits, then the doorbell rang, making me jump. I looked at my watch. Goodness, it was 10 o'clock, it must be Lynne and Dave.

I opened the door and let them in, just as a sleepy Christophe emerged into the hall, behind me asking where the bathroom was, kissed me 'good morning' and went upstairs with his bag.

We made small talk until he came back down, showered, shaved and in fresh clothes and I gave him coffee and biscuits, explaining why there was no other food. I added that I'd better go to my flat and change, since we were going out for lunch and Christophe said he'd come with me.

Dave offered to take us in his car, so I left Lynne with mother's front door key, promising not to be long. Then Christophe and I went up to my flat, leaving Dave in the car, and I think he was quite shocked by just how tiny, and cramped, my living space was. He opened the glass door and went out onto the balcony.

Leaving him to enjoy the sunshine, I put on fresh clothes and make up, poured orange juice for us both, and took it, and a couple of bananas, out to my tiny balcony table, where we quickly ate. Then, just as we finished and Christophe leaned over to kiss me, the doorbell rang.

Thinking it was Dave, I sighed and went to open the door, discovering, to my horror, that it was Rosie and Jules.

'Hi just passing, late work start today, so thought we'd like call in and see how you're doin' babe,' and they tried to come past me, into the hall, then, before I could say anything Christophe appeared.

'OMG, is he drop dead gorgeous or what?' Rosie squealed and swayed against Jules who, open mouth agreed with idiotic nods. 'No wonder you're tryin' to like get rid of us,' (big wink), and she introduced herself, as they both stood gazing at him.

'Christophe Richarde,' he said and kissed each of their hands.

Rosie turned to Jules 'Oooh, and he's like très Français as well,' she cooed. It was so embarrassing. 'So this is why you had to stay in France for like six weeks is it?' wink, wink.

'I think someone's been telling porkies,' Jules said.

Christophe was looking confused, by the Rosie/Jules babble.

'We have to go Christophe,' I said, 'Sorry girls, but we have a lunch date and our chauffeur's waiting downstairs.

I grabbed my handbag, locked the patio door, shepherded everyone onto the landing and pulled my front door closed.

'Don't suppose you want us to like tag along do you?' Rosie grinned revoltingly, even leeringly, at Christophe.

'No', I said firmly. 'We're someone's guests, we can't possibly take you as well.'

Then I looked at Christophe's face, horror that I even knew Rosie and Jules was written all over it.

We all got into the lift and went downstairs, with the girls ogling Christophe, and looking questioningly at the bag he was carrying.

Christophe and I said goodbye to the girls and got into Dave's car, but then, on the way to my mother's, I suddenly remembered my appointment with John Harverson!

Immediately we arrived I explained this, and Dave again offered to act as chauffeur, with Lynne reminding me that we still needed to talk, so it was agreed I'd call them so they could pick me up when my meeting finished, and we'd talk over lunch.

Christophe said he'd come with me and, arriving dead on time, we were shown straight into John's office. He kissed me on the cheek, asked how I was, then said 'I need to see you on your own Fay,' looking pointedly at Christophe.

I sat down. 'Are you afraid he's a foreign gigolo I picked up, who's only after my money?' I laughed.

It was clear from his embarrassed expression that was exactly what he thought.

'How long have you known Miss Barker?' he asked Christophe, trying to make it sound like a casual, conversational enquiry.

'How old are you now, 26?' Christophe asked me, and I nodded, 'then I've known Miss Barker for 26 years'.

'Oh,' a slightly deflated John responded 'and your relationship to Miss Barker?'

'We're soon to be married.'

John, trying not to show his surprise, looked to me for confirmation. I, trying not to show my own surprise, nodded.

'Yes, a few things to sort out, but that's the plan,' I agreed happily – well actually ecstatically!

'I see,' he said, but he still looked unhappy. They both sat down.

'You can look him up on the internet. He's a well-respected architect in France, not a fortune hunter. Anyway, I don't have a fortune to hunt.' John raised an eyebrow, I frowned.

Christophe handed over his phone, which showed a photograph, and details of his considerable architectural success and his status as a Director of an Architectural company in Paris.

Reassured, John opened a folder and explained the complications of my parents' wills.

I'd never seen my father's will, but I believed half of the house had been my mother's, and half my father's. I assumed my father had left his half and the rest of his estate to my mother, when he died, and I understood my mother had made over her half to me before she died.

However, John said it wasn't as straightforward as that, and we needed time for him to explain properly, and I kept looking at my watch.

I apologised and asked why it was complicated.

'I don't think your father wanted you asking too many questions. A secret perhaps.' He replied and, from his shuffling of his papers and avoiding looking at me, as he said this, I was sure he knew more.

I took a deep breath, 'I've learned recently that I may not be his daughter,' I said.

He nodded, showing no surprise at all, so this was probably not the secret.

'and do you know who your father is?'

'I believe so, we're having lunch with him and his wife, I'll know more then,' I looked at my watch again.

'Well, in that case, we'll call this a preliminary meeting Fay. I assume you'll be with Miss Barker for lunch?' Strangely, John seemed reassured when Christophe said 'yes'.

Was he now concerned that it was Dave who was after my money, such as it might be?

'We'll finish now Fay, with the one item that needs your urgent attention.' He took a deep breath. 'As well as the house you lived in with your parents, your father had a property elsewhere, to be left to another woman., not your mother.

'What!' I exclaimed and he put up a hand to stop me, before I could say more.

'Another complication,' he continued, 'is that his will didn't leave his half of the house to your mother, but 'temporarily' also to the other woman.' Again he put his hand up to stop me speaking.

'However, that half of the house was to become yours on the death of your mother, but what you must decide, and immediately, is whether to contest the other property, which was left to this woman.'

'Do you know who she is?' I asked, bubbling angrily inside.

'She's Dutch, and I understand he spent part of each year with her.'

OMG. More secrets. The long visits to Holland on 'business' trips!'

I was now remembering the foreign woman at his funeral. I'd asked her who she was, and she'd said she was from the Dutch company my father did a lot of work for. I remember thinking that he must've been highly thought of, for them to send a representative, but it had been yet more lies!

John hesitated again, then continued, 'As your mother hadn't worked since she married, she had no personal pension plan, so your father had made a number of investments in her name. He invested wisely and they've grown significantly over the years.

Because she couldn't touch these until she was 65, and sadly, she never reached this age, they remain untouched. So, together with the house, you've inherited estate well in excess of,' he took a deep breath, 'A million pounds.' He studied the reactions of us both., adding 'I would suggest you mention none of this to the people you are lunching with'.

My eyes had opened like saucers, and I was speechless and gaping like fish!

'There's much to be discussed, but you can see now,' he looked at Christophe, 'why I was cautious about your credentials. I hope you understand?

'Of course,' Christophe nodded, 'and no doubt we'll appreciate your advice on managing this bequest'.

John looked relieved.

'I thought you were joking about me coming into money,' I said, adding 'or perhaps not', when I saw his unsmiling face, clearly horrified that I might think him capable of such levity.

'May I ask, Monsieur Richarde, what your financial circumstances are. You've shown me that you are a successful architect, but . .'

I protested.

'Non, ma petite, it's a perfectly acceptable question and I'm pleased that monsieur 'Arverson is so diligent. My financial position sir, is that I own one third of the Company I'm a Director of. I also have an apartment in the very best part of Paris, on which I owe no money. Then, I have financial investments in a number of other Parisian properties,' he looked at me and added, 'plus there is the Chateau.'

'The chateau?' I stared at him in amazement, 'you own the Chateau Richarde?'

'The very same,' he smiled. 'I bought it from my father when he decided they would to spend most of their time in Paris, and the rest on Réunion. My older brother, Romain, did not want it and my younger brother, Stèphane, had no money, so I bought it to keep it in the family, and told Stèphane that he could live there.'

That wasn't quite how Stèphane had told it, but I suppose it didn't matter.

'So that that was why Stèphane did as he was told, when you gave him orders, and why he felt he had to go to Paris, and tell you that he wanted to marry me.' I said, adding 'He couldn't just move me into the chateau permanently, not without your permission?'

John Harverson by this time was looking totally confused.' You were going to marry Monsieur Richarde's brother?'

'Long story' I laughed, 'perhaps another time.'

'Yes, another time,' it was John's turn to look at his watch. 'Where are you meeting for lunch?'

'We're not, they're picking us up here, as soon as I call them,' and I took my mobile out of my bag. 'Their car is in your car park, and they've gone for a walk.'

'In that case, I'd very much like to meet them.' John said so I called them, asking them to come up to John's office, and his secretary ushered them in a few minutes later.

I introduced them to John, who said, 'I understand you've told Fay that you believe you are her father?

'Well, we'd agreed to tell Fay the full details at lunch time, but yes, that is so, however, it's based on more than a belief.

Then he told us how my mother had contacted him, when she knew she was terminally ill, saying she was certain he was my father. She'd asked that he have a DNA test to confirm it and, since I'd have nobody when she was gone, she'd could die happier, if she knew he'd be there for me if I ever needed help.

I was shocked and humbled by her love and concern.

Dave continued, 'Naturally, I talked to Lynne first, she agreed, then I did a DNA test. Fay's mother, somehow, got a DNA sample from her, and the results confirmed it. There's no doubt. I have the results here,' and he produced a piece of paper, which he handed over to John, although I couldn't help thinking it should've been given to me.

Phew I breathed, so there it was, he absolutely and totally is my father. I looked at Lynne and wondered how she really felt. Her face gave nothing away.

Looking at John she said, 'I was always fond of Fay as a child', then she turned to me 'and, since none of it was your fault, I saw no reason to object.'

'DNA is a fascinating topic,' John said, conversationally - and a bit weirdly I thought. 'If I were younger, I'd train in medical research. As it is, the study of DNA has become my hobby, in fact, I often ask clients if they'd mind giving me samples – for my research,' he looked quizzically at us.

'I have no problem with that,' Christophe said.

Lynne and Dave offered theirs too, but, having just learned that I'd been tricked by my own mother, I was more reluctant. Why hadn't she just asked? Although I had to admit that I'd have probably thought she'd lost her marbles, so maybe she did the right thing.

So I agreed to the sample, after all, what harm could it do?

Swabs done, John said Christophe and myself must make another appointment, to discuss "what we'd talked about earlier," referring to my inheritance I supposed.

'I have to return to Paris, later today, so it'll be Fay on her own,' Christophe said, and the two men shook hands, while I looked at Christophe in horror. Going back to Paris today? No!

But all I said was 'And I want to get my mother's house sorted out, and on the market. It is completely mine now isn't it?'' (I thought I 'd better check.)

'Yes indeed' John confirmed. 'There'll be death duties of course, and there' still the decision to be made regarding 'the other property' I mentioned. The rest can wait for the moment.

'I can give you my decision immediately, regarding the 'other property', I want nothing from the Dutch woman.'

For a moment I thought Christophe was going to challenge my decision, but, since it had nothing to do with him, I ignored this.

 John thanked me and we said our goodbyes, he kissed me on the cheek and we left.

We were all very quiet in Dave's car. I was thinking over what John Harverson had said, and Christophe was probably doing the same. I also knew now why Christophe had brought his bag with him, when he left my flat.

'When do you have to leave?'

'My flight is 5 o'clock this afternoon.' He held me close. 'It won't be for long, I promise.'

We studied the restaurant menu then gave our orders to the waitress, after which Dave recounted how my mother, who'd been unable to conceive for some reason, went to babysit his and Lynne's children. Lynne was visiting her elderly mother, and Dave was away working but he finished early, and came home later that evening.

'I can make no excuses for my behaviour. Lynne and I had been going through a tricky patch, and your mother tempted me into having sex on the sofa. I'm sorry if that sounds like me blaming her, but that is how it was. I've often wondered if it was pre-planned. I suppose now we'll never know.'

I kept looking at Lynne, while he was speaking, but she seemed quite calm about it.

'Not long after that, your parents went to France and when they returned your mother was pregnant. I knew that it could be mine, and I was appalled, not least because I thought Lynne would leave me if she found out. But your mother behaved as though it was her husband's child, and I was relieved, and of course, as far as I knew then, it could well have been his.

Lynne and your mother's friendship carried on, and I decided to forget about what happened, but, one day your father and I were replacing some fencing together, while your mother and Lynne had gone shopping. They were both 6 months pregnant. Your mother with you and Lynne with Tom.'

Lynne winced as he said this, which I thought a bit odd, but Dave didn't appear to notice and carried on.

'Stupidly I said 'not long now,' and your father said "No, more's the pity."

'Oh, come on, you must be looking forward to being a father,' I said, and he replied, "I'm not going to be a father".

My heart nearly stopped, then he followed up by telling me that he'd had tests done and they proved that he couldn't father a child. I was pretty certain then that you were mine.

I asked if your mother knew about his test results, and he said, "No I thought she'd leave me, she's so desperate to have a baby, but I didn't think she'd go with someone else to get one. I was thinking adoption."

I was horrified. I felt both sorry for him, and as guilty as hell.'

'So no-one wanted me then?' I said quietly.

'Your mother did, desperately, and your father changed when you were born. He told me that he couldn't love you more if you were biologically his child. I was relieved that he'd had such a change of heart, and thought that was the end of it, although every time I saw you, I looked for tell-tale signs that you were mine.'

'So, what changed?' I asked, because it all sounded as though it was leading up to something.

'Well, when you were eight, I was at your house, waiting for your father to come home from work, to ask him if he'd give me a hand over the weekend. You were in the garden, and I never saw him come in, because I was too busy watching you through the window.'

'When I turned, and saw him, I was sure he'd guessed. This was reinforced when I mentioned needing a hand at the weekend and he said, curtly, that he was busy, and showed me to the door.'

A few days later your house was empty and you'd gone.

'I was devastated,' Lynne said. My closest friend and her family just upped and left, without saying a word.'

'Lynne was beside herself and kept asking over and over, why? She became convinced it was something she'd done and got quite depressed. In the end, I had to tell her the truth.'

Christophe was holding my hand.

Then Lynne spoke, 'I was so relieved that your leaving was not my fault, nothing I'd done, that I agreed to forgive Dave. Things were pretty rocky for a while, but I've never regretted that decision. I did, and do, love him very much'. By now they too were holding hands.

'It still didn't make me your child,' I said, in a detached manner. 'There might have been other men.'

'No,' Dave replied. 'She was a good and decent woman, just desperate for a baby.'

'Anyway,' Lynne added, 'As we told your solicitor, Dave has the DNA test results to prove it.'

Dave produced an envelope 'This is a copy of the results, both of yours and of mine, and the conclusion the experts reached.'

Without opening it I put it in my bag. I didn't thank him. I wasn't even sure how I felt.

CHAPTER 11

There was a difficult silence, then Christophe said to Lynne 'Madame, I think you are a truly great woman. Your understanding, and acceptance, is extraordinary and you sir,' he addressed Dave 'I hope you appreciate that fact'.

'I certainly do,' Dave replied, looking chastised.

I took a sharp intake of breath. Something wasn't right here. Despite misgivings, I was glad Dave had been frank with me, about my mother and him, but I certainly wasn't happy at Christophe professing his opinion. If anyone was going to say what they thought it should be me.

There was more silence then I said to Lynne 'It's strange, but when I was small I sometimes felt you were more a mother to me than she was, the time you spent with me, sewing clothes and baking plus knitting squares to make blankets for charities and I remember painting on blouses and t-shirts, it was you who taught me to do them all, well you and Nana Molly. My father's mother' I explained to Christophe, adding that she'd died when I was seven.

'I remember her well,' Lynne smiled.

'I think I looked on you as a second mother' I continued. 'I was really upset when we moved away, but only for a few weeks, then I was given a puppy.'

We all laughed at this children's logic, and another over-emotional situation was diffused, but then I added, addressing Dave, 'I'm sorry but I just can't call you 'dad', even though you taught me how to play chess and other board games.'

He smiled understandingly. 'You were an excellent pupil.'

A waitress appeared with our food,

'So, what now for you two?' Lynne asked brightly. 'Did you say wedding bells were on the cards?'

'Yes, and the sooner the better. I'd like to say three weeks?' Christophe replied, then he looked at me, with that winning smile, and I went weak.

'Three weeks,' I repeated?

'Oh, I'm sorry, is that too long?'

I play punched his shoulder, and he feigned injury, and we all laughed, but I thought Lynne and Dave looked concerned. Strange how anyone watching would have thought we were just a normal family out for lunch, when we were anything but!

'You haven't actually asked me to marry you,' I reminded him.

'That's because you might say no,' Christophe replied, and again we laughed. 'Ok, ok' he held up his hands at my expression, 'Ferelith Barker will you marry me?'

'Of course I will,' I breathed, but why did he make me feel I'd forced him into asking?

Lynne and Dave congratulated us, Christophe leaned over and kissed me, and a bottle of champagne arrived at our table.

'There's a condition to my acceptance'

'Anything, anything at all,' Christophe said earnestly.

'You promise,'

'Of course.'

'I still want to try and find the lost treasures.' Christophe's face fell.

'You just promised' I reminded him.

Christophe looked cross, as though he thought I'd trapped him into agreeing, and, again, I found this disconcerting.

Lynne changed the subject by asking ''So, are French weddings very different to English weddings?'

Up to this point I hadn't even considered that they might be.

As we ate our main course Christophe said, 'I've never been to an English wedding, so it's difficult for me to say, but I suspect they're more informal here.

Then he explained the strict protocol in France, how a couple announce their wish to marry and a betrothal party is held, so that the families of both couples can meet and get acquainted. This is usually a whole weekend, sometimes longer.

Lynne and I looked at one another. 'Are you thinking what I'm thinking?' she said

'That if it happened here, most engagements would be off?' I said and she nodded, and we both went into helpless giggles.

'Ah, le weekend,' I laughed, then explained to Lynne and Dave that the French, not having a word have adopted the English into their language.

'Informally, not officially I think,' Christophe added pompously.

'Well anyway that bit's easy,' I smiled, 'since I don't have a family', then I saw Dave's face.

'I'm so sorry, I didn't mean, Oh…'

'It's o.k.,' Lynne patted my hand. 'it's going to take time to get used to the situation, we understand that. You may not even want to see us again, and we'll accept whatever you decide.'

Christophe then carried on with his description of a French betrothal, telling us that both families must be happy about the engagement, if they aren't then the bride to be doesn't wear her ring. The families must then talk until they reach harmony.

'You're not serious?' I said in amazement.

'Of course I'm serious, although perhaps not so much is decided by the families at our ages.'

'When all is well, the girl can then wear the ring the man has bought for her, and, in return she gives him a watch' Christophe continued, adding 'For us that is not necessary, as I have several watches.'

Again, decision made for me. I frowned.

Christophe continued with the French wedding ritual, telling us that, next, pre-invitation letters are sent, with the date. Then guest lists are made, and, once the ceremony is booked, the witnesses are chosen and the formal invitations sent out.

I learned that even there are two sorts. One to close family and friends, plus the bride and groom's personally chosen supporters, inviting them to the ceremony, which is conducted by the Maire, in the Commune, where the wedding is being held, and where either the bride or groom must have been living for 30 days before the ceremony.

Still thinking of the chateau I protested, 'but neither of us will have been living in the commune for 30 days If we're to marry in three weeks' time.'

Christophe frowned. "I live in Paris, we marry in Paris, it's not a problem".

My face fell. Paris! So my dream of a wedding at the Chateau was not to be - decided for me again!

Christophe didn't even notice my disappointment, and continued, with the complicated French ritual, but I'd stopped listening.

I came back to his explanation to hear him saying that It's usual for marriage formalities, at the Mairie, to take place in the evening, the couple are then legally married, and the reception is usually held the following day.

'You do not do this here?' he asked when he saw Lynne and I looking confused.

I explained to him that marriages in Britain usually include all of the guests, both the service and the reception, which are often the same place, perhaps a stately home, or an hotel.'

Then we learned that such things were not possible in France, as all ceremonies must take place at a Mairie, or Hotel de Ville (town hall).

'Except church weddings,' Lynne remarked, but then we found out that church weddings were not legal in France, but just for the blessing of a couple. My head was spinning. There was far too much to remember.

'What about bridesmaids?' Lynne asked and, again, Christophe looked blank. I explained what they were, only to learn, yet again it's quite different in France.

'The attendants of the bride are small children only, called flower girls and flower boys, who walk in front of the bride,' Christophe told us.

Well that ruled out Rosie and Jules. They might behave like children, but they were most definitely adults. Then he started to explain about the bride and grooms' supporters, and I asked him to stop.

'You need not concern yourself my love;' he answered, stroking my hand reassuringly. 'I will organise everything, and I think, with your mother's death so recent you'll want to keep it as small and informal as possible?'

It was said as though it were a question, but yet again, I felt Christophe had already decided.

'I need to think about it,' I replied, but it all felt too rushed and I'd rather wait a little longer, so we could be married at the local village Mairie, with the reception afterwards at the chateau. Paris didn't figure in my planning! Stupidly, I said none of this.

Thinking I'd be on safer ground I asked casually, 'Will Stèphane be your best man?' but this only added more confusion, and we learned that there is no best man at French weddings!

'So who do you go to the Mairie with?'

I nearly fell off my chair when he answered in all seriousness, 'The groom arrives with his mother' – (not even his father) – his mother!

It was difficult to know what to say, especially since he'd forbidden his mother from attending!

'Will your friends come to our wedding do you think?' Christophe asked, trying to sound casual. He could only mean Jules and Rosie, and his tone conveyed that he hoped not.

'I'm not sure,' I replied, but I was actually thinking "It will be my decision."

'I believe you have two brothers?' Lynne said. Christophe nodded and the conversation became more general. Lunch was soon over and it was time to take Christophe to the airport.

It broke my heart to say goodbye, but before we did, he asked me to wait, then he disappeared into an office, emerging a few minutes later, with some pieces of paper in his hand. He looked triumphant as he announced that he'd just downloaded the necessary forms for our wedding.

'Just put your signature on these my darling, you don't need to waste time reading. It's only bureaucratic paperwork, and he smiled as he looked into my eyes. 'Full name, and place and date of birth, where I've put the crosses, and your signature at the bottom, and I'll fill in the rest.'

My stomach did somersaults. It was really happening, I still couldn't believe it, then, not wanting to argue with him, I signed the forms and Christophe kissed me and was gone.

'What are you going to do about everything, if you're intending to live in France?' Lynne asked, as we left the airport.

I wasn't sure what she meant, so she said 'Your mother's house, her clothes and other belongings, your flat, your furniture and your car, things like that?'

'I haven't thought about anything like that. In fact, I don't think I can cope with it all,' I wailed, my spirits dragged down by Christophe's departure.

'Look, Fay, I don't want you to think we're interfering, but we'd be happy to lend a hand if it would help. I had to deal with everything for my own mother, so I know what's involved, and it's emotionally challenging to do it all on your own.'

Relieved, I grabbed Lynne's offer with both hands.

So, the following morning we began the onerous task of disposing of my parents' lives – which was the only way I could see it.

Thankfully Christophe had called last night, when he got back to his Paris apartment, and again this morning. I missed him so much that I ached, but hearing his voice made it more bearable. I told him my plans, and he sounded pleased that Lynne and Dave would be with me.

'You'll clear the house quickly, and your flat, and then sell them both? He asked, then he enquired about the selling process in England. I told him what I knew, and then we said goodnight.

So, all I had to do now was tie up all the loose ends and go to France and marry Christophe. At long last I could look forward to a settled and happy future. . . . . .

CHAPTER 12

Next day, Tuesday, Christophe called me before he went into his meeting, then I met Lynne and Dave at what was legally now my house.

Lynne suggested I begin by calling a couple of estate agents, for valuations. They came later that morning and both thought it a good-sized family home, with huge garden, perfect for a growing family. Then the first suggested a good price, without me doing any work, but the second thought we should paint it right through and suggested a lower price.

I told Lynne and Dave that I just wanted to be shot of it as quickly as possible, not hang about painting, so I'd decided to let the first agent have it, but I'd decided to hang onto my flat for now.' They thought I'd made the right decision, on both counts.

It was all so calm. Conversations with my mother had always turned into arguments, and my father had always treated me as though I wasn't old enough to decide anything for myself.

Over the next few days, using Lynne's wonderfully simple system of black bags for rubbish, green for recycling/charity shops and boxes for stuff to be kept, the sorting went well.

I was grateful that Lynne tackled the upstairs, as I couldn't face sorting my mother's stuff. Dave did the shed, garage and garden, going periodically back and forth in his car, disposing of the full bags at the relevant places.

I undertook the task of sorting my mother's desk, where much needed careful checking. It seemed to take forever, but at last I got it down to just two boxes to keep. One of old photographs, and the other of important paperwork, including several large brown envelopes.

Dave had been going out for fish and chips or sandwiches each day, and Lynne had been a rock.

One day I'd watched them together realising that if, at this moment in time, they said 'Would you like us to take over as your parents?' I'd probably say yes. Weird or what?

The desk finished, I sorted my bedroom, then together, Lynne and I sorted ornaments, glassware and books. Apart from one or two volumes of sentimental value, the rest went to the charity shops.

Later in the week, as we sat having a cup of tea, Lynne told me she'd put some of my mother's possessions into a box, for me to sort once I was settled in France.

Then Dave asked me to tell them about the chateau's 'hidden treasures,' so I told them briefly how finding the treasures could save the chateau, as selling some would pay for the desperately needed repairs. Then I explained the leaning turret problem.

'Did you say you have some paperwork?' Dave asked, adding 'I'd love to have a look at it, sounds fascinating, but as you say, if no-one's found it in all this time. …'

This prompted me to tell them about my foray into the silver mine, my subsequent fall, which had caused my leg injury, and how I thought I saw something shining in the roof.

'Christophe thinks it was probably a vein of silver ore, but I don't think so. It sounds silly I know, but it was as though I could see it "through the roof", you know through cracks, rather than actually being part of the roof.'

'I don't know why' I told them earnestly, 'but I'm convinced the answer to finding the treasure lies with 'The Coffin Tree'. However, Romain, Christophe's older brother, thinks whatever the 'Coffin Tree' is, it brings bad luck to the chateau and because of this he won't even visit. When I go back to France I want to see if I can learn any more about the old woman who mentioned; 'The Coffin Tree', in case it helps.

I sat drinking my tea as Lynne and Dave both looked at the paperwork, then Lynne said thoughtfully, 'What a shame the chateau's in France Dave, or you could've had a look at it.'

I frowned so Dave explained that he was a surveyor, adding that he'd been involved in major repairs on several structures suffering from water associated problems, including bridges, the work on which had to be carried out under water.

We got back to the job in hand and, as I worked, I wondered what to say to Jules and Rosie about the wedding. Since I' been back I'd found the way they spoke, and behaved, really irritating, and was horrified to admit to myself I'd been the same, thankfully changing when I went to France.

I know that makes me sound disloyal, when Jules and Rosie have been such good friends over the years, often getting me through the bad times at home. I sighed, they'd been really embarrassing in front of Christophe, and I could see, all too clearly, what would happen if I invited them to our wedding. They'd drink themselves stupid, and probably jump in the swimming pool fully clothed. I shuddered.

Then I realised there'd be no swimming pool, because we wouldn't be at the chateau, unless I could persuade Christophe to change his plans, but deep in my heart I knew he'd probably not agree.

However, since Lynne's earlier revelation about Dave and his work, I wanted to take them both to France so Dave could assess the chateau damage, but how could I achieve this?"

Then, unexpectedly, the opportunity presented itself!

Christophe emailed to say he'd be in a Meeting all evening and would Skype the following morning. When he did so, I told him the house was nearly finished, so I'd be coming to France and he replied that, as a result of the previous evening's Meeting, he now had to go to Barcelona on Sunday, for a week, so I should postpone my trip until his return.

My initial reaction was bitter disappointment, but then I saw the opportunity to take Lynne and Dave to the chateau - without Christophe knowing.

Late, because of Christophe's Skyping, I arrived at the house to find the kitchen emptied and cleaned.

'The last of the

furniture goes this afternoon, when you've confirmed that's ok?' Dave said, and I assured him again there was nothing I wanted to keep. Anyway, there's no room in my flat for anything extra.

Oh! My flat, of course I wouldn't be there, as I'd be living in the chateau, hopefully, but then I shivered at the thought that we might still lose the chateau. Paris? Permanently? I groaned.

I looked around. In just a few days we'd dismantled my parents lives and thrown, or given, their every possession, away. I should feel sad, but my only sadness was that I didn't

Then I told Dave and Lynne that Christophe was going to Barcelona for a week, and so the three of us could go to the chateau, assuming they'd like to, adding, 'Then perhaps you could stay for my wedding?'

'We'd like that very much', Dave said, after looking enquiringly at Lynne.

'First, there's a favour I'd like to ask you Fay,' Lynne said, and I held my breath.

'We'd really love you to come back with us, only for a day, two at most, to say hello to the boys. They know all about you, have done for years, and are asking to see you again.'

I breathed a sigh of relief that it was something so simple.

'Of course,' I replied. Well, what else could I say, after all the help and support they'd given me over the past week? However, learning their sons had been aware of my existence for years, I couldn't help feeling a bit resentful that, although I'd been the main player in this story, it felt like I'd been the only one who'd not known the truth.

'We'd better get finished here then sort out somewhere to stay in France, perhaps there's a small hotel nearby?' Lynne asked, and I laughed.

'The chateau has masses of rooms, I don't know how many, and, since it belongs to Christophe, I insist you stay with us. We'll all have to muck in with the housework, as long as you don't mind that?'

'I don't mind at all,' Lynne said excitedly, 'but I thought you said it was a small chateau?'

'It is, compared to the chateaux of the Loire,' I laughed.

'Right then, we'd better get on. There's just one job left here, and I knew what she meant.

I'd been putting off opening the large brown envelopes. For two pins I'd chuck them in the bin. I just wanted to leave this life behind me. I had a new life to go to, sharing it with the man I love.

I intended to forget all about my parents, although of course, strictly speaking, Dave is one of my parents. Still can't get my head round it., but I now know that I want him and Lynne to have some part in my new life.

Lynne carried the five envelopes over. 'You might as well use the table, while we still have it. I'll make some tea,' and she went into the kitchen.

I already knew what was in the 'Certificates' envelope, so put it straight into the box and, of the other envelopes, one was marked, "The Last Will and Testament of George William Henry Barker. Copy," I sighed. I didn't want to look at it now, so into the box it went. Another," The Last Will and Testament of Elizabeth Jane Barker, Copy," went into the box too,

A third was labelled 'Insurance' – 'There may be something to claim', Lynne said, when I showed it to her, and the fourth one, marked 'Investments', Lynne thought was for the solicitor to deal with.

Perhaps this was going to be easier than I thought, after all. However, the final envelope, in my mother's writing said sinisterly, 'To Fay, to be opened only after my death'. Lynne and I looked at one another. I'm sure we were both wondering if this letter would finally tell me that Dave was my biological father. I put it into the box.

The doorbell rang several times, as the charities arrived to collect the furniture, but the final caller of the day, to my surprise, was John Harverson.

'You're almost impossible to get hold of Fay,' he looked at Lynne, 'Can't you explain to her that there are certain things which …..'

Lynne held up her hand to stop him. 'It's all taken care of', and she took the 'Investments' and the 'Insurance' envelopes, and handed them over to him, saying 'There you are you see we're onto it. Now, is there anything else?'

He hesitated, 'Well yes, actually there is, and I would appreciate a moment alone with my client.'

Lynne immediately left, closing the lounge door behind her, and John produced an envelope, from his inside pocket and handed it to me.

It said simply "Fay," on the front of it, in "my father's" writing.

I looked up sharply. 'He's been dead 6 years,' I said. I'd gone quite cold all over.

John stood looking at me for a moment or two, before he said 'Yes, but I believe that you'll understand the delay when you read it, although of course I don't know what it says. All George said was that I was to keep it, only giving it to you on the death of your mother.

Unless it's terribly personal Fay, I'd appreciate seeing a copy of it. It's possible that there may be something in it, which seems unimportant to you, but could be significant.'

What on earth was he talking about. Did he think I was stupid?

However, I just nodded and followed him into the hall, then Lynne appeared and gave him a piece of paper, with the address of the chateau on it. He thanked her and left.

'Well then I guess that's it', she said, just the cleaning to finish, so, since, it's getting late, I suggest we leave it for tomorrow.

I put my father's letter into the box with my mother's, on the windowsill in the dining room and drove home, but I had a dreadful feeling of foreboding.

CHAPTER 13

When Christophe called, I told him I'd invited Lynne and Dave to our wedding. He said 'ok', but then asked, 'and the girls I met?'

'I haven't decided. I don't want to hurt or upset them, but ....', then he cut me short saying 'I must go, we'll talk about it, later peut-être.'

No, we wouldn't "talk about it later", they were my friends, so I would decide, but instead of telling him this, I said that Dave and Lynne had invited me to visit their house, where I'd see my brothers, and I'd accepted.

'That sounds a good plan, then you'll come to Paris next weekend?'

'D'accord,' I agreed. What I didn't say it was that we'd only be at Dave and Lynne's for two days, then we'd go to the chateau, and I didn't tell him because I was certain he'd forbid it.

I justified this by telling myself that, Christophe didn't need to be told, because we were only going to the chateau so Dave could assess the condition of the collapsing tower. Hopefully it would then be a lovely surprise if I was then able to then tell him that the damage was not too serious and could be repaired at reasonable cost.

I also hadn't faced up to telling Christophe, that I wanted our wedding date postponed. The date he'd chosen was now little more than two weeks away!

"It's all too rushed," my brain screamed, whilst my heart said "but I'll be with Christophe", then it added "but in Paris!"

This was to be the last day at my mother's house, so I quickly sorted my room, while Dave and Lynne finished cleaning the rest of the house, then Dave cut the grass, a van came to collect the last of the stuff and that was it!

'Shall we wait in the car, while you to have a last look around by yourself?' Lynne asked, thoughtfully.'

I shook my head and went upstairs and stood at my bedroom window, remembering the day we came here, when my father told me that it was an adventure, as though it wasn't permanent.

I looked down on the orchard, the stream, the little bridge, the huge gardens. As I surveyed the scene, my eye caught the small cross, which marked the spot where 'Molly' was buried, The adorable mongrel dog, named after my late Nana Molly, whom I'd adored.

Molly the puppy became my best friend. In fact, for a time, my only friend, and this was why I mustn't shut out Jules and Rosie now. In those early days, when I wasn't accepted by most of my new class, arriving as I had in the middle of term, wearing the uniform from my previous school, Jules and Rosie had turned on the bullies who'd taunted me, and they made me their friend. Only eight years old and in a new environment, I don't know what I'd have done without them.

I quickly turned away before I succumbed to tears, not only for my beloved pooch, but for the unhappiness this house held for me. My parents cool and aloof with one another, each over indulgent with me on occasions, as though they were competing for my love and attention. My father away a great deal of the time. My mother left alone, in an isolated spot – with only a bicycle.. There wasn't even a bus route.

I suddenly realised that I'd hated it here, the house, the situation, the way my parents behaved, even the school, although I'd done remarkably well, using exams as my passport away from all of this.

Even then my father had tied me to them by buying me a flat only a mile away. It was given to me on my eighteenth birthday, with the proviso that if I sold it, while either of them was still alive, the proceeds would go into a fund, managed by John Harveron, until my 30th birthday!

He also paid my Uni fees, but the strangest condition attached to both the Uni fees and my flat, was that I must not go to France!

Of course, I now I realised the reason for this – since he must've died still under the impression that Monsieur Richarde was my father, so I went downstairs and tore open the envelope with his writing on it.

"My dearest Fay, since you are reading this, I must be dead. I hope my death was peaceful and that you were at my side."

I smiled wryly. A motorway pile up in Holland couldn't be further from that wish.

"If I died before your mother it's possible that she's already told you that I'm not your biological father" – so there it was in my father's own hand – "and, in case you had any doubts, it's true."

"When I married your mother, I couldn't have loved her more, but she let me down and betrayed me, so I punished her by making her as miserable as she'd made me."

I couldn't believe what I was reading. This was the man I'd loved, as a daughter, thought highly of and cared about. I read on.

"We'd been married a number of years and your mother became quite neurotic about having a baby. We had tests done and hers were fine, but I never told her that mine had proven, beyond any doubt, that I couldn't father a child.

I still loved her back then, and I was terrified she'd leave me if she knew the truth. I thought with time perhaps she'd accept that it wasn't meant to be, or we could even consider adoption.

I was still thinking like that when we went to our holiday home in France, for an Autumn break. However, a month or so into our holiday she excitedly told me she was sure she was pregnant.

I couldn't tell her it wasn't possible, without admitting that I'd known I couldn't father a child, so I went along with it, pretending to be pleased, whilst hoping she was wrong.

We returned to England, her pregnancy was confirmed by our own doctor and I tried to work out who the father might be, but she never gave anything away. However, once when I saw them exchange glances, I had a feeling that it might be David Broome. The following July you were born.

Believing my hunch to be right, I was cut to the bone as he'd been my friend, and the only person I'd ever told about my inability to father a child. Then I began to wonder if he'd told your mother and also agreed to make her pregnant, but I was still desperate not to lose her, so I said nothing.

When you came along and, because I still wanted to make her happy, I made sure that she had a baby." Odd wording, I frowned and continued, "and I came to love you as much as if you'd been mine. I couldn't forgive your mother but I made the best of it.

Then, one day, when you were eight, I caught Dave Broome looking at you as you played, and, in that instant, I thought he'd guessed." I read on, "Afraid that he might try and take you from us, I took you both and your mother and hid you away in an isolated house, with no neighbours, telling your mother we'd had to move for financial reasons. I got rid of her car and gave her a bicycle, so she couldn't go too far! I even kept her without a telephone for two years, so she couldn't contact him."

By this time I was beginning to feel sick, and a chair would've been good, but they'd all gone, anyway, I might as well read on and get it over with.

"We continued to holiday in France and I even considered moving us all over there permanently. You got on well with the boys at the chateau, and I could keep a close eye on your mother. However, everything fell apart when you were fifteen, and you became infatuated with Christophe Richarde. I was concerned you'd go the way of your mother, and get pregnant, but I soon found I wasn't the only one with concerns.

Madame Richarde had noticed Christophe was attracted to you also, and she sought me out, saying that because of the possible situation that could develop, she felt obliged to tell me that she believed her husband to be your father.

I can't tell you how I felt, and I certainly can't tell you why," I frowned at the wording again "but I sold the house immediately, and we never visited France again.

This was why I put the clause in the ownership of your flat, that you must not visit France. I had to keep you away from the chateau, so you never learned the truth.

It was an irony that I'd moved your mother 150 miles away from Dave Broome, but continued to take her to France, where the man was who'd really made her pregnant!!

Moving you away was cruel, to both Dave and Lynne Broome, for reasons you'll never know," I sighed at yet more confused wording, "but at the time I thought I was punishing both him, and your mother

You're a pretty resilient young woman and I'm sure you'll take all this in your stride. I've always loved you as my daughter and will continue to do so in death.

Your ever-loving 'dad'."

My first thought was to tear it into shreds and throw it in the last rubbish bag, but, because some of it didn't make sense, I resolved to read it again at a later date.

His letter had sickened me, not least because it had shown how little I'd known about him and what a hideous monster he'd been, taking pleasure in making my mother's life a misery.

I'd been reading so intently that I'd not seen Lyne and Dave standing in the doorway watching me.

I looked up and silently handed them the letter, then I tore open the one from my mother.

"My dearest "baby Fay", silly I know, but that's always been my pet name for you, anyway, I think should know the truth, so I'd like to tell you myself.

I loved your father, but I was desperate for a child. I don't know whether you'll understand or not, but I felt so unfulfilled, so empty, and all the holidays in the world, nice clothes, cars, or anything else couldn't fill that void.

We had tests done and mine were fine, no problem at all. Your father said his tests were fine too, but that he'd read somewhere there are people who just don't conceive. I became very depressed.

Anyway, one night, I'd offered to babysit overnight for Lynne, who was my closest friend. She went to visit her mother, who wasn't well, and Dave was away working. However, he came back unexpectedly, and I was only in a flimsy nightie, and one thing led to another, and you were the result.

I never said anything to Dave, so he no doubt assumed that George Barker, was your dad, which was just as well.

As for your father, he seemed to have assumed the same, but then suddenly one day he moved us away, and began treating me like a criminal, or even worse.

I know you loved him so I don't intend to criticise, suffice to say I had a pretty miserable life from then on, except when we went to France, and everything was different. However, that too came to an end when you were 15, and he did the same as he'd done before, selling up without warning.

For the following five years I felt I was being punished daily, in one way or another and, it might shock you, but it was a relief when he was killed. I truly hope you don't hate me for saying that.

However, I soon discovered that his hatred of me extended beyond the grave, when I learned that I didn't get his half of the house, (as most widows would have) but that he'd left it to his long-term mistress in Holland.

You probably assumed that I'd been left the house, and I couldn't bear to tell you the truth, so I said nothing.

'O.M.G.' I cried out loud. I looked up to find both Lynne and Dave looking concerned.

"I'll tell you later', I said and continued reading, but now I knew why my mother had kept my father's will from me, and I'd always thought it odd that she didn't sell up and move.

'The house had been like a prison to me for 12 years! I'd have loved to get away, perhaps to a cottage by the sea, bought a little run-around car, and lived for myself, for the first time in years. Enjoying what was left of my life, although I didn't expect that to be cut short too."

Tears were running down my face by this time, and Dave gave me his big 'man hankie' to dry my eyes.

When I became ill, and learned that it was terminal, I was really worried about you being alone in the world, with no-one to turn to, so I contacted Dave. I told him the situation and asked if he could find it in his heart to keep an eye on you after I've gone. I'd really like to tell you all this before I die, but I'm not brave enough.

Anyway, I began "putting my affairs in order", as they say, sorting through accumulated paperwork, including some of you father's, and I came across the results of tests from the hospital, more than 25 years before, which said that George could never father a child. I was devastated.

It meant he'd always known you weren't his, and he could've freed me long ago and let me make a new life for us both! But he'd taken some kind of perverse pleasure in torturing me.

You'll probably think we were equally guilty, but I think, under different circumstances you and I could have had a happier life, and I'm sorry for you for being denied that. However, I'm not sorry I had you. In fact, you were probably the only good and happy thing that happened to me, in the thirty years I was married to your father.

Now you know the truth, so go out there and live your life. and be happy, and above all, when you find someone to settle down with, be honest with each other at all times. I think if your father hadn't lied to me, and I to him, we might have found a path through.

Perhaps you should go back to France and see what happened to Stèphane Richarde. He was a lovely young man, perfect for you I thought, before we were wrenched away, for whatever reason. You were both far too young then, of course, but in time, who knows what might have been?"

'Who indeed', I murmured. Strange how she'd written Stèphane, when she must've known it was Christophe I cared about.

I handed that letter over to Lynne and Dave also.

They read it together, as they had my father's, then Dave turned to me, looking thoughtful, "So now we do know that your mother hadn't planned that evening, when she baby sat. I'm really glad, but there are some parts of your father's letter than I couldn't follow.'

'I'm relieved too, to learn you mother didn't plan it,' Lynne said. 'She really was a wonderful friend, but of course, once Dave told me what had happened, I was glad you'd all moved away, because our friendship could never have continued, and you living so close would've been too much.'

The doorbell rang, for the last few bits to be collected and now the house really was empty.

We had one last check through, then I was finally able to shut the door, for the very last time. I locked up and we went to the office of the agent I'd appointed, where I signed the necessary paperwork and handed over the keys.

I also learned that he'd have no trouble letting my flat, furnished or unfurnished, If I removed my personal stuff.

'I'm ravenous, time for a late lunch,' Dave said decisively. So, I left my car in the estate agent's car park, and Dave drove us to a pub.

Dave and Lynne were brilliant at lifting my spirits, and soon we were chatting and laughing, and no-one passing our table would ever have guessed at our shared story.

Straight after, lunch we went back to get my car and found the estate agent waiting for us and wanting to know what I was intending to do with my car, if I was planning to live permanently in France. When I said I had no idea, he asked if he could buy it for his daughter. He then took it for a quick spin, was happy with it and we shook hands on the deal. Another problem sorted.

Dave then drove Lynne and I to my flat, so I could sort and clean it, ready to let, but all the while I avoided asking myself why I felt the need to hang onto it at all.

I quickly sorted through my stuff, using Lynne's 'bags and boxes' system. What I was keeping went easily into the two large suitcases I'd brought from my mother's house.

Meanwhile Lynne sorted and cleaned my tiny kitchen, while Dave went to the launderette with the stuff used over the past couple of days. I also gave him the file of papers on the chateau to take with him, to read, while the machine went through its cycle.

On his return he picked up the stuff for the tip and charity shops, and by the time he came back again, I'd packed everything and Lynne had finished the cleaning.

So, that was that.

CHAPTER 14

We took everything down to Dave and Lynne's car, which thankfully was a large estate, and pushed it in tightly, which hardly left room for me. Then, just before we started our journey, Rosie and Jules turned up. I was horrified, as I'd overlooked saying goodbye!

'Whatcha doin' babe?' Jules asked, looking both shocked and distrustful.

'Packing to go to France'

'What like you were just doin' another runner, without like sayin' goobye – again!' She looked cross.

'No, well not really', I floundered. 'I'm getting married, but it's all been such a rush, having to clear my mum's house and everything.'

Rosie squealed 'Married! To the fit one?'

'Yes to the fit one. The wedding's in two weeks' time. I was going to email you when I got there, to invite you over.'

'Coo, you're like getting married in Paris right? One of them posh jobs? Love Paris babe, yeah we'll like be there,' Rosie squealed again.

Then they looked at each other and said in chorus 'Hats! Love hats.'

'Posh weddin', posh hats', Rosie added.

I glanced at Lynne who interpreted my anguish. 'Sorry to disappoint you girls', she laughed gaily,' but the wedding is going to be very small, not posh, and may not be in Paris. It could be in the office of a local Maire, in the French countryside. Like our register office I suppose' she added.

I could've hugged her, but I felt guilty, as I watched them deflate.

'So it's like a short jobbie, in an office, and not posh, ya?

'Ya,' Lynne and I said together, 'pretty much,' I added.

'Well of course we'd like to be there, cos we're your best friends right'?

My heart stood still, what would Christophe think? But then Jules added, 'We've got a lot on. Two weeks you said, not sure if we can like make it babe. Better check diary. Will you like forgive us if we can't come?'

'Of course,' I said, perhaps a little too eagerly, but neither of them noticed, in fact they couldn't get away fast enough, but as they left Jules asked, in a whisper, who Lynne was.

'She's my second mother,' I laughed, as I hugged them goodbye, possibly forever.

'Two mothers, cool! Well she's an improvement on the first one,' Rosie said, not realising just how insensitive her remark was, and they were gone.

'You ok?' Lynne asked.

I assured her I was fine, and just wanted to get on our way, then, knowing she must have overheard what I said, about her being like a second mother, I added 'I hope you didn't mind?'

'Of course not. I'll let you into a secret, when you were tiny, and I looked after you for your mum, I sometimes pretended you were mine. I always wanted a daughter, but we won't dwell on that' and the same shadow passed over her face, as I'd noticed that day in the restaurant.

So this was it, we were ready. I squeezed into what was left of the back seat, and we set off. My busy week soon caught up with me and I fell asleep, and the next thing I knew, we were approaching the town where I'd spent the first eight years of my life.

As we pulled into the drive to Lynne and Dave's house, the door opened and three young men came out. I suddenly felt shy.

After initial hugs from their sons, Tom, Paul and Jack, Dave and Lynne each put a hand on my back and brought me forward, 'You remember Fay don't you boys,' and then they were hugging me too.

They were very good-looking young men, and Tom, although the shortest, was probably still six feet tall. He looked very like Lynne, but had blue eyes, like mine and Dave's. Paul had Lynne's slim build, and was the tallest of the whole family, and I couldn't help noticing that his small nose flared out at the bottom, just like mine!

Jack was very like his father, and our thick, dark hair was the same shade. I turned to look at Dave; perhaps Lynne was right, I do have his almond shaped blue eyes. I certainly have his slightly too wide mouth. How very strange it all seemed.

We went inside, and there were so many other people that I was immediately lost in the introductions.

'Stop, you're confusing your sister,' Dave said. They'd told me of course, that the boys had known about me for years, but it was the openness of it I found amazing, as though it was quite normal for me to just appear again after all this time, in the role of their half-sister.

'Let's do this sensibly, so Fay at least has some chance of remembering', Dave said. 'Paul is now 32 (he pulled a face) and this is his wife Juliette', an extremely tall elegant fair haired young woman, dressed mostly in black, stepped forward and kissed my cheek. These are their three children, twins Mandy and Ella, aged 10, and little Bobby who is 3.

He moved on, 'And here's Jack, who's now 29 and this is his partner Mike, probably the next wedding, and he winked at me.

Last but not least Tom, the same age as you of course, although you were born the day before, his partner Samantha, and their son Mark, who is 4, and his sister is due in 3 months' time.

Samantha was a feisty looking redhead, who looked really friendly, and I took to her at once.

'Goodness', was the only thing I could think to say. It was all quite overwhelming.

I was ushered to a chair in the sitting room, where photos of the family were everywhere.

The boys soon surrounded me. 'We want to hear everything,' they demanded.

I noticed Lynne and Dave ushering the partners, and their children, out of the room.

'Oh you don't, you really don't,' I laughed. But in no time we were chatting, and catching up. Having learned a lesson in openness from

Dave and Lynne, whereas even a week ago, I would have kept everything to myself, now, I shared pretty well everything with them.

I was astonished how easy it was, no secrets, no lies, no cover ups.

They told me what they'd been up to, then I had to ask, 'You don't mind me being your sister?'

They looked confused. Why would they mind?

It was Jack who spoke. 'I suppose we've known for so long, that you've always been a part of this family, albeit "in absentia"'.

'Oh get him 'in absentia' – guess who did Latin' Tom laughed.

'Can't do medicine without it,' Jack replied, and hit Tom with a cushion.

'You're a doctor?'

He nodded, but Paul chimed in, 'He's a surgeon, I'm just a humble GP'

'Wow! Medicine too,' I was impressed

'They're the brains, I'm just a humble web designer', Tom said.

It was my turn to use the cushion, and I got Tom squarely in the face, 'There's nothing humble with being a web designer, that's what I am,' I laughed

'And there's nothing humble about being Tom,' Paul added, and we all collapsed with laughter.

As we chatted, I looked around the beautifully furnished room, which, for all its elegance, was still comfortable and homely, then we eventually wandered outside, to find the others.

It was a lovely warm evening, as we sat in the large, well kept, garden, while the boys barbequed, the girls fetched and carried, and the children plied me with questions. Lynne and Dave oversaw everything, and kept the drinks flowing.

Everyone wanted to know about France, Christophe, and the chateau I had a feeling they were expecting to be invited to the wedding.

'We've all got the date in our diaries' Tom said expectantly, but, when I still didn't say anything, Jack added, in an American drawl, 'An invitation would save us gate-crashing. "Bein' family an' all".

They were a great bunch of lads – and they were my brothers!

I smiled at them, then explained that Christophe was away in Barcelona, but when he returned, I was going to suggest we postponed the wedding, just a few weeks, so we could have our reception at the chateau. They accepted this without comment.

Then each of their partners came and sat with me, so I had a chance to get to know them individually, but, although it looked casual, I was sure it was all being carefully choreographed by Lynne.

I occurred to me that she'd have made a great wedding organiser, if Christophe hadn't taken over doing everything!

I shivered at such a hostile thought and that was it! in that instant I decided that Christophe rushing me into a wedding in Paris in just two weeks' time, with no say in any of it, was not what I wanted.

It was only 9pm, and, despite dozing on the journey, I was suddenly overcome by fatigue, but my overnight bag must still be in the car? And where was I sleeping?

Dave noticing my exhaustion, called for quiet and said, 'It's been a long day for all of us, so I think we'll wrap things up now. Lunch at the Lamb tomorrow o.k. for everyone, then we'll be leaving for France? There were murmurs of agreement from all.

'That ok with you Fay?' Dave asked.

'Oh yes, I'd love us all to be together again tomorrow,' I said and then I burst into tears. Tears of exhaustion, happiness at being here, but sadness that I was now about to postpone my wedding to Christophe. It had all got the better of me.

'As a GP, I prescribe a hot milky drink and an early night,' Paul smiled.

As soon as they'd all gone, Dave brought me my overnight bag and I went up to bed, absolutely shattered. I was sure I'd sleep well, but a couple of hours later I awoke, physically still tired, but with my brain buzzing.

How was I going to persuade Christophe to postpone the wedding and, probably even more difficult, agree to us marrying in Poitou Charente, and having our reception at the chateau?

I lay there, unable to get back to sleep. It was quite bizarre being here, as the house was pretty well identical to the one I was brought up in, only a road away. Then I had a really weird thought - based on what was in my mother's letter; my life had begun in this house, this was where I'd been conceived. Creepy or what?

I got out of bed and went quietly downstairs, surprised to find Lynne sitting at the kitchen table. She too had been unable to sleep and suggested we have a cup of tea and, while we drank it, I told her what I'd decided about Christophe, and why.

She nodded, diplomatically making no comment, other than to ask if we were still leaving for France the following day?

'Oh yes we'll still go to the Chateau, so Dave can have a look at the leaning turret, and we can all think about the "missing treasures" I replied, carefully omitting that Christophe knew nothing of these plans.

I decided I'd wait until Christophe returned from Barcelona, to tell him I want to postpone our wedding, marry in the village and have our reception at the chateau..

'How do you think Christophe will feel about this?' Lynne asked.

'If he truly loves me, and wants me to be happy, he'll agree,' I replied naively - Lynne said nothing, then, overcome once more by fatigue, I went back upstairs.

However, before I fell asleep I thought about Stèphane. I'd not been in touch with him myself, as Christophe said he was in daily contact his brother and I'd been both pleased, and relieved, to learn that sales were fine, and that there'd been no problems at all with the website.

But, the following morning, when I contacted Stèphane, to say Lynne, Dave and I were coming over, he was really cross, and told me the site had been playing up, orders had been lost, and his customers upset. He said he'd been shocked to hear nothing from me, not even replies to his emails, so much for the help and support I'd promised!

I couldn't make sense of this but assured him I'd sort the problems as soon as I got there, adding that Christophe didn't know about my visit, because I wanted to surprise him. I don't think Stèphane believed me, but he was relieved that I was going over.

After breakfast Lynne suggested a walk and, when I saw my old house, I felt surprisingly indifferent, other than to regard it as the place where we'd been happy, and from which we'd been removed, and, I now knew, my mother's life of hell had begun.

We went on down to the park, where I'd played, then on to both the infant and junior schools I'd attended, even going inside, with the caretaker's permission.

'Oh yes, I remember this room,' I laughed. 'I sat here near the front and Tom sat further back. He used to flick rolled up paper at me, with his ruler, and I used to get into trouble for squealing.'

'That sounds like Tom,' Lynne laughed.

After that we wandered back, and found Dave putting a tarpaulin over a small trailer.

'Not enough room for all of our cases in the car, plus your boxes of stuff, so I've put everything in here,' he explained. 'It'll be more comfortable for travelling. I'll hitch up the trailer when we come back after lunch, but first I'd like to have a chat about the chateau paperwork, and the hidden treasures.'

It was still only mid-morning, so we had plenty of time before we went to the pub to meet the rest of the family – my family! A little shiver ran down my back. I felt so lucky.

Lynne made coffee, and we sat at the kitchen table, where Dave spread everything out and I shared my hunch that the 'The Coffin Tree', whatever it was, held the key to where the treasures were hidden.

Dave nodded, as I then explained that I planned to visit the graveyard, and see if I could locate 'the old crone's' grave, hoping in the hope that I might learn something from it, although I'd no idea what.

'That sounds a good starting place,' he agreed.' Perhaps it will all make more sense when we get there. As for the turret, these plans and maps are all helpful, of course, but a site visit is essential.

I was thrilled that he thought my theory worth following, although, except for the paperwork Christophe had lent me and which I'd copied, I didn't know what ideas had already been exhausted in the past.

Lunch was a rowdy affair, as the boys plied me with questions about the chateau. I told them what I knew of the history, including the 'story of the hidden treasures' and how finding them could pay for essential repairs.'

'But Fay has a plan, so if it proves fruitful, the chateau may now be saved,' Dave told them, as I

explained that part of it was in danger of falling down.

'Is that where we're going to sleep, in the bit that's falling down,' a little voice asked. It was one of the twins.

The poor child looked terrified.

'No Mandy, you will be in the best bit, I promise,' I reassured her.

'Thank you,' she replied with a cheeky grin, adding, 'and I'm Ella'.

'No Mandy, you are not Ella, you little minx,' her father laughed, and she pulled a face at him.

Then I remembered the photographs of the chateau I'd taken on my phone, when I was planning Stèphane's website, so I was able to show them exactly what it looked like.

They all loved it, then Tom asked for Stèphane's web address and looked it up. 'Wow' he exclaimed, 'you designed this for him? It's awesome, love the 3-D effect.'

They all craned their necks to see the gently rotating chateau and jewellery, and agreed that they could hardly wait to see it for real.

I was torn between wanting the time to fly, so I could be at the chateau, and not wanting the family lunch to end, but end it did, and all too soon we were saying our goodbyes, and heading back to pick up the trailer.

Soon we were en route to Portsmouth, with our overnight cabins booked. It seemed like no time at all and yet, weirdly, also long ago, since I'd done this same trip, after my mother's funeral.

We arrived and checked in around 9pm and it felt very déjà vu, watching all the vehicles come off the ship. So much had happened since then, so very much.

We boarded and went up to our adjacent cabins, then ate in the restaurant, after we sailed at 10pm.

'Excited?' Lynne whispered afterwards, as we went back along the corridor to go to bed.

'Very,' I whispered back.

'Me too, I've never been to France before. Goodnight.'

CHAPTER 15

I snuggled down thinking over Lynne's final remark; because it was so close and we'd spent so much time there, I suppose I'd assumed that everyone had been to France. Anyway, the bed was comfy, the sea was calm, and I was soon rocked to sleep, awakening at 6 a.m. when we docked.

I'd told Dave and Lynne about breakfast on my last trip, and they liked the idea of doing something similar but if they'd never been to France, I thought I'd better make sure, before we left the ship, that Dave was ok about driving in France. If not, I guess it would be down to me.

'Oh, I've driven all over Spain and Portugal', he laughed, 'it can't be much different, as long as you know where we're going.'

I assured them I did and that, because this was their first visit, I wanted them to see rural France and had chosen my route accordingly.

As we drove, I told them about Brittany, the cauliflowers, the wine and the seafood, and we stopped to have coffee and fresh croissants, sitting in the sun, much as I'd done before.

'I can see why you love it', Lynne said, looking around her at the gently rolling countryside and, later in the morning, we stopped again, for a light lunch followed by another break a couple of hours later, to give Dave a rest from driving and all of us a chance to stretch our legs.

Having parked, we walked to the village bakery, which we caught, just before it shut for the afternoon break; it would re-open later, with freshly baked bread for evening meals.

Dave and Lynne were impressed the fabulous range mouth-watering pastries on offer and, disarmed by the friendliness of the locals, who passed us as we sat in the village square. Then back in the car, we continued our journey, and as we neared Niort, I described my experience at the Tour des Cloches to Lynne and Dave and we all laughed happily.

'Not far now', I said, my voice shaking slightly, and an hour later we turned up the drive to Chateau Richarde, and Stèphane appeared at the front door.

He seemed hesitant, but after I'd introduced him to Lynne and Dave, he gave me a hug and all seemed to be ok. However, just as he and Dave took our cases inside, Monsieur and Madame Richarde appeared also.

I was stunned! I'd not been expecting to see them in France, let alone here at the chateau, especially after Christophe's description of his visit to Reunion.

They greeted me civilly, but now that I knew Madame Richarde had had a large, and negative, influence on how the last eleven years of my life had gone, I was not so kindly disposed towards her. As for Monsieur Richarde, I felt I didn't know him at all, and, curiously I could feel no animosity between them, which seemed at odds with Christophe telling me that they weren't speaking to one another.

My negative feelings must have shown, and Stèphane made no secret of his displeasure at my coolness toward his parents, especially considering I'd been his guest for several weeks. I quickly realised my mistake.

'Monsieur, Madame', I forced a smile and kissed each of them on both cheeks, then I introduced Dave and Lynne, who'd picked up on the atmosphere, and were looking concerned.

'This is my natural father, Dave, and his wife Lynne', I said as though it was the most normal thing in the world, surprising even myself.

They all shook hands, but Stèphane looked extremely distrustful, of Dave, in particular.

And I looked at Stèphane and thought, "Well that's how I feel about your mother!"

This wasn't going at all as I'd expected.

As I was soon to be Christophe' wife, and he was now the chateau owner, I reasoned that made me "The Lady of the Manor", so as their hostess, I'd planned to put Lynne and Dave in the room with the bathroom, however, not surprisingly, Madame and Monsieur Richarde were already installed there.

Annoyingly, Madame Richarde took Lynne and Dave to my old room, where I'd intended to sleep and I was shown, to a smaller room, with the only thing to commend it being its proximity to the main bathroom. It had a single bed (which in itself seemed like a statement) a very small wardrobe and tiny chest of drawers, with a mirror perched on top, and very little else.

I was fuming, but what could I say, or do? I was certain Christophe would also be furious that his mother was here, in this house, after what he'd said. To make matters worse, she was actually behaving as though they still owned the chateau. The cheek of it and, just to compound my misery, because I'd kept my return a secret from Christophe, I couldn't contact him and tell him any of it. Also, when he Skyped, later that evening, I had to make sure he didn't guess where I was!

By the time he returned from Barcelona, if I had good news from Dave about repairs and had also learned more about 'Eloise Chevron, the old crone who'd muttered "The Coffin Tree", I was sure he'd forgive my deception.

However, when I turned on my tablet, I found I'd missed Christophe, but he'd sent an email, saying he'd left for Barcelona and would Skype the following evening.

I looked out of my window and could see Stèphane and his father, preparing food for a barbeque, and chatting with Dave. Well it was France, and hardly likely to be a Sunday roast!

As I watched them, I wondered what to do next. Stèphane's website needed attention, I needed to tell Madame Richarde, in no uncertain terms, what I thought of her, and tomorrow, I must visit the Mairie, and advise them of my residency status, in preparation for my wedding.

Above all, I must behave exactly as I'd intended before we arrived, which was that, as Christophe's fiancée, I was now mistress of the chateau and would set my own rules, so I put on my swimming costume, and a towelling robe, went downstairs and got into the pool.

It was lovely and warm, so I swam several lengths, then, just as I was just about to get out, I heard Stèphane.

'What do you think you're doing?' he demanded.

'I'm having a swim,' I replied, and began another length.

'Get out – now!'

'You can't tell me what to do,' I responded

'I can when you are insulting my parents. They've prepared a meal, for you and your guests, and you are swimming!'

Put like that he had a case, so somewhat deflated, I climbed up the steps, and, a few minutes later, I joined everyone else, but with head held high. I did not apologise.

The group were already seated and clearly waiting for me, but the worst part was the atmosphere my behaviour had created. Lynne and Dave seemed very ill at ease and I felt really bad about that and wished I could go back an hour or so and forego the swim.

I offered to help clear up afterwards, thinking this might help, but was politely declined, so I walked back towards the house. However, as I passed his workshop, Stèphane came from behind, opened the door and pushed me inside. Then, after closing the door, he pulled me through into his studio.

'What the hell do you think you're doing?' I shouted at him.

'I'm making sure you listen to me. Sit down Fay.' He was clearly very cross with me, and I cared what he thought.

I sat down on the chair he'd pointed to.

'You 'ave come here, with your friends' – he held up his hand when I was about to interrupt- 'at your own invitation. You do not bother getting in touch, to ask how things are going and, when I was desperate for 'elp you ignored my emails. I think that you made empty promises, and all since you met Christophe again. So, If this is what marrying my brother is going to do for you, then I do not want you even as my friend. As soon as you marry I shall leave the chateau, although I doubt Christophe will ever live here, or let you do so. 'E 'as no time for it, never 'as 'ad.'

I was shocked by everything he'd said.

'Stop it Stèphane, you're not making sense,' I wailed 'I haven't had any emails from you, and Christophe said he was in touch with you every day, and that everything was fine with the website. He said sales were going well, and there were no problems at all. And, since the Chateau now belongs to Christophe, why would he not want to come here? That would be ridiculous.'

Stèphane was looking at me in astonishment and something approaching hatred.

Then a voice said, 'So that's what Christophe's told you?' and Madame Richarde appeared in the doorway. She held up her hand to stop Stèphane saying any more, then turned to me.

 'I think you and I must talk, but not now. Tonight, I think Stèphane's problems are more important. Perhaps you will see to them at once?'

It may have sounded like a request, but it was clearly a command.

What should I do? If I agreed, I'd be giving away my newly-assumed status, but I couldn't bear the thought of falling out with Stèphane.

I'd been up since 6 a.m. had had a long journey and was shattered, and I desperately wanted to go to bed, albeit in that hideous little room where his mother had put me, which now felt like a punishment for seemingly abandoning Stèphane and his website.

Stèphane didn't offer a way out, but instead leaned over and turned on his p.c. and Madame Richarde left.

I forced myself to concentrate, while Stèphane told me what had happened.

He explained that the site worked well to begin with, but, after I left, it no longer displayed the 'sold out' sign, but just kept on accepting orders, way past the maximum of 10. This meant that poor Stèphane now had very angry and unhappy customers, who were demanding he fulfil their orders, but he couldn't, or it would break the promise of each piece being produced only 10 times.

'I tried to put the site right myself,' Stèphane said, miserably, 'but I just made it worse. It still keeps on accepting orders, but now it no longer asks for payment!'

O.M.G. what a bloody mess! If only I'd known, I could've done it all remotely, taken the site down and put up "Site Undergoing Maintenance", while I did the repairs.

I got my laptop from Dave's car, opened up Stèphane's website, accessed the maintenance area and took it off-line.

The fault was comparatively easy to locate, and soon corrected, however, there'd been sixteen orders accepted for one of Stèphane's designs, and fourteen for another!

They were in date and time order, so, thankfully, it was easy to see who should have their orders fulfilled, and who should not.

I printed out the extra orders, together with contact details, then checked on the orders for the other two designs. One had eight and the other five and Stèphane ought to be ecstatic, which I'm sure he would've been, without the website problems. However, now uppermost in my mind was, "why had Christophe lied to me?"

I now systematically checked the financial area of the site, and located the glitch, which had been triggered when Stèphane had played about with it. Thankfully, within a couple of hours it was all put right, and back up and running again.

'But what do I do about the un'appy people?' Stèphane asked woefully.

I wanted to hug him and say, "it'll all be ok" but obviously I didn't.

'I'm terribly sorry Stèphane, and I feel like it's all my fault, but I genuinely didn't know.' I was trying to think of a solution as I talked, and hopefully I'd find one.

I told him that, because we needed to make his unhappy customers happy, perhaps we could offer them priority viewing on Stèphane's next collection, maybe even at a special price. Obviously, since it was my error I'd make up any financial shortcoming.

'My mother has left me rather a lot of money,' I added, to prove that I was financially equipped to do this.

'I thought she might have,' Stèphane said, rather strangely I thought, but dismissed it.

It had been a very long day and was now past midnight and I was close to tears, but determined not to let it show.

Then, ever tuned in to how I was feeling, Stèphane stood up and pulled me to my feet. 'I know it's because of you my work is selling. You 'ave made me successful, and I am very 'appy about that. There will be no further talk of money. Now come Fifi, you must sleep', and he led me up the stairs by the hand. At the top, he was about to open the door to the room I'd had when I stayed here last time, so I stopped him

'Your mother's put me down the corridor,' I whispered and we went along to my room.

'This one?' he said, sounding surprised, even shocked, I thought. nodded and turned the handle. 'Goodnight Fifi', he whispered and leaned down to kiss my cheeks, just as I turned to say goodnight to him, and our lips met. I don't know who was the most shocked. He disappeared off down the corridor, the short distance to his room, and I rushed into my mine and closed the door behind me.

I looked in the mirror, my face was glowing red with embarrassment, and I suspected that Stèphane's was too.

CHAPTER 16

My bed wasn't very comfortable, but it was going over my conversation with Stèphane that kept me awake; that and our accidental kiss!

I thought back. Christophe had definitely said he was in daily contact with Stèphane, who'd assured him the website was working perfectly, and orders were coming in without any problems. Why had he said any of this, when it quite clearly wasn't true? And why hadn't I received Stèphane's emails?

 Not surprisingly, I overslept and it was Lynne bringing a cup of coffee that awoke me. She put it down on the bedside table.

'Do you want to talk?' she asked.

I said "Yes, but later and not here", and I put a finger to my lips, to convey that we could be overheard.

'I have to finish sorting out Stèphane's problems first,' I said and got out of bed.

'Ah yes, Stèphane,' she said thoughtfully adding, 'the Stèphane your mother referred to in her letter?' I nodded and she left.

Soon after, whilst eating my breakfast, in the chateau kitchen, Dave told me that he and Monsieur Richarde, or Maurice, as he was now calling him, were going to spend the day examining the turret and the watercourses, to see what could be done.

I then learned, to my surprise, that all the adjoining fields, and woodland also belonged to the chateau. Dave said that this land was let to a local farmer, so in view of the area to be covered, he and Maurice would be using the chateau's small tractor to survey it.

I wished him luck and took two mugs of coffee over to Stèphane's studio.

'Bon jour Fifi'.

'Bon jour' I replied.

'I've been thinking about', Stèphane began, and my heart did a flip. Oh no, surely he wasn't going to talk about what happened when we parted last night, but thankfully, he carried on, 'what you said last night, regarding the disappointed customers.'

I breathed a sigh of relief.

Then he told me that he had a number of pieces which he'd made only once, so each was unique. Maybe each of the disappointed customers could each be 'allowed' to choose one of these pieces at half price.

I told him I liked his idea, as long as we 'bigged up' the pieces, making them sound really special. Stèphane laughed heartily, and I relaxed. We were back on track.

'They'll need special packaging' I continued, 'In fact all your pieces will, boxes and small cards of authenticity', I'll knock up a design.

'Parfait!', he grinned. For a moment I thought he was going to hug me, and yesterday he probably would've, but something had changed last night, with that kiss. I could sense it and it saddened me that we might lose the easy-going relationship we'd always had.

Stèphane found the pieces he'd be happy to include in the 'exclusive offer' and, while he did this, I used the contact details I'd downloaded the night before to ring each of disappointed customers, in strict time and date order.

I was relieved that all but one spoke at least some English, so, with 'Franglais speak', I managed to convey that I was the website designer, and the error had been mine. I then told each that Monsieur Richarde, being of artistic temperament, was cross with me, and devastated for his customers. I laid it on thick, ending with, "to make amends, Stèphane would, personally, like to offer each of them the opportunity of buying a one-off exclusive piece."

A price reduction seemed pointless, as I doubted that money mattered to any of them, but the "devastated artiste, suffering for the mistake", did – well they were French, they understood these things!

By mid-afternoon, I'd photographed the 'special' pieces, and sent personal emails "from Stèphane", then I waited until each customer had made his, or her, choice, before sending the next. I wasn't going to risk another cock-up, with more than one customer ordering the same piece! By 6 p.m., it was all sorted.

'Thank you Fifi', Stèphane sighed, and sank back in his chair and closed his eyes.

He looked like a weight had been lifted from him, and so it had. When he opened his eyes, I told him about Dave being a surveyor and structural engineer, and that he and Monsieur Richarde had been out for the day, to assess the turret damage and watercourses, to see what might be done.

'You really love the chateau don't you?' he asked, and I nodded.

'So, did you ever care about me at all, or would you 'ave stayed here, perhaps even married me, just so you could live in the chateau?'

I was shocked at his bluntness, then to make it worse, he added, 'And, since you believe Christophe now owns the chateau, is that why you're going to marry him?'

I was stunned and had to pick my words carefully. 'I've always cared a great deal about you Stèphane, and the answer's no, I wouldn't have married you solely to live in the chateau. As for Christophe, I agreed to marry him before he told me that he now owns the chateau.'

 'Anyway,' I added, knowing it was a dangerous route to take, 'Since we're asking such personal questions, it's my turn.' He raised his eyebrows.

Why, when you asked me to stay 'forever', which I assumed, meant we'd marry, did you never even kiss me properly?'

It was Stèphane's turn to look unhappy. 'It's complicated,' he replied.

'Yes, I'm sure it is, but tell me anyway' I persisted.

'OK. I wasn't sure 'ow you felt about me, but I was more concerned 'ow you might feel about Christophe. When I said 'it's always Christophe' you thought I meant that all my life 'people' 'ad chosen Christophe,' he smiled wistfully, 'but I meant it was you who'd always chosen Christophe. Whenever there was a choice, who to sit next to at barbeques, who to race against in your piscine, who to pair up with for anything, you always chose 'im.'

'Well it never got me anywhere,' I replied thoughtlessly.

'Perhaps not, but I was afraid that if 'e asked you to go, you'd leave me, even if we were married.'

I was shocked, not just because he thought this, but because he might be right.

'Also' he continued 'you brought 'im into the conversation too often for me to be 'appy about it, "'As Christophe called at all? How often does 'e come down to the chateau? Is 'e in a relationship?" and on and on. I don't think you realised just how often you said 'is name. That's why I was reluctant to kiss you.'

'I'm so sorry Stèphane.' I didn't realise.

He nodded. 'All my life Christophe 'as taken things off me, and it would've broken my heart, if you agreed to marry me, then 'e came 'ere and took you. I think much of what he does is just proving that 'e can, not because 'e cares.'

Alarm bells rang.

'So,' he continued 'I decided I must find out and went to Paris, to tell 'im you were 'ere and that I intended to marry you. Either 'e'd congratulate me, or 'e'd immediately come down 'ere, work his magic and take you away, but I 'ad to know.

What I didn't expect was that 'e would tell me you were my sister. I was devastated that I'd lost you after all, but at least it meant 'e couldn't have you either.

After that you 'ad your accident and 'e came and took over, and then, because he knew I didn't totally believe 'im, he went to Reunion to ask our father to confirm that you were his daughter. I gather papa was astonished, and angry, that mama had said such a thing. Of course, once 'e knew you were not our sister, 'e decided, as I'd been worried 'e would, that 'e wanted you for himself. So I lost you anyway.'

He bowed his head and his shoulders slumped.

I felt awful. 'But what about Justine?' I asked

Stèphane frowned, 'Who's Justine?' he asked.

I suddenly went cold all over. 'Christophe told me she was your long-term girlfriend and wanted to marry, but you'd never commit. She lives in Paris and hates the countryside, so she's never been to the chateau, instead you go to Paris to see her.'

Stèphane looked astonished!

'I don't have a girlfriend in Paris. I don't even know a girl called Justine'.

It was my turn to look astonished.

'Perhaps Fay, by telling you such a thing Christophe's intention was to make you believe Stèphane was cheating on this girl, and so would cheat on you.' Madame Richarde's voice said.

I wheeled round, how long had she been in the workshop? My look must have conveyed this.

'I've heard much of your conversation – and why not?' she said defiantly, 'although I only came to say that supper is ready. However, since I'm now part of your discussion, but not by choice, I'll tell this to you Fay, I love Christophe very much, he is my son, but I'm not blind to his faults. Stèphane is right that as soon as he has something, Christophe wants to prove he can take it off him. It has always been so.

Christophe is an Adonis, an extraordinarily handsome man. He's also a talented architect and a successful business man. Women fall at his feet, and he discards them without a second thought. It's not Stèphane who would cheat on you, nor would Stèphane ever tell you lies.

What you choose to do is up to you, as long as you remember Fay that you were warned, by people with your best interests at heart, as I had, all those years ago, when I could see that you were infatuated with Christophe. I could also see that Stèphane cared about you too, and this made Christophe want you more.

As for what I told Christophe then, about you being his sister, I had indeed seen your mother with my husband, but, if I'm completely honest, I never really thought he was your father.' I gasped and so did Stèphane, 'However, it stopped Christophe from hurting you – and believe me, that's what would've happened.'

I was speechless, but found it weirdly fascinating that Madame Richarde, like Christophe, could pronounce "h's", when Stèphane could not.

I came back to the conversation.

'Sadly, it meant Stèphane lost you too, because your father, or rather, the man we'd all thought of as your father, sold your maison-secondaire and we never saw you again - but at least you were safe from Christophe.'

Poor Stèphane looked acutely embarrassed, and I think we were both shocked at how this woman had chosen to manipulate all our lives.

Would this nightmare, that my life had become since my mother's funeral, never end?

'I might as well go back to England,' I sighed, exhausted. 'It's all too much.' Stèphane looked concerned, Madame Richarde did not!

Instead she said, I understand you have some thoughts about the hidden treasures, perhaps you'd be kind enough to share them before you leave?' and she left the room.

Hidden treasures, who cared about the hidden bloody treasures! For two pins I'd put a sodding bomb under the chateau with all of the Richardes inside it! I guessed I must've looked really angry because Stèphane said, 'Does this mean you're going to the plan d'eau again, my swan?'

I turned to him in astonishment. 'How can I when I haven't even got a bloody car?!'

'I could always lend you mine, or I could take you, and we could both stamp around the lake, or whatever you did last time.'

His suggestion was so ridiculous that we started to laugh, then I began to cry, and, once again, Stèphane consoled me, then he said 'I think we should swim before we eat, to wash the cobwebs away'.

I didn't tell him he was mixing metaphors, instead I said, 'first to do 20 lengths buys champagne, and I ran out of the workshop, over to the house, and up to my room to put on my costume, drying my tears as I went'.

Annoyingly he was already in the pool when I went down.

'Seize,' he called out, as he reached the far end of the pool.

'Don't tell fibs, you have not done 16 lengths, anyway I wasn't even here, so it doesn't count.' I shouted, as he turned and swam towards me

He got out of the pool and took up a diving posture, waiting until I did the same, alongside him.

'Prête?' he asked

'Yes, I'm ready.'

'Trois, Deux, Commencez!' and in we both went. I did well for about 6 lengths but then Stèphane pulled ahead and, in the end, won by 2 full lengths and a bit. I tried to convince him he'd made a mistake on the counting, and I'd won really, but he was having none of it.

We sat on the side of the pool panting, then he pulled me to my feet and said 'We must eat,' and threw me a robe and espadrilles.

'We can't join the others dressed like this,' I protested.

'I think if we delay any longer mama will put us on the barbeque.'

I giggled, fully believing she might do just that.

Lynne looked surprised when we appeared in bathrobes. 'Swimming,' I said, and she smiled.

'I won,' Stèphane announced victoriously.

'Only just,' I protested

'two lengths and an 'alf' he replied pompously, and everyone laughed.

Over our meal Dave told us how he and Maurice had traced a number of water courses, appearing from different directions, and joining together around the damaged Turret. He then professed the belief that it couldn't have been like that long ago, when the chateau was built and must have altered over time.

"So we must divert the water courses and dry out the foundations, but slowly, otherwise the turret could collapse," he then explained.

Whilst Dave was speaking I studied the Richardes, they were a very handsome couple, no wonder they'd produced such good-looking offspring.

Madame tall, slim and elegant, wore minimalistic statement jewellery, her fair hair swept back into a loose chignon was tied with a blue silk chiffon scarf, which perfectly matched her eyes.

I'd given up long ago trying to emulate the seemingly effortless elegance of French women, putting my lack of success down to growing up playing with three boys, both in France and England, exploring, climbing trees, lighting bonfires and riding bikes.

 Monsieur Richarde was taller, with broad shoulders and chiselled features, his dark hair flecked silver at the temples. They were handsome perhaps, but I found them cold and unapproachable, I always had, and all that talk of "protecting me" I believed really meant, "retaining control of my sons".

'Tomorrow Dave and I will finish our survey, and hope to have a solution,' Monsieur Richarde said, adding 'As to cost?' followed by the Gallic shrug.

After that talk was more general, then I popped into Stèphane's studio, checked that his website was running perfectly, and went to bed. I was shocked when I realised that I'd barely given Christophe a second thought all evening!

O.M.G. Christophe!

 I'd completely forgotten our Skype rendezvous. But why then hadn't he called?

Of course! It was because he didn't know that I was here, at the chateau, and my mobile was turned off, almost permanently these days!

Truthfully, I wasn't sorry to have missed our nightly conversation, because I hadn't decided yet what I was going to say. After Madame's outburst, earlier in the day, Paris was now definitely off, and I knew this wouldn't be received well.

The following morning, there was no-one about, so I swam before breakfast. Stèphane was already at work in the studio and afterwards I breakfasted on the patio, with Lynne.

'I'm not surprised you love it so much, everything, the chateau, the village, France generally,'' she sighed and closed her eyes adding 'Have you spoken to Christophe this morning?'

'No, we agreed to only speak in the evenings, because he'll have meetings all day, but I completely forgot his Skype call last night.'

Lynne raised her eyebrows. 'And he hasn't contacted you some other way?'

I then had no option but to admit he didn't know we were at the chateau, and that my mobile was turned off.

'So where does he think you are?' Lynne asked frowning and I shrugged, then I went to Stèphane's studio and checked the website again.

'You're sold out of another 2 pieces,' I told him, 'soon they'll all be gone.'

'I know, I still cannot believe it. I really thought you 'ad asked too much cost. I also thank you for making things ok with my un'appy customers.'

'Least I could do, when I'd let you down'

'Ah, well, "C'est la vie,".

'C'est la vie indeed,' I agreed.

Stèphane looking thoughtful added, 'I cannot thank you enough for what you've done for me Fifi. I am so 'appy now, to be following my passion and finding that other people, discerning people, love my work. My only concern is,' he hesitated, and looked directly at me.

'Go on' I encouraged and he continued, 'My concern is that, when we began this venture together, you said you'd be 'ere, to deal with customers, and 'elp with my forward planning, but soon this won't be possible for you.'

I wanted to say that perhaps I could come down from Paris, by the fast TGV train, for one day each week, but I just knew that Christophe wouldn't agree.

So I replied, 'I can deal with almost everything remotely', but I knew Stèphane meant he wanted me there, physically, in his studio, to discuss and photograph, and share it all with him.

'Alone the pleasure is not the same,' he said, confirming my thoughts.

'Perhaps we could look for another web person?' he added after a moment or two.

Did he really think I could be that easily replaced? Anyway, I didn't want someone else sharing it with him. O.M.G, I had no right to think like that, what was the matter with me?

I went up to my room and shut the door. I needed to be alone to think.

CHAPTER 17

I thought about Madame Richarde, an intelligent woman, who'd just told me that eleven years ago she'd acted in the best interests, not only of her sons, but of me, by lying about my mother and her husband.

It had made me see that I neither liked nor trusted her and that these feelings were probably mutual. However, I'd also realised that I must change her attitude and feelings toward me, if I was ever to be a part of this family, and the only way I see, to achieve this, was to find the hidden treasures.

After all, surely, if the woman had spent more than 30 years looking, she had to think I was wonderful if I found them?

However, it was extraordinary that Madame Richarde truly believed she'd been justified in what she'd done, but in my eyes, it turned her into as big a liar as her middle son seemed to be!

'O.M.G'. I couldn't believe what I'd just admitted to myself about Christophe, and when she'd remarked, with reference to him owning the chateau, "So that's what he's told you is it?" it was as much a statement of "That's a lie," as possible, but was she accusing me of making it up, or Christophe of telling lies?

Other things she'd said were striking unwelcome chords too, hinting that Christophe would cheat on me. I might've dismissed her words, except that Stèphane had made no attempt to stop, or even discourage her. This in turn led to my thinking back to the hospital, when I realised that Christophe was something of a "babe magnet", when I wondered if I could've coped with it had he not been my brother. So, could I cope with it now?

I shivered again.

Christophe had said his father was angry and his parents weren't speaking, but there'd been no sign of this, and why were his parents back from Reunion and here at the chateau anyway?

But the biggest question of all was, did Christophe really only want to marry me because Stèphane did? There was a light knock at the door. I didn't answer. Then the handle turned and my brain screamed "go away". The door opened and Lynne came in and sat down beside me.

'I overheard some of what Madame Richarde said earlier, is that why you're shut away up here?'

I nodded, then it all poured out in an unstoppable torrent. The doubts I'd already begun to have, the way I felt Christophe had been manipulating me, and deciding everything for me, just like 'my father' had done to my mother.

The fear that I might not be able to stop him doing this. The anger at him planning the kind of wedding that I didn't want, and didn't feel a part of. It could've been anyone's wedding, it certainly didn't feel like mine!

He'd even stopped me from inviting my friends, with his looks of horror, and disapproving remarks. None of this was what I wanted, in fact Christophe may not be what I want either!

There, I'd said it!

'So, what now?' Lynne asked calmly.

I shook my head forlornly, 'I don't know', I admitted.

'Okay, well, since I'd love to do some sightseeing whilst we're here, perhaps a few more days might help you decide the path to take. What do you think?' Lynne asked and I knew she was right . A bit more time should sort out my head and help me to make the right decisions.

'I'm here for you whenever you need to talk Fay, now, shall we go and see how the menfolk are getting on?' and Lynne pulled me to my feet, and I followed her downstairs.

We located Dave and Maurice, (as Lynne was also now calling him) by the leaning tower, and I warned Lynne to be careful walking near the boggy ground.

'It would be embarrassing to get stuck in front of the men,' I whispered and she laughingly agreed.

Once there, we learned that the first priority was to create a pond, in the field over the hedge, then divert the watercourses into it.

Apparently, the farmer who rented the land had offered to excavate the pond, using his digger, in return for a couple of rent-free months. How French!

I looked at Monsieur Richarde, in checked shirt and jeans. Long ago, even when barbecuing, he'd never worn jeans.

The men went off to see the Maire, an old friend of Monsieur Richarde, who'd know where to get quotes for the rest of the work, although Monsieur thought any price would probably be prohibitive.

Dave had nodded understandingly, but advised that, even if further repairs proved too expensive, slowly draining the area should still help stabilise the tower, and protect the rest of the chateau.

We watched them go.

'Dave's been at a bit of a loose end since he retired. He's in his element here, doing what he knows and loves',' Lynne said, smiling fondly at her husband's retreating figure. I smiled too.

In the evening I went to my bedroom, for Christophe's Skype call, ensuring a blank wall was my backdrop. It was a strange conversation, totally about his meetings, his successful talk, his design proposals. Him, him, him, him, him!

He never asked what I'd been doing, and I felt it was because he wasn't interested. This made me wonder again why he wanted to marry me, and, for the first time, neither of us said we loved the other. I also had a strange feeling there was someone with him, perhaps someone female? Had Madame been right about that too, or was I allowing her to manipulate me again?

After supper, I sat on the terrace with the men, drinking coffee and cognac, and looking at the myriad of stars in the black velvet sky before retiring late.

The following morning, just as Dave, Lynne and I were about to go out together for the day, Stèphane suggested he come too, then we could also pick up the jewellery boxes he'd ordered, made to my design, which he'd loved. We'd then be able to send out the pieces to the previously disappointed, but now delighted, customers.

Only too happy with this suggestion, we piled into his car and drove to

Niort where Stèphane dropped us off, and Lynne and I headed for la Gallerie Lafayette.

Lynne was tempted into buying a beautiful silk dress, the colour of coral, then we wandered along the narrow side streets, until we reached the covered market. Here we bumped into the menfolk and Stèphane suggested we have lunch at a little place close by.

The Proprietor was an old school friend who welcomed us warmly, asking after Stèphane's family. He said that his parents were currently at the chateau and Romain and family lived near Paris and were well. Until then the proprietor was friendly and smiling, however, when Stèphane mentioned Christophe, the man's face changed. He grunted, handed us the menus, and left.

It was a lovely meal, after which we strolled back to the car. Lynne and Dave were a little way ahead so I took a deep breath, 'Are you going to tell me why your friend changed when you mentioned Christophe?' I asked.

'I think it best I do not,' Stèphane replied, and began walking faster, so I was almost running to keep up with him. I managed to catch hold of his arm. 'Slow down Stèphane and tell me - or I'll scream.'

At this he stopped dead and his face broke into a huge grin, clearly remembering when we were small, and that, if the boys ran away I'd scream, saying they'd left me on my own, and they'd get told off.

He shrugged, 'OK I'll tell you, but remember you made me. Christophe had an affair with the man's wife, and it broke up their marriage. Now, did you really want to know?'

I didn't reply, but actually yes, I wanted the truth, because I was realising that there's Christophe I think I'm in love with, then there's – what? The real Christophe? The other Christophe? Madame's words about him cheating echoed in my head once more.

We reached the car, Stèphane opened the boot and showed me the boxes. 'Parfait' I nodded, absent-mindedly. Christophe was not mentioned again.

Stèphane then took us to visit a small vineyard, owned by one of his many friends, making me realise that Christophe had never mentioned any friends. Colleagues yes, friends, no.

At the vineyard we received another warm welcome, and clambered aboard a tractor and trailer, to be taken on a tour by the owner. As we went round Stèphane explained the main types of soil, the grapes that could be grown on each, and the different wines they produced. I was both surprised and impressed.

'A vineyard is my dream for the future,' he leaned over and whispered.

Wow! I'd never have guessed

Tour over, we saw the pressing machine, which would soon crush this year's grapes, and the vats where the liquid would then be stored and fermented, before being transferred to oak casks, until it was ready to be bottled and sold.

Dave and Lynne bought both red and white, and I chose a bottle of sparkling wine.

'I never gave you the promised champagne, when you won the swimming,' I whispered to Stèphane, and I handed it over.

He thanked me, kissed me on both cheeks and said, 'We'll celebrate the success of my website with this,' then, looking into my eyes, he smiled and something inside me melted.

However, when it was time to pay, the owner insisted bottle of 'bubbly' was a gift.

'So, you still haven't "bought" me champagne, or even sparkling wine' Stèphane murmured in my ear. 'perhaps you'll have to stay until you do.'

'Ok, but what if I never buy it' I asked coyly?

'Well I guess that means …' Stèphane shrugged expressively. It was as though we'd both forgotten all about Christophe.

My heart was beating too fast, my mind was in turmoil and I was glad to reach the chateau, get out of the car and away from the close proximity to Stèphane.

I hurried upstairs for Christophe's Skype call, turned on my tablet and he appeared, then he frowned and asked where I was. I answered evasively, but what had made him ask?

Then I realised, in my rush I'd not positioned my tablet accurately, so maybe he could see part of the chateau window. I gently moved the screen until I was sure it was out of shot.

It was a short call, and again quite impersonal. I did not sleep well.

CHAPTER 18

The following day I spent in the village churchyard, where I made some interesting discoveries about 'Eloise Chevron. I also spoke to Josef, the gravedigger, about a theory I had, and was delighted when he confirmed I could well be right.

I returned to the chateau feeling pretty pleased with my day's efforts, almost certain that I was on the verge of solving the 250-year-old mystery. Then suddenly, while we were having coffee after dinner in the salon, I glanced across, at the painting of the lady on the horse, and in that moment, I finally solved the riddle. I knew where the treasure was!

'That's it' I almost shouted and everyone stared at me, 'I believe I know where the treasure is!'

Monsieur's face became taut and he sighed, but Madame became animated, like I'd never seen her before.

'It's in the painting.'

'What are you talking about?' Madame asked crossly and, just for moment, I wondered whether to tell her I was going to withhold the information as a punishment for her behaviour, but I just couldn't contain my excitement.

Everyone was staring at the painting.

'Could you explain please Fay', Dave asked.

'Yes' I replied, 'But I must tell you the whole story, so that you will see what I can now see,' then I began.

'I visited the village graveyard today, to see if I could find out anything out about 'Eloise Chevron, the crone said to have chanted "The Coffin Tree" and 'Thirty Metrès", and what I found was excellent and contained much useful information.'

They were all totally silent, even Monsieur Richarde looked intrigued.

'By studying the headstones, I discovered 'Eloise Chevron was born in 1810 and her maiden name was Michelle. She was the daughter of one gravedigger and the granddaughter of another. Then I thought, who better to hide something than someone used to digging deep holes, and who more likely to have been told the secret of where it was buried than the child of the person who'd hidden it?

Her grandfather, Daniel Michelle, died in 1820, and her father Jean Michelle, in 1822, so 'Eloise would have been old enough to remember what she was told, which, but, because she was a child it was likely to have been kept simple, i.e. "The coffin tree" and "30 metres" or in French "l'arbre de cercueil" and "trente metres".

'How does this help?' Madame Richarde asked crossly, making me want to deck her. I clenched my fists and took a deep breath.

'Did you know that the current gravedigger, Josef, is the grandson of 'Eloise Chevron's grandson?'

The Richardes all shook their heads. 'Well he is, I said and continued, 'Josef even personally knew 'Eloise Chevron's grandson, Philippe Chevron, who was his great grandfather, as he only died in 1970, aged 95, and Josef was born in 1950.

Josef says that Philippe was a teenager, when his grandmother, 'Eloise Chevron died in 1885, but she'd told him that must he must remember 'The Coffin Tree' and '30 Metrès' because it was very important. Sadly, she never said why, probably because she didn't know, so, like everyone else he thought she was senile, but he still never forgot what she'd said.

Anyway, moving on, because coffins are often made of oak, I asked Josef if the term 'coffin tree' could perhaps refer to an oak tree and he said, yes, it was a long time ago, but he had heard the term used that way – Result!

Now we know that Emilie Richarde, when she returned to the chateau, after the revolution, was told where the treasure was buried, but decided not to recover it straight away. She must have been a very clever lady, because I believe that, rather than risk writing down the details of the location, which could have been found by anyone, she had this painting done.'

Everyone looked again at the lady on the horse, but still no-one was seeing was I saw.

'The clue is in her journal, where she pointedly describes the picture, as "A Treasure", an odd description, but without doubt this descriptions was intended to alert the reader to go and study it.

I've always thought the painting strange in that it includes so much relatively uninteresting scenery, so my belief was that perhaps the small stone marked the grave of a child, or treasured pet, and this was why she wanted it included. However, I'm now certain that the tree to her left is a young oak, i.e. 'A Coffin Tree', and it was essential to include the small gravestone on the far right of picture, as I believe it is 30 metrès away, and marks where the treasures are buried!'

'Mon Dieu!' Madame exclaimed, her hands tightly clasped and her eyes fixed on the painting. 'I believe you could be right'.

Even Monsieur was muttering that it could be so, as he too had always thought the painting a strange construction.

'I see it now', he said. 'The viewer looks at the lady on the horse, then is immediately drawn to the small headstone on the far right. My only reservation is would they have dared, during the revolution, to engage the services of a mason to produce such a stone?'

'Ah, I have the answer to that', I smiled, 'Madame Chevron's father, Daniel, was a stonemason, as well as a gravedigger, so they didn't need to involve anyone else. How clever is that? And, what could be more likely than for the gravedigger and his son to bury the treasure, probably in a coffin, and mark the spot with a small gravestone?

'Eloise Chevron's apparent ramblings now make perfect sense,' I finished triumphantly.

'Wow' Stèphane interjected. It was the first sound he'd made, adding 'all we have to do now is find the tree and the stone, but I don't recall the stone and there must be dozens of oak trees in the chateau grounds.'

'Well the Josef tells me that, assuming it has survived, the oak will now be enormous and about 250 years old. He says he can date trees fairly accurately and so I think we should ask him to look for it, but I was must admit I was hoping one of you would have seen the small gravestone' but apparently they had not.

Monsieur Richarde and his wife were still staring at the painting, then Monsieur said

'I do believe I know that tree, and that the scene in this picture is on the rise behind the chateau, not far from the silver mine. My wife has always said that she felt the tree was watching her, and she wanted me to chop it down.'

'Perhaps it was trying to tell you something,' I suggested and she shivered and whispered, 'Perhaps you're right.'

She went very quiet but then she said 'Fay, I am French and we're a nation of romantics, but I cannot see how a young woman, who is clearly as intelligent and clever as you, could be stupid enough to fall for Christophe's charms.'

I was too stunned to speak!

Dave, also shocked by this outburst, quickly changed the subject by asking Maurice Richarde if he could have a copy of the detailed map of the mine, and also the chateau grounds, the following day?

So, first thing next morning Monsieur ran off a duplicate of each and gave them to Dave. He then fetched Josef to the chateau and showed him the relevant tree, leaving him to study it and any others of the right age in the vicinity.

Poor Francoise had been horrified to see the grave-digger, taking it as some sort of omen. She shivered, made the sign of a cross and disappeared into the pantry, as though keeping busy would keep her safe.

Later that morning the Richardes, plus Dave, Lynne and myself, gathered in Madame's office, so Dave could explain the relevance of the two plans, however, before he could begin, I saw a car coming up the drive and Madame asked me to see who it was.

I went to the front door and opened it, forgetting I was holding a plan of the chateau grounds and was shocked to see Christophe get out of the vehicle. He came striding towards me with a face like thunder and I quickly whispered to the others that it was Christophe, and he didn't look very happy. Madame Richarde signalled that they would all remain quietly in her study, out of the way.

'So you are here!' he said, throwing down his bag, just missing my leg, the one which had been injured. 'I guessed it was one of the chateau windows, when we Skyped. What are you doing here? You neither told me, nor asked my permission.'

Then he saw the plan in my hand and, snatching it, he tore it up, and threw it on the ground.

'You can pick up the pieces, and then pack your bags. I'll instruct the car to return and we'll go to Paris.'

'I'm not picking up your rubbish, and I'm not going to Paris,' I retorted angrily.

'You'll do as I say', and he grabbed my wrist. 'I wasn't giving you a choice.'

'I'm here at the chateau, because, when you asked me to marry you, I made it a condition that I could look for the lost treasure,' I declared

'And I didn't give that permission. In fact, I didn't answer your request, but the answer is no, you will not, now or ever, waste your time looking for the supposed lost treasure. My mother was stupid enough to waste her time, I'll not allow you to waste yours.'

I saw my chance. I'd already told them that Christophe had said he owned the chateau, but, after Madame's remark, which I felt cast doubt on him having said this, I wanted him to repeat it.

I was very conscious of the silence in Madame's study, and guessed they must all be listening intently.

'Oh yes of course, you own the chateau now, I'd forgotten,' I said, to encourage him.

'How could you forget. It's not possible that you forget that it's now mine. You're a liar. I'll give you ten minutes to get enough together to take to Paris and Stèphane can send the rest, after Francoise has packed it. At least he does as he's told.'

'You're arrogant Christophe' I returned. 'You've put together a wedding I don't want, in a city where I don't want to marry, in fact I realise now that I don't want to marry you at all!' There, I'd said it!

He went white with fury. 'It's too late. It's all arranged, for a few days' time.'

'Too bad,' I said, 'Now let go of my wrist' his grip tightened, 'You're hurting me Christophe. Let go or I'll scream.'

He curled his lip and laughed at me, 'And who are you expecting to protect you? Not Stèphane I hope, because he is weak and stupid.'

At that the door beside me flew open, Stèphane rushed into the hall, and before I knew what was happening, he'd punched Christophe in the face.

Christophe fell to the floor, and was now on his hands and knees, with blood pouring from his nose.

'You'll pay for that Stèphane, in fact, you can pack your bags and get out. Now!' he shouted 'Or I'll throw all of your rubbish jewellery trinkets in the poubelle.'

To have his life's work referred to as rubbish trinkets, fit for the rubbish bin, made Stèphane even angrier and, as Christophe stood up and sneered, and then laughed in his face, I shouted 'Go Stèphane, go,' and Stèphane knocked him down again.

The boys were fighting! It was like being 15 again! I applauded loudly.

'Suffi!', Monsieur Richarde said angrily, as he joined us, followed by Madame.

If Stèphane's punch hadn't floored Christophe, I think the sight of his parents would've.

'I left you in charge of the chateau Christophe,' Monsieur said quietly. 'I did not give, or sell it, to you, nor did I give you authority to throw Stèphane out.' He had his arm tightly around his wife, who, for the first time, in all the years I'd known her, had lost her composure and was close to tears.

'I'm sorry you feel I wasted my time, searching for the lost treasures Christophe, it was to save the chateau for future generations,' Madame said.

'And I understood, and applauded that,' her husband added.

Then his mother wearily picked up Christophe's bag and gave it to him, 'Now please call your car back, and leave. You're not to set foot in the chateau again,' and she opened the door and showed him out.

To everyone's astonishment his parting shot to all of us was, 'You've no idea what it's like being so
clever, so good looking, so talented, so perfect. The expectations from

everyone are enormous."

His mother shut the door firmly behind him, then she and Monsieur Richarde apologised.

'My hero,' I whispered in Stèphane's ear.

'I feel the need to drive to the plan'd'eau,' he said, and held out his hand.

I took it and we ran through to the back of the house, got in his car and off we went, waving to Christophe as we passed him in the drive, where Stèphane missed him, quite deliberately I imagine, by only a few inches.

The car windows were down, and I heard Christophe shout 'It's not over Fay, you'll pay for disobeying and humiliating me.'

A few minutes later we were sitting looking at the water.

'Don't say anything', Stèphane bade me, so we sat in silence.

Eventually he said, 'You didn't answer properly last time, but you can tell me now, did you want to marry Christophe because he told you he owned the chateau, or because you loved him?' he sat staring straight ahead.

I felt as though I'd been slapped, but I also thought I probably deserved his comments.

'I think I was star-struck, that someone so handsome, gorgeous, and successful, wanted to marry me. Someone I'd worshipped since forever. I believe I was blinded by his looks, and blind to his faults.'

'And now?'

I frowned. What did he mean?

'What will you do now?'

I relaxed. 'I said I'd stay and help you run your business and I will, if you still want me to?

He didn't answer at once, then he replied, 'Fay, I'm going to say something I think you'll not like, but I still must say it.'

I waited, concerned, because whatever it was didn't sound as though it was going to be good.

'I know you love the chateau, and for me, it's been my home since I was born, but for you it's like an obsession.

Despite your protests, I still believe that that at least part of you wanted marry Christophe as soon as he told you he owned the chateau.' He held up his hand when I tried to protest.

'I also equally believe you'd have married me to live at the chateau, perhaps even convincing yourself you were in love with me, but, if I went to live in Paris tomorrow, and the chateau was sold, you'd go straight back to England to live.

You don't love me Fay, certainly not in the right way, and never will. I know that now and you could never persuade me otherwise, not that I think you're silly enough to try.'

I was too shocked to speak because, over the past few days I'd become more and more certain that it was Stèphane I loved. So, ironically, my mother had been right after all, when her letter said Stèphane, and I thought she'd meant Christophe. It was also realising how much I loved Stèphane that had given me the strength to tell Christophe it was over.

Stèphane was speaking again, 'I've always loved you, and perhaps part of me always will, but now I'm going to put it behind me and move on with my new life. It's a life that you've created for me, and for which I'm truly grateful, but which can't include you.'

I was already reeling from this shock when he dealt the body blow

'My mother has found me someone who can look after my website', he added, with a firmness and resolution in his voice which said there was no room for discussion.

'Please Stèphane, don't do this. I do love you, I know that now.'

'I think we've finished with the plan d'eau,' he sighed, started the car and drove back to the chateau.

I was now too stunned to speak, and I think Stèphane was glad to get home, so he could get away from me.

As we arrived and parked at the rear of the chateau, Madame Richarde came rushing out of the back door. 'Josef, the grave digger, we'd forgotten all about him. Where is he?'

I pointed out that he was around the corner, talking to Francoise, who seemed to have overcome her dread of his being on the premises, in fact, she was chatting away, animated like I'd never seen her before.

'Well, who'd have thought it,' Stèphane muttered. The next wedding?'

Before his recent heartfelt comments at the plan d'eau, Stèphane and I would've gone into fits of giggles over this, which is a huge part of why I love him so much. But now all I could manage was a wan smile.

I felt lost and asked Stèphane if he wanted to swim, but he shook his head.

'Perhaps you're exhausted from fighting Christophe?' I half-heartedly teased him, trying desperately to salvage something from the situation.

He stuck his chest out. 'Certainly not. In fact it's given me an inner strength. He's always made me feel inferior, but never again. I should've punched him in the nose, and knocked him down, years ago.'

Strangely, we both laughed and then, since everyone seemed to be busy, we began preparing lunch. I made some salad, whilst Stèphane made omelettes. The atmosphere was a bit strained, but we coped.

Immediately after lunch, warmly dressed and wearing boots, gloves and hats, and each with a large lantern, Dave, Stèphane and his father, set off, with the dogs for a foray into the mine. Apparently, Dave wanted to see exactly where I'd fallen, so that he could mark it on the mine plan.

Two hours later they returned to the chateau.

'I'm pursuing your thoughts Fay, which, look promising.' Dave said and I frowned, not totally following. He then marked, on the mine plan, where I fell, and the laid this plan on top of the one of the chateau grounds, then he looked up, beaming as we all gathered round the large dining table.

'When Stèphane found Fay, in the mine' he began 'she told him that she'd seen something shining, through cracks in the roof. So, using our lamps, we studied the roof above where Fay fell and there did seem to be a dull metallic glow.'

'Josef has confirmed that the tree, which we asked him to study, is of the right sort of age, so I've marked its position with a green blob, and he held up the plan of the chateau grounds, for us all to see, then he continued.

'So, by laying the two maps, one on top of the other, I've been able to pinpoint on the top map i.e. the chateau grounds, where Fay fell in the mine below and I've marked this with an X.

Now, if I draw a 30 metre circle around the green blob, which marks the position of the oak tree, you'll see that the place where Fay fell, in the mine below is right at the edge of the circle i.e. she fell 30 metrès from the oak tree. Now, without wishing to get too excited, it is just possible that what she saw, from below, was buried treasure.

I've used a wooden peg on the surface to mark this spot and, again don't get too excited, just in case, but I had difficulty pushing it into the ground, because I hit what I believe to be the remains of the small tombstone.

Everyone gasped.

So, based on all of this, we've arranged for Josef to return in the morning, when we shall carry out a test dig. We can't be certain our search will prove fruitful, but it's all quite a coincidence otherwise.'

Madame Richarde looked as though she could barely contain her excitement, and Monsieur poured us each a stiff drink, then, as if lured by some strange magnetic force, we all gravitated into the salon where we stood staring at the painting.

However, although there was now much excitement over the treasure, I could feel no joy, because I couldn't stop thinking that the chateau was no longer important to me, and I could happily live in a tent, as long as it was with Stèphane.

Sadly I'd realised all of this too late!

CHAPTER 19

The following morning, Josef arrived early, with his son and we all made for the place where Dave had pushed the peg into the ground. Once there we stood silently watching as, appreciating the importance of excavating with care, the men slowly began removing the soil. They worked as they might have on an archaeological dig, or, as Josef explained it, as carefully as if they were exhuming a body!!

Josef found and removed the small gravestone then explained that he thought they'd probably have to go down at least as far as for a normal burial, possibly deeper. However, the roots of the oak tree didn't help.

The first shout, heralding a find, came at 11 a.m. Something resembling a coffin had been located.

'I hope it doesn't contain a body,' Stèphane whispered in my ear. I shuddered.

Trust Stèphane to say such a thing and, just a short time ago I'd have clung to him in trepidation, and he'd have hugged me tight, but those days were gone., so, with a heavy heart, I just ignored him.

The coffin was in bits, "split by the tree roots as they spread", Josef explained, and soon pieces of silverware were being carefully passed up, one at a time, to an accompanying gasps from us all.

I was handed the first one, by Dave who kissed the top of my head and said 'This is what you saw from the mine below, my love, well done.'

Monsieur Richarde hugged me, 'After more than 200 years, you've found the hidden treasures Fay, and saved the Chateau Richarde,' he said then handed the piece to his wife.

Everyone turned back to watch as piece after piece was handed up, together with what they supposed must be rolled up paintings, wrapped in material of some sort. All were laid carefully on the grass. Now the question was, were there more coffins?

Certainly, the porcelain, glassware and most of the paintings were still missing, and, having seen the damage to this coffin, it was the paintings that were the biggest cause for concern.

Josef and his son cleared away more earth, but found no more coffins, or anything else.

Francoise appeared with the strong, washable cloths, used to cover the tables at the Fête du Pain, which seemed so long ago.

The silverware was placed on these and carried indoors, the paintings were moved separately and the Richardes took the decision not to unpack them, but to send for an expert from Paris. He or she could decide how to proceed, because for all we knew they could disintegrate at the slightest touch.

Josef had explained that, because the coffin had been buried on the top of the slope, where the ground was comparatively dry, it had minimised damage over the years. We'll never know whether this site had been chosen by accident or design, but Josef, not unnaturally, was certain it had been a deliberate, and very clever, choice by his ancestor!

That evening Monsieur took us all to the Moulin Blanc, to celebrate the discovery of the 'lost treasures', although Madame thought they should wait until the rest was found.

'You'll love the Moulin Blanc,' I told Dave and Lynne, as the taxi collected us. I hadn't been there since Stèphane took me in July, for my birthday.

Pierre welcomed me as though I were an old friend, partly because he'd known my parents, but more, I suspected, because I was with Stèphane.

As ever, the meal was wonderful, and, because it was probably the last time I'd dine here, I was determined to enjoy it, but try as I might, I just wanted to leave, even though Lynne kept sending encouraging looks my way.

As we left Pierre caught my arm and held me back, 'I was hoping this was to be a celebration for you and Stèphane,' he said quietly, with a question in his voice.

'If only', I replied wistfully, adding, 'I'm afraid that'll never happen. I'm leaving soon,' and I turned to go.

'No, you must not do this,' he said, with great concern, which was rather touching.

'It's not my choice Pierre, Stèphane has asked me to go,' and, fighting back the tears, I left.

Dave and Lynne were waiting in the car, the others having already left, including Stèphane, even though he'd travelled to the Moulin in the same car as us. This hurt too.

The following day Francoise was in her element, cleaning the silverware and, later in the day, an excited art expert arrived from Paris. He warned us that the pigment in the oil paint would almost certainly have cause the colours to darken, having been stored for so long. However, this should not be a cause for concern, as these pigments should recover, when the paintings were brought into the light.

He also admired the silverware, which was very ornate, and remarked that they'd obviously dined in style, here at the chateau, in the 1700's.

Everyone seemed to be busy doing something, and I'd have loved a swim, but the weather was much cooler, too cool for swimming or even sitting outside.

Madame, although thrilled that we'd found some of the treasure, never even thanked me for my input! 'Of course the paintings are far too valuable for us to keep,' was all she said, 'so we shall have copies made and sell the originals. These copies will be hung on the landing, upstairs.'

So with the repair money now available, the creation of a land drain, to channel the water away from the chateau tower could begin in earnest and, the following morning I watched as the work on the drain begin. The turf was removed and stored, for replacing when the work was finished, then the fall of the land was calculated. A channel was dug and the bottom filled with fine shingle after which a perforated plastic pipe was laid, wrapped in geo textile fabric, to let the water seep in, but keep soil out so it didn't silt up the pipe.

Next, the plan was to support the tower, allow the ground to partially dry out, and then pump suitable material, under pressure, which would force it underneath the tower. All this would be done slowly, to avoid further damage. Gradually, the tower should become level, once again.

Sadly, our find had not satisfied Madame, who'd become even more obsessive than before about finding the rest of the treasure, and Monsieur was nearly as bad.

Still feeling low and at a loose end, I suggested to Lynne that the two of us go out for the day. She was keen to do some more sightseeing and so we used Dave's car to drive to the Marais Poitevin, a huge wetland area, in the area known as Charente Maritime. Once there, we propelled ourselves around the delightful waterways in a flat- bottomed boat, taking pictures of birds and other wildlife.

As lunchtime approached, we moored the boat and walked the short distance to a picture postcard café, with Provence blue shutters, which was set amongst weeping willows.

We sat down, then, after ordering local seafood salad, Lynne asked me when I was going to reveal my real reason for our outing. I sighed and asked how she knew.

'Because, since before the treasure was found, you've looked like a wet weekend,' she smiled.

'It's Stèphane,' I began and Lynne visibly relaxed.

'You surely didn't think it was Christophe?' I exclaimed.

'I couldn't be sure,' she replied, so, while we ate, I told her how I was now certain it was Stèphane I loved and wanted to spend my life with, but that he'd recently made it quite clear the subject was a no-go area. He'd also made it clear that I couldn't stay at the chateau.

'His mother has even found a replacement for me, to look after his website' I wailed, and now he's told me I'm obsessed with the chateau, so he can't trust anything I might say about caring for him.

'So, in an ideal world what would you like to happen?' Lynne asked.

'Well now that I've got my feelings straight, all that matters is Stèphane, but I think I may have lost him forever, and don't know what to do. I'm desperate for him to change his mind, let me stay, and give me a chance to prove that it's him I love, not the chateau.'

'Well it sounds like that's not going to happen, Fay, nor would it be a solution if you think about it, because he's right, he'd always have it in the back of his mind that the chateau was the attraction.'

Sadly, I knew she was right, then she asked, 'So, what would happen if his parents sold the chateau?'

'Oh, I think, from things he's said, that he's quite philosophical. As long as he has a workshop for his jewellery making, and a studio for his painting, he'd probably be happy somewhere else, but it would have to be in the countryside, like the chateau is.'

'Then I think you have your answer.' I frowned and she continued, 'You have the money from your mother's house, which I understand is now sold?'

'Yes' I replied, having almost forgotten about it in amongst all that been happening. 'A developer offered a great cash deal for a quick completion, so I accepted.'

'Well then, why not prove you could happily live somewhere else, by buying a property for the two of you. You know Stèphane well, so you should be able to find something that you'd love, and that you're sure he'd love too. Once you show you're perfectly happy elsewhere, and no longer want to live at the chateau, I think you'll find everything will fall into place, so give him some space and time - don't rush it.'

'I think that's a brilliant idea', I breathed, looking at her in wonder.

She looked thoughtful. 'Maybe it would be wise not to buy anything too near the chateau?' Then she asked 'How long does the buying process take over here?' and I had no idea.

At that point Lynne thought we should start by finding out, so we took the boat back and drove into Niort, where we bought a map, sat down at pavement café, spread it out and decided on a search area.

She then suggested that, since Dave was busy with the work at the chateau, everyone else would just think she and I were sightseeing, so we could start house hunting immediately?'

'Oh yes' I breathed excitedly. She'd given me back hope and my dark mood had been lifted – for now.

It felt strange, property hunting in France, but Lynne was encouraging and asked the first agent we called on, to explain the purchase procedure. Much of the process was the similar to the U.K. but there were one or two notable differences. Legal fees and taxes were more expensive, at ten per cent of the purchase price, and, once a property was chosen, an offer to buy was made - in writing, which was binding If the Vendor accepted the offer. The other difference was that both parties usually used the same Notaire.

The agent seeing my concern about the binding contract, reassured me by explaining that Vendor and Purchaser saw the Notaire, together, almost immediately, to begin the procedure. However, I'd then be given a seven-day cooling off period, during which I could change my mind. After that there'd be no going back, and ten per cent deposit would be required at once.

We discussed what I was looking for, and the agent gave me some details to look at, but I was disappointed by how brief French house details were. No fancy brochures and write ups, just a small picture of the house, the square metreage of the largest rooms and others not mentioned! Even gardens were in square metres or hectares, with no description of lawns, flower beds herbaceous borders, or anything like that!

The young estate agent was keen, and suggested she take us to see a few properties immediately. I was equally keen, so we headed off into the countryside without delay.

I'd requested a minimum four bedrooms, outbuildings for Stèphane's workshop and studio, and a studio for myself, plus a bit of land around the property.

The first house, although lovely, only had the potential for four bedrooms, they'd not yet been created in the enormous roof space. I knew this was common in France, not developing space unless it was necessary, as Habitation Tax, similar to our Community Charge, is only payable on useable rooms, not on undeveloped space, even if it has a staircase and flooring.

Unfortunately, the agent became pushy, and began to annoy me. The house was too close to a busy road, not near a community and didn't already have four bedrooms! So, lovely or not, I didn't want it! Nor did I want a cross examination as to why, or her insisting it would be perfect for me!

Sadly, nothing she showed us was suitable, and we parted, with her thinking I was difficult to please, and me thinking she'd wasted both her time and ours. She promised to let me have future property details, and, as Lynne pointed out, it was good experience and we'd learned a lot.

Unfortunately my enthusiasm had been dented to discover that finding my ideal property wasn't going to be as easy to find as I hoped.

'Never mind, at least you've seen what's on offer around here and how the system works,' Lynne reassured me, and I knew she was right.

First thing the following morning, Lynne and I checked the progress of the groundworks. They were coming on well, and Dave thought another 7-10 days at most, should finish the job and the turret would be upright once again, supported on its reinforced foundations. And, do you know what? I couldn't bloody well care less!

Lynne and I set off for another day of house-hunting, but hadn't gone far before Lynne asked conversationally, 'So what happened to upset you, as we left the Moulin Blanc the night before last?' and I repeated Pierre's words.

She looked thoughtful. 'Interesting, yet another person who thinks you two belong together.' Then we drove into Civray, called at a couple of agencies, picked up some details and sat outside a café, studying them.

I was mindful of having been told that east of the N10 motorway was said to be cooler, so, when none of the properties appealed, I dumped the details in the nearest street bin, took the area off my search list and we decided to head for the area around Angouleme.

As we drove, the properties became more elegant, probably meaning prices would be higher too, but the rolling hills covered with vineyards really appealed to me, and I thought they'd appeal to Stèphane too.

We picked up some property details in Angouleme, then went on to Cognac, where we got some more.

'I like this area very much, and Cognac is a delightful town,' Lynne said, 'and I have a feeling that you'd be very happy here, both of you.'

I'd already been thinking the same and agreed with her, totally.

We were having a late lunch, after spending the morning with an entertaining estate agent called Jacques, who did his best, but just couldn't come up with anything that suited.

I felt a bit down, because I still didn't 'love' any of the properties we'd been shown that day, and I sighed as we set off back.

'Oh Lynne, I'll have to leave the chateau soon and I really hoped I might find something quickly. Do you think I'm being too fussy, or do you agree that the properties we've seen aren't right?'

'You're going to spend a lot of money Fay,' she replied, 'and must be sure of what you're buying, so I think you're right to be fussy.'

I then moaned that I might end up trailing round houses, day after day, desperate to find what I wanted, but not succeeding, so Lynne suggested that perhaps I should rent somewhere for a while. This would mean I could move out of the chateau and house-hunt without pressure.

Yet again she'd found a perfect solution, and I relaxed, but almost at once, my mobile rang. It was Jacques, the agent from earlier in the day.

'We have a property, just come to us I think it may be what you're looking for', he told me excitedly. 'Is it possible you can come at once, before anyone else sees it?'

'Not really, we're on our way back to where we're staying', I said, also relaying the conversation to Lynne. She pulled over, telling me to ask where it was and, as soon as we learned it was only a few kilometrès from our current position, we agreed to go and see it.

So, ten minutes later, we met Jacques in the square of a nearby small town and followed him to the hamlet, where the property was situated. As we drove into the little cluster of houses, I loved it instantly, and, when Jacques turned in, through wrought iron gates, which opened automatically, I gasped at what I saw.

I couldn't wait to get out of the car, as we parked in the huge immaculate, gravelled courtyard, with a fountain playing in the centre of a circular raised pond, then I turned to the property and stared at it I awe – I loved it!

The house was detached and three storey, with a large single storey wing on either side. Then I looked around the courtyard, at the numerous outbuildings, and became worried that the property for sale might be one of those. It surely couldn't be everything?

'If this is as good as it looks, then my decision's already made,' I whispered to Lynne.

'Then fingers crossed,' she whispered back.

'It's what's called a Maison de Maitre,' Jacques explained. which means 'House of the Master'. The huge vineyards that surround it, as far as the eye can see, used to belong to this house, so he'd have been master of all he could see. However, the property is for sale now without the vineyards, just the house, the courtyard and these outbuildings', and he waved his arms around as he spoke.

So it was everything – wow!

'It's a four- bedroomed house, as you request, but also with potential to create more on the top floor.'

It seemed absolutely perfect, then I realised he'd not mentioned it having a garden and, if it didn't, then it could be the perfect house, but in the wrong plot. So, holding my breath and crossing my fingers tightly, I asked if there was one?'

'Yes, there are superb gardens at the back' Jacques replied, 'together with a large terrace and a very large heated swimming pool, with changing room,'

I nearly passed out. It all sounded too good to be true. Was I missing something?

'It'll sell very quickly, probably to Parisians,' Jacques said. 'They're always on the look-out for elegant maisons-secondaires such as this. They're not interested in farmhouses, or cottages and certainly not in properties to renovate.'

He opened the front door with a large ornate key, which reminded me of the one at the chateau. I shivered with excitement.

We entered a huge hall, with fabulous curved staircase, superb polished wood floor, and high ceiling, and I looked at Lynne, who could sense my excitement.

'It's beautiful,' she smiled.

Then we went through ornate double doors, into an inner hall, with a reasonable sized room either side, perhaps a potential study and snug.

Beyond the inner hall were more double doors, which led into the single storey wing, the whole of which was a magnificent reception room, overlooking the courtyard at the front, and the gardens at the back. The ornate plasterwork, on both the ceiling and the walls, was dazzlingly white, and the main part of the walls were china blue. I loved it!

I walked over to the rear window. The grounds were beautifully landscaped, with magnificent shrubs in circular beds, amid the huge lawned areas. Tall glass double doors led out from this room, onto a terrace, which went the length of the house.

'How is it looking?' Jacques asked.

By this time, I'd become so emotional that I could hardly speak. 'Wonderful,' I croaked.

Across the main hall, the rooms were a mirror image of the first side. One was a kitchen, quite small, which surprised me, with a utility room, then there was a large dining room, which looked over the courtyard.

So far, the only surprise, I couldn't even say disappointment, had been the kitchen, but I could live with that.

I said this to Jacques, who replied, 'Ah but you haven't seen the summer kitchen yet', and he unlocked a door into a room the size of the blue sitting room I'd seen earlier. This was the other single-storey wing.

'Wow,' Lynne and I chorused. It was huge and the units looked lost in it, but the main feature was a large copper still.

Lynne asked why he'd called it a summer kitchen and Jacques explained, 'Because it would've mainly been used through the summer, for feeding workers who toiled in the vineyards, including harvesting the grapes in October, then it would've been locked up for the winter, and the smaller kitchen used.

'I walked over to the copper masterpiece. Is this a real still?' I laughed, 'it's amazing'.

'Ah yes but not usable, because It's no longer registered for legal use. Customs men will have visited and disabled it by punching a hole. They do this at the back, so the look of it isn't spoiled. Would you keep it?' Jacque asked.

'Of course,' I answered without hesitation and he looked pleased.

Next, he opened the glass back door and we went outside, where we saw the swimming pool, changing area and hot tub.

Jacque's 'phone had rung twice, since we started our tour, and both times he got agitated, but, because he spoke so fast, I couldn't tell what he was saying.

'We go up now', he said and we followed him up the magnificent staircase, to the landing, where the far-reaching views became apparent.

'Stèphane would love this I know he would', I whispered to Lynne.

'I'm absolutely certain you're right' she whispered back.

I can't say the upstairs was a disappointment, but the only thing exciting was the views. The rooms were very large and light, but rather bland and there was only one bathroom. However, I was sure I could make the upstairs as stunning as the downstairs, so it wasn't a problem.

Upwards again, and the top floor was a vast open space, above all the rooms below, beautifully floored, with polished oak boards, and the views, because of the extra height, were stunning.

The space had great potential, possibly two huge artists' studios, one each?

I could just imagine the 'Maitre' coming up here to survey his vineyards.

'You like?' Jacques asked.

'I like,' I agreed, 'but what's the price?'

He hesitated. This was it, I knew there'd be a downside.

'I bring you here because I think it's exactly right for you, and I think you feel the same, but it's more money than you said.

There'll be little if any price negotiation with the owners, and I have to warn you that the two calls I've received have been from my office. Other people wanting to view. I've said no, however, I think Catherine does not listen to me, someone might come anyway.'

No, no, no! my brain screamed. I was not going to lose this house, but I dreaded him telling me the price.

'You said you budget was 350 – 400,000 euros', I nodded. 'I'm sorry but it's 500,000 euros'.

it took me all of 10 seconds to say, 'I'll take it'.

Lynne gasped 'Are you sure? It's a lot more than you planned?'

'I've never been so sure of anything in my entire life,' l said and shook Jacque's hand, 'It's sold,' I announced firmly.

He looked delighted 'Then we must quickly see the outbuildings and get back to the office before anyone else can buy it. Such properties rarely come on the market and there are those who will purchase without even viewing'. Then he called the office with my decision.

'Someone else is on their way, to look,' he said with concern, whether this was because I might lose the house, or he might lose the commission I wasn't sure.

'Then let's go to your office without looking at the outbuildings,' I suggested.

'No you must look, I give you the keys,' and we left through the front door which he then locked. 'Don't let anyone else in, then come to the office, as soon as you're finished. I'll have the offer papers, ready for you to sign, then we give them to the owner.'

I couldn't believe it, an hour ago I was despondent, and now I'd bought my 'Stèphane House', as I shall think of it.

The outhouses were great, one converted into a Housekeeper's apartment. Then there were other stone buildings, with arched openings, probably where carts and perhaps a small coach might've been kept. No doubt the horses to pull them would've been stabled in the adjacent stone barn.

As soon as we'd seen everything, I locked up and we got into the car as two other cars came through the gates. The passengers got out and began arguing, presumably over the house, so, without hesitating, Lynne drove off.

Back in his office, Jacques had called the owners and been given authority to accept my full-price offer, as soon as I completed the paperwork, so having had it explained to me, I signed at once. An appointment was then made with our joint Notaire, for two days' time, at

11a.m.

I'd suggested an early completion date, and, since the property was empty, Jacques said that this shouldn't be a problem. I couldn't believe how happy I felt as we drove back to the chateau.

CHAPTER 20

Next day, Lynne and I, together with Dave who'd taken the day off, went to La Rochelle, where we strolled along the quaysides of the marinas, and chose our 'gin palaces'. Then we had a seafood lunch, in one of the myriad of eateries close to the beach. It was now late September.

While we ate, I took the opportunity to tell Dave about my house purchase. He was somewhat surprised, and asked if I'd mind him attending the signing at the Notaire's office, tomorrow.

I was delighted, because I knew he was used to dealing with contracts and agreements, so his presence would be reassuring. Dave then added that he'd welcome a chance to see the property first, if that were possible, so I rang the agent and we arranged to meet, at the house, the following morning, before we went to see the Notaire.

After lunch we strolled casually along the seafront, but Dave wanted a brisker walk and went on ahead, having arranged to see us back at the car.

I remarked to Lynne that I thought it was good that Dave was having a break as he'd been looking tired recently. Whether she'd have told me otherwise I'm not sure, but she then said that the day before, while she and I were out looking at houses, Dave had had a very unpleasant altercation with Madame Richarde (I noted the first name use had been dropped).

Lynne said that two concrete lorries had arrived and Dave had needed to speak to Maurice Richarde, on a matter of urgency about something he'd discovered. However, Madame asked if it affected the stability of the tower and, when he said 'No' she'd said 'Well just get on with it then – NOW!' as though he was some sort of servant.

He tried to say he wanted to discuss it first, but she insisted he go back to the lorries.

'Get on and pour the concrete and don't trouble us further,' she'd commanded, throwing after him, 'Hopefully you'll soon go back to England and take your daughter with you, we don't want her here either!'

She'd wave him away and walked off, but she'd made an enemy of Dave, who was now out for revenge!

I was now angry too. 'How dare she, after all Dave had done for her,' I declared.

Lynne nodded in agreement, 'So you're right, he did need a day off – and away from the chateau.'

The following morning, we left the chateau at 8 a.m. I was both nervous and excited as we got nearer, but, when the Maison de Maitre came into view once more, I knew for certain I was doing the right thing.

Dave was absolutely knocked out by the house, but still checked it over with his "surveyor's hat" on. 'It's a beautiful property Fay, I can see why you've been tempted to buy it, but why do you want something so big?'

There was no way I was going to tell him it was because I planned for Stèphane to live here one day, so it had to outshine the chateau, that was my, and Lynne's, secret.

'It's not that big really, I said lamely, then I had an idea. 'I was thinking I might run it as a Chambres d'hote, you know, a bed and breakfast. That would cover the costs and give me a small income.'

He laughed. 'O.K, sounds like you've got it all worked out. Can I ask the price?'

I told him and he whistled.

'It's not that expensive for what I'm getting, I said defensively.

'I'm whistling because I think it's amazingly good value,' Dave explained, adding, 'Anyway, it's your money, you can spend it as you choose, and I think you've chosen wisely.'

'Merci mon chèr papa,' I laughed, and he looked slightly abashed, but very pleased that I'd called him 'papa'.

We arrived at the Notaire's office in plenty of time. John Harverson had transferred the deposit money to my current account, and I'd brought my passport and other requested details with me.

'I shook the Notaire's hand and introduced Dave and Lynne as, 'Mon père, Monsieur Etienne Broome et son femme, Madame Lynne Broome, then we all went through to another room, where a number of chairs were set out.

'It's a sale upon death', the Notaire said, seeing me eyeing the chairs, 'with many beneficiaries. It has been in the same family for 200 years, so all will be straightforward. I've done all the usual checks, to safeguard you. Everything is satisfactory so, if you are satisfied, we can proceed as soon as they get here.'

At that moment an outer door opened, and in came a group of men who could've been out of a pantomime. I stifled a giggle and didn't dare look at Lynne, as Grumpy, Noisy, Ugly and Argumentative took their seats, along with Smelly (straight from a farm I guessed), and still wearing his grubby salopettes! He obviously saw no need to make an effort for the occasion.

Then there was a sixth member, who looked out of place with the others. He was taller, good looking, and smartly dressed, so I nicknamed him Smartie.

We were introduced, but when the Notaire said the family name of the group was Clouseau, it was almost my undoing. I excused myself, ostensibly to visit the loo, and once there I laughed uncontrollably.

This pantomime cast couldn't possibly be called Clouseau, like the inept Police Inspector in the Pink Panther films. it was too much. How was I going to keep a straight face?

Lynne soon joined me, she knew exactly what I was thinking, and she was laughing too.

'We couldn't have dreamed it up,' she giggled, and I agreed, but someone knocked on the door, so we had to compose ourselves and go back to the office.

Once there the Notaire gave me a dossier and Smartie, who seemed to be the Clouseau leader, received one as well, then each page was explained, in both English and French, and signed by both Smartie and myself.

When we'd finished, we were given a copy to take with us, and a date of six weeks' time was set for completion. I had seven days in which to change my mind.

In spite of the Notaire describing it as straightforward, it had taken nearly two hours, so I couldn't imagine how long a complicated contract would've needed.

We shook hands, and that was it, although Dave remained behind in the Notaire's office, joining us a few minutes later.

He gave no reason for this, but I wasn't at all bothered, in fact, I was jubilant as we left the office and went to celebrate over lunch. Then Lynne took Dave on a distillery tour, and I wandered around the delightful shops of Cognac, choosing all kinds of things which would be perfect for the 'Maison D', as I'd taken to calling it, not buying anything, but making copious notes.

Dave was now in the final stages of the Chateau repairs, so they'd soon be going home and I'd miss them terribly. Also, although I didn't want the Richardes to know about my house, I still wondered if I could, somehow, stay at the chateau until my purchase completed. Then I recalled Madame's comment, that she expected me to be going back with Lynne and Dave to live in England.

Sadly, I knew that was probably Stèphane's wish too.

****

The seven days cooling off period passed, so, knowing the balance of the money would soon be required, I emailed John Harverson, to release my mother's house proceeds into my account, but strangely, his reply email told me he was reluctant to do so.

Angrily, I took my 'phone outside, where I couldn't be overheard, and called him, confiding that I'd signed the contract on a property in France and needed the money to complete the sale. However, instead of accepting my instructions, he insisted that there was an urgent need to discuss my financial situation, and asked when was I coming home.

'This house will be my home, I'll be living in France,' I replied, thinking, not for the first time, that he was a terrible fusspot. I then repeated my instructions, terminated the call and switched off my 'phone, then I went back indoors, joining Lynne and Dave, who were having coffee in the kitchen.

We'd seen very little of either the senior Richardes or Stèphane recently, and I was feeling more and more unwelcome, despite all we'd done for them!

To compound this, my replacement, to look after Stèphane's website, was working out well, so no chance of using that to stay on now.

Next day I was restless, so I found Lynne, who was reading in the salon, and suggested we go and do some 'proper shopping'. She was out of her chair in a shot, and soon we were on our way.

Several hours later, I'd ordered a bed for me, and two more for visitors, plus a sofa and two large comfy chairs for the snug, a huge kitchen table and chairs, and numerous other items, all to be delivered on completion day.

I kept Stèphane in mind when making each purchase, and I was feeling pretty pleased, until I tried to buy some tableware and cutlery and my card was refused.

I was embarrassed and angry. John Harverson had obviously not transferred the money I'd requested. How dare he ignore my instructions?

'But why would he?' Lynne asked.

'I don't know, but I'm sure as hell going to find out!'

I'd been feeling really happy until then. We'd even visited the hamlet and peered at my house through the gates before we shopped, but now my day was spoiled.

The chateau was eerily quiet when we got back, and Dave said Stèphane and his parents had gone out, without saying when they'd be back, so we to ate at a small bar restaurant in a nearby town. John Harverson would have to wait until tomorrow!

It was very late when we returned, the chateau was in darkness and so we'd gone straight to our rooms, however, by doing so we'd missed a note, left on the kitchen table. It was therefore something of a shock, the next morning to learn that John Harverson was arriving, in a few hours' time.

'What? Here, in France?' I said. It seemed so unlikely. 'Are you sure?'

'Yes, quite sure,' Monsieur replied. 'He's travelling by TGV, and I'm collecting him at Poitiers railway station at 12 noon,' then he added, 'I understand he's your mother's solicitor?'

'Yes,' I sighed. 'I expect it's only something to do with her will. More papers to sign.'

'He didn't say, only that he'd not be travelling alone.' I frowned.

'I suppose we'll have to offer them beds for the night,' Madame said, but her tone made it clear that it would only be out of politeness. This compelled me to apologise for the inconvenience.

'It's of no matter,' Monsieur said, Madame glared at him and the two of them went out of the back door.

Lynne and Dave came into the kitchen and I told them about John Harverson. They seemed rather serious, but I didn't want anything to spoil my happiness over buying my "Stèphane House", so I didn't ask why.

However, Dave said, 'Look Fay, it may just be Maurice's interpretation, that John Harverson needs to see you urgently, but he's asked that we be there as well.'

I was suddenly alarmed. Then I thought about the refused card, the day before, and fervently hoped this wasn't linked to his visit. Not being able to buy tableware was one thing, but the money had to be available for my house completion.

'Perhaps I'm not wealthy after all', I said, thinking out loud. 'It did sound too good to be true. But at least I have the money from my mother's house, to buy the Maison de Maitre." I added quietly.

'Your mother asked me to keep an eye on you Fay, so Lynne and I will do just that. Whatever the problem is, we'll help if we can, but sadly, I'm inclined to agree with you, that your promised fortune may not exist after all.'

Monsieur appeared during the latter part of the conversation and replenished our coffee cups, from the large pot on the hob.

'I couldn't help overhearing,' he said, 'and we'll make sure you receive a share of the treasure. 'It's the least we can do. Later he left to pick up John Harverson in Poitiers, and I sat in the salon, looking longingly at the pool, wishing it was still warm enough to swim.

I pretended to read a book, but I was really thinking about John and his mystery guest. I was cross that he thought he had the right to turn up here, at the Chateau, but I had to admit I'd ignored his 'phone messages, assuming them to be unimportant.

Well I'd soon know, but I wasn't going to let it bother me too much, after all, whatever he had to say was hardly going to be life changing!

I went upstairs to have a shower and change and, when I came down, I found Madame waiting for me at the bottom of the stairs, together with Lynne and Dave.

"Monsieur Harverson had arrived and was waiting for me in Madame's office", I was told.

'We don't know what it's about,' Dave said, adding 'but I think you'll be shocked by his travelling companion, but we'll be with you,' and he squeezed my shoulder reassuringly.

'O.M.G. he surely hasn't brought Christophe with him?' I whispered to Dave, who shook his head and I added, 'Then he's going to say George Barker's not really dead?'

'No, but there is a connection,' Dave replied mysteriously, reaching out his hand protectively and leading me in, with Lynne following close behind, but at the door I turned.

'I've not forgotten what you said, but I want you with me for this. Please,' I whispered to Stèphane, who was in the hallway. He nodded and we all went into the office and I introduced Stèphane to John.

Then I turned to John's companion. I didn't recognise her at first. She'd looked different at the funeral, all in black, and with the half veil on her hat hiding part of her face. I gasped!

'What on earth are you doing here?' I demanded. Even though I now knew George Barker wasn't my father, I still felt contempt for this woman, who must've made my mother's life miserable, and I couldn't think of one reason why John would bring her.

'Please sit down, all of you,' John said, and gestured to the chairs, including the one he'd just added for Stèphane, 'I'll explain the reasons for Ms Rindt's presence later,' he said to me.

'This is going to be a very difficult conversation, and I'm still struggling with the best way to tell you why I've come here today. There are two reasons, and it's difficult to know which one to begin with, so I'll start with the one least life-changing.'

Then he looked at Stèphane who had, comfortingly, moved his chair closer to mine.

'I wasn't anticipating you being here', John said to him, 'and I'm not sure it's appropriate.'

'Stèphane is my oldest friend,' I stated.

'So was Christophe, if I remember rightly?' John frowned. 'So perhaps we should begin with why Stèphane is here, and not Christophe?'

'I broke off my engagement to Christophe and haven't seen him since,' I explained, feeling no emotion, 'and Stèphane lives here, and my father, Dave, has been supervising the renovation and repair of this chateau, which was in a desperate state, and that's why he and Lynne are here.

John nodded, adding 'I still don't think Stèphane should be present'.

'Stèphane is staying, so just get on with it please John, and I want to know why you never transferred the funds I asked you to yesterday.'

'Oh no,' he sighed deeply.

Good grief it couldn't be that bad?

'Very well, we'll start with the transfer of funds. I did it as soon as you asked Fay. If you're saying there are no funds in your account, then it only confirms what I was dreading, and why I've been begging you to contact me.

By ignoring all my desperate e-mails, and the messages left on your phone, you left me no alternative but to come here.'

'I hardly use my mobile, and I've only had a couple of emails from you, and I didn't see any reason for them to be urgent' I retorted.

'Fay I've come here because I believe your system has been hacked. I grew more and more worried each time you asked for money to be transferred, especially when you didn't confirm you'd got it, despite my requesting you do so.'

'But I've only asked for funds a couple of times John, so how do you mean "each time I asked for money".

John said nothing, but sat looking at me, frowning and rubbing his chin, then he looked again at Stèphane.

'Fay, have you ever divulged your passwords, for your email, or any of your bank details to anyone?'

'No of course not' I replied indignantly. Then I froze.

'Christophe!' I whispered 'O.M.G.'

Stèphane was shocked. 'Why on earth would you give Christophe those details?' he asked.

I turned back to John, 'After my fall, I was told I had to pay for my treatment before I allowed to leave the hospital, however, in order to be able to do this, I needed to transfer extra funds into my debit card account. Unfortunately, the use of mobile 'phones was forbidden inside the hospital, so I wrote my details on a piece of paper, which Christophe took outside, with my mobile, He accessed my account, transferred the funds, then returned and gave me back the piece of paper - so he didn't keep the information.'

'But he could've copied it?' John asked.

'But why would he?'

'Why indeed? Over the past few weeks I've been asked to make numerous transfers of money to your bank account, and that's without your most recent request. It's all been by email, supposedly from yourself, but you say you've not sent them and received none of the money?'

'No, other than ten thousand pounds I asked, for just after my visit to your office, another sum ten days ago, which I did receive, and a large sum the day before yesterday, which I did not receive.'

I looked at Stèphane who was as white as a sheet.

'Oh Stèphane' I stammered, 'that night as we drove past him, the night you punched him, he said he'd make me sorry.'

John had raised his eyebrows.

Stèphane and I looked at one another, recalling how we'd laughed at him en-route to the plan d'eau.

'Fay, I'm so sorry. I knew he was capable of cruelty. But this …….' And he left the room.

I suspected he was going to tell his parents about Christophe.

 We all sat in shocked silence.

'Perhaps we should leave the second reason for my visit until later?' John said.

There was a knock on the door and Monsieur Richarde came in.

Monsieur sat down next to me. 'Stèphane has told us. It's terrible. If you wish to call the police then you must do so. Christophe has committed a crime, but whatever you decide, the money will be returned to you, in full.'

'If he still has it,' John observed. 'Do you know why he might have needed it so badly that he was prepared to steal it?'

'Yes, I'm afraid I do, you see Christophe has a gambling habit. We've had problems for many years. If we'd realised you had such money Fay, we would have warned you, although I'm not sure you'd have believed us. Madame and I will give it back to you ourselves if necessary.'

He was right, until the bust up I thought Christophe was pretty well perfect, and I'd have probably thought it was his mother trying to stop the wedding.

'I can't possibly let you pay me back Monsieur Richarde, since it's not your fault, but thank you for the offer.

Madame had come into the room, 'Oh we'll just take it out of

Christophe's share of the proceeds, from the sale of the chateau treasure,' she said.

I could've slapped her. It was like saying "we wouldn't have offered otherwise".

Her husband glared at her.

Then she said, 'I told you Fay that I couldn't understand how someone as intelligent as you could be silly enough to fall for Christophe, but I certainly can't believe you could be stupid enough to give him your password and account details.'

She was as good as saying it was my own fault and I deserved what happened. This was war!

Lynne came over and put her arm around me protectively, then she said 'And you Madame, and your husband, are such charming people, that I can't believe you could be so stupid as to bring your son up so badly!'

Lynne had expressed just what I was thinking, except my version would've had contained 'bastard' and a few 'f' words!

Monsieur hurriedly ushered his wife out of the room, saying he'd bring us coffee.

'Christophe must've planned it right from when had my accident,' I whispered, because that was when I told him I had my mother's house to sell, and what it might be worth. He also asked if I used the same password for my emails. That must be why I never received those from Stèphane. Christophe must've been intercepting my emails for weeks.'

Surprisingly, it was Madame who brought the coffee. I could hear Stèphane's voice in the distance and asked when he'd be returning.

'He won't' Madame said, 'We have something of a family crisis,' and she left. I was disappointed, but I'd have been far more had I realised that I might never see Stèphane again.

****

Lynne calmly took over, poured our drinks and handed them round with those lovely little oblong biscuits the French serve with coffee.

Once she was seated, back with Dave, we waited expectantly, but John said nothing more until we'd finished and put our cups back on the tray.

None of us could think of anything else he might need to talk to us about, but he now took a deep breath and began on his second reason for this visit.

****

'When you were in my office, back home, I persuaded you all to supply DNA samples. I think you, Mr Broome, guessed there was more to it than my idle curiosity, and a hobby involving DNA studies. In fact, I actually needed them, to send away for professional testing.'

Dave nodded, 'Yes, I thought at the very least you were checking that my DNA results letter was genuine, but I was happy with that.'

 John nodded and continued, 'The sample from Christophe Richarde was likely to be irrelevant, and proved to be so, but it would've looked odd if I'd left him out.'

 'And mine was irrelevant too, of course,' Lynne said.

Weirdly, John didn't answer her, but turned back to me and said, 'My request for samples was based on something your father, or rather George Barker, said to me, several years ago Fay.

At the time I dismissed it as ridiculous, possibly because I didn't want it to be true. Had I believed what he said I wouldn't have known what to do with the information, I'd have been bound by professional conduct rules of course, but morally . . . . .' he tailed off.

Now we were all confused.

'Fai, I asked you for a copy of the letter your father had left with me, because I wanted to see whether he gave you any clues, or even perhaps told you, what he'd confided to me.'

'And did he?' I asked, pretty sure he hadn't.

'Well actually he did, but so subtly that probably, neither you, nor anyone else would've picked up on it.'

 'Fay let us read the letter and we thought some of the wording was a bit odd,' Dave said.

'What in particular?' John asked.

'He said that "his wife had to have a baby, so he made sure of it", or something like that. It was peculiar wording, made no sense. Then there was also something about "being sorry for me, once he was told that Monsieur Richarde was Fay's father". It was all most peculiar.'

John Harverson was nodding, 'As I said, the clues were there, then Ms Rindt, and he gestured towards our extra 'guest', (whom I'd almost forgotten was in the room) came to see me a few days ago. She'd been searching unsuccessfully for you Fay, but we'd met at George's funeral and she remembered this, and managed to trace me to my office.

Then when she confided her reason for trying to find you, I wasn't as shocked as she'd expected, since it was the same story I'd heard from George Barker, years before and dismissed.'

I felt like saying 'For God's sake John just get on with it! Spit it out!', but I didn't, thankfully, as it turned out.

'The results of all your DNA samples arrived on my desk the following day, and they confirmed everything,' he said mysteriously.

'Everything?' we said in chorus

'Yes everything. Now, I'm choosing my words very carefully, because none of your lives will ever be the same again, after I impart this information, and I have no way of knowing how any of you will deal with it.'

What was he chuntering on about?' "What a drama queen" I thought.

'But what could the DNA results show, that was so different from what we, who were involved expected?' Dave asked, perplexed.

John was clearly struggling, and, for the first time, I began to get alarmed, especially as he turned his full gaze on me.

'What they told me Fay, is that not only is Dave your father, but Lynne is your mother.'

We were all stunned into silence. Lynne had gone very pale.

John turned to the Dutch woman. 'Perhaps you would tell us what you know Ms Rindt?'

So the smartly dressed interloper began, in a quiet, but clear voice, looking straight at me.

'Your father, or rather George Barker, told me that when his daughter, Ferelith, known as Fay, was born at 8 o'clock in the evening, all seemed well. He was still very much in love with your mother and, seeing her overwhelming joy at your safe arrival, was prepared to pretend to the world that the baby was his. His mother Margaret, although I believe you called her Nana Molly, arrived, thrilled at the arrival of her first grandchild.

George remained at the hospital, throughout the night and his mother stayed too

Meanwhile, Mrs Broome, just after midnight, i.e the next day, gave birth to twins, a boy and a girl.'

'Yes, and my baby girl died,' Lynne whispered. Dave put his arm around her and held her close. I gasped, this explained the shadow that had crossed her face a couple of times in past conversations.

'No, it was Ferelith Barker who died,' Ms Rindt said quietly, but firmly.

Now there were gasps all around the room.

Ms Rindt continued, 'George told me that the babies were all in the nursery, so he and his mother sat with his wife, who'd fallen asleep.

All was quiet and they couldn't help overhearing a nurse, who clearly had severe financial problems and was 'phoning round all her friends, trying to borrow money. He said she sounded desperate.

At about 3 a.m., his wife was still asleep, and George and his mother tiptoed into the nursery to look at Ferelith. The Broome twins had also been brought int the nursery by then, but when George and his mother leant over Fay's cot, they were shocked to find she wasn't breathing and was quite obviously dead.

George was frantic, because he knew that Liza, as he called his wife, wouldn't be able to cope with losing the baby Then his mother saw the nurse with money problems and she took over.

Margaret Barker told the nurse what had happened, and promised to pay the nurse £5,000, if she'd help them. She told the nurse what she wanted

200

her to do, then she wrote the cheque and waved it under her nose.

When the nurse hesitated, George Barker joined in, promising to add another £5,000, in cash, the very next day. All she had to do was immediately switch anything that identified the babies, wristbands, ankle bands, clothes etc. Seeing a way out of her troubles, the nurse gave in and went ahead, making all the changes.'

 At this point Ms Rindt turned to Dave and Lynne who were clearly in a state of horrified shock.

'George and his mother returned to Elizabeth, with the 'switched Ferelith'. The nurse then waited a short while before' finding' your daughter, Christine dead, when actually it was Ferelith, in Christine's clothing. '

'And that's what he meant in his letter by "making sure his wife had a baby",' John said. 'He did, but it was yours.'

Ms Rindt then said to Dave. 'George told me he saw you watching Fay one day, years later and he thought you were coming close to guessing that Fay was actually Christine. That's when they left their home and went into hiding.'

I was horrified. It was so awful, so shocking, that I ran out of the room, through the house, out of the back door and up through the undergrowth to the 'Coffin Tree', where I pounded the tree with my fists.

'You bring bad luck to everyone', I told the tree. 'No wonder Romain thinks you're evil. Everything bad on this estate has probably been caused by you, the problems with the chateau, Christophe being a little shit, my accident, Stèphane telling me to go away. Even pointing us to the treasure has turned out to be bad, because of the way the bitch Richarde has behaved since. And now this. My beloved Nana Molly stole me, how could she?

 I'm Ferelith, but Ferelith is dead, and you deserve to die too. I lay on the ground, silently weeping, I don't know for how long, but then I heard sirens, and flashing lights lit up the sky.

CHAPTER 21

The sirens and lights came closer and closer, but I ignored them and lay, shaking, on the grass, still trying to cope with what I'd just learned.

Eventually, I heard Monsieur Richarde calling my name. I didn't move, or make a sound, but still he found me. 'Fay, you must come. Lynne has collapsed. She's been taken to the hospital. I'll drive you in my car.'

'O.M.G.', I clutched my chest area. 'There you are - it's all your bloody fault again,' I muttered, as I stood up and kicked the coffin tree, 'Die' I hissed at it' again, then I ran down to the house.

Going into my automatic "Cope in an Emergency mode," I knew Lynne wouldn't have taken her bag, but it would be the first thing she'd asked for, so I put it, plus her hairbrush and a lipstick, into a carrier bag. Then I ran along to my own room, grabbed my own bag and went back downstairs. It was very quiet.

'Where are Stèphane and Madame? I asked.

'They're not here,' Monsieur replied, evasively, as we got into his car.

'And Mr Harverson and Ms Rindt?'

'They've gone too. Neither of us spoke again after that, and we arrived at the hospital in Poitiers some 45 minutes later. A nurse took us to a waiting room, then Monsieur said, 'I must get back, I'm sorry', and he left.

I felt so alone, in a foreign country, with a father I hardly knew, and a new mother who'd collapsed, and my darling Stèphane had abandoned me.

I waited, in the sparely furnished room, just a few wipe clean chairs, a bench and a coffee table with a pile of French magazines. Apart from a couple of nondescript pictures, the walls were bare. Not even a clock!

My watch said 10pm. I wished someone would come and tell me what was happening, but no-one did and, eventually, I lay down on the bench and fell asleep.

It was 5 a.m. when I awoke, stiff and aching, amazed I hadn't rolled onto the floor in the night, then I realised I wasn't alone.

Dave and Lynne's middle son, Jack, the surgeon, was also in the room.

'Hi' he said,

I sat up and asked how he got there so quickly, and he muttered something about a friend with a private plane.

'Have you heard anything?' I said hesitantly and he replied that Lynne was in theatre, undergoing surgery. We'd know more later.

'Where's your dad?' I asked. He didn't correct me that Dave was 'our' dad.

'He's having a wash and shave. He'll be here soon.' I nodded. 'I understand the attack was brought on by discovering you're her daughter?'

I nodded sadly, then he came and sat next to me. 'I don't suppose it was any less of a shock for you Fay. Pretty unbelievable story. How could anyone do what George Barker and his mother did?'

I shook my head, thinking that George must've really loved his wife back then. Sadly, it was never apparent to me.

'Ah you're awake', Dave said as he came into the room, with two coffees, and Jack immediately went to get one for me.

'Was it my fault it happened?' I asked.

'If you mean, did learning the truth cause her collapse, the answer is yes, but it was in no way your fault. How could it be? You're just as much the innocent victim in all of this as Lynne and myself.'

Jack returned with my coffee. 'I've just seen the theatre nurse. Mum's in the recovery room, until she comes round. Everything went well, and the surgeon will come and see us soon.'

Dave visibly relaxed. Poor man, He'd probably sat here, frantic with worry, while I slept.

'Useful to have a surgeon on our team, he can interpret, when we're told the surgical bit,' Dave winked at me, and I smiled wanly, then he suggested we have some breakfast. Suddenly, I felt ravenous, then remembered that I'd brought Lynne's things, so I handed over the carrier bag to Dave.

'Oh you angel, she can't live without her 'lippie,' Dave laughed. 'She'll love you even more now, if that's possible'.

I registered what he said, 'love me even more,' and it felt good, so good.

In the canteen, I tucked into scrambled egg and croissants, with hot chocolate from a large insulated jug. The French do love hot chocolate with breakfast.

Then we returned to the waiting room, and a nurse came to tell us the surgeon had been delayed, and that Lynne was drowsy, but awake. She could soon have one visitor.

Dave and I both thought it should be Jack, as he could assess her medically and, after a few minutes he returned, looking relieved. Then Dave saw her next and after that, it was my turn. She lay smiling at me. 'I'm so happy, so very happy,' she said, as she reached out and touched my face.

'Really?' I asked and she nodded. I was now very happy too.

Later in the morning, when I was alone I the waiting room, Madame Richarde suddenly appeared and gave me two pieces of plastic.

'Hotel keys' she explained. 'I've booked you and your father into adjacent twin rooms at the Mercure hotel close by. It'll be very convenient for the hospital.

You'll find all your belongings there, including the boxes which you stored in Stèphane's studio.

Her underlying message was crystal clear – "Here's all your stuff – now get out of my life!"

'Monsieur Harverson gave me your bank details, for the refund and also a reward for the treasure find, (she seemed to have trouble saying this last bit), before he returned to le Royaume Uni. He'll talk to you when you are settled back there with your family, and Ms Rindt has returned to les Pays-Bas. There'll be no need for you to come back to the chateau, so I'll say goodbye.'

I stared at her in utter disbelief. What a spiteful old hag! Charming and elegant she may be, but she was a charming elegant old hag!

'I'll return to the chateau - to see Stèphane,' I said firmly.

'No Fay you won't,' she replied, equally firmly. 'He flew to Reunion last evening, where storms have caused severe damage to our property. He'll be there, probably for many weeks, supervising repairs. His new assistant is handling everything at the chateau.'

She said a lot more, but the gist was that I wasn't needed, or wanted and I was to blame for the disintegration of her family. So much for my belief that finding the lost treasures would make me flavour of the month!

Just for a moment she looked unsure how to say goodbye, then she turned on her heel and left.

Jack, happy with his mother's treatment, returned to the UK after a few days, and we all began adjusting to the shocking news which had caused Lynne's collapse that awful evening.

I'd already been getting used to having three half-brothers and a new father, so to find they were "full" brothers wasn't much different, except it felt weird that I was a twin. I was half of a pair!

When not visiting Lynne, I spent time changing my passwords and sorting through the boxes Madame Richarde had brought.

As I sorted, I chose pictures for Dave and Lynne, charting that part of my life they'd missed out on, and I wrote notes, to go with these. This gave them a photographic timeline as I grew up, and seemed to comfort Lynne enormously.

She and Dave said they'd do the same for me, and I could collect it at Christmas, when I went over to spend the festive season with them all.

Lynne took to calling me 'her baby girl', and we reminisced how, when I was small, she'd sometimes pretended I was her little girl, and I'd sometimes wished she was my mum. Perhaps deep down something inside us had always known?

John Harverson began sorting out the legal side of my situation, and together, Lynne and I agreed, that, since I'd always been known as "Fay", it was easiest to keep that as my new registered name. Ferelith Elizabeth Margaret Barker would be legally registered as deceased, and I'd legally become Fay Christine Lynne Broome.

Madame transferred the stolen money to my account, but not before she'd tried to force me into agreeing never to bring any charges against Christophe.

I instructed John to tell her that I couldn't agree to this, and what's more, I'd definitely prosecute if I didn't have the full money, by the following day,

Why should I let him off the hook so easily? The spoilt brat should be punished, and I could only do this by terrifying him with the threat of bringing charges, which would appear in the newspapers and ultimately destroy him.

I was immediately reimbursed in full, plus another 5,000 euros, my 'reward' for finding the millions of euros worth of 'lost treasures'! Another slap in the face!

The estimated value of the paintings alone had been in excess of 3.5 million euros, which the Richardes were going to divide between themselves and their three sons. Therefore, Christophe's share would be in the region of 700,000 euros. I'd been refunded the 500,000 he'd stolen, but It still left him 200,000, which he'd presumably gamble away!

We said nothing to Lynne, but Dave was furious. 'You saved their chateau, provided a comfortable future for all of them, and that's your thanks; less than .2% of the estimated value. Even the auctioneers, who'll do precious little, will probably get 15%!'

The money didn't bother me and I really didn't care if that's all they thought I was worth. However, I now understood the emotion Christophe had felt, when he'd said he'd make me sorry, because that's how I felt now about his mother. I wanted to make her very sorry indeed, for the spiteful things she'd said to me, and how she'd denied me any chance to see Stèphane ever again!

Taking Lynne's advice to heart, I shall spend some time working on the Maison D, and then I'll get in touch with Stèphane - and this time I won't mess it up. I'll win his heart back somehow and then let's see how his bitch of a mother copes with that!

Once the stolen money was safely in my French bank account, I called the Notaire, asking if the buying process could be speeded up, as I'd now become homeless.

He immediately contacted the vendors, who, surprisingly, said I could move in at once, as long as the full balance of the sale figure was deposited with the Notaire, ready for payment on the due date. I'd be responsible for any damage, and must pay heating, water and other bills. Naturally, I agreed and transferred the balance to the Notaire's account immediately.

I couldn't believe it. I could move in, well I could if I had any furniture, so ! I got straight on to the suppliers and was able to bring forward delivery, of all the items I'd ordered, ready for the original completion date. All I had to do now was buy stuff like pots and pans, crockery and cutlery.

'Oh I'd so love to see everything we chose together, in place in your new house' Lynne smiled wistfully.

'Well perhaps you can,' Dave said mysteriously. 'I've just been told you can leave hospital in a couple of days, as long as you to stay fairly close, at least for the first week. I was going to take you to the hotel, but I'm wondering how Fay would feel about having visitors?' He turned to me.

'Oh I'd love that,' I grinned broadly, 'We can do some more shopping - but on line,' I added quickly, when I saw Dave's concerned face. 'Should we have one of the beds downstairs?'

'Not necessary, Doctor says walking and stairs are good heart exercise - in moderation,' Dave replied. So, a couple of days later we collected Lynne and we all moved into the Maison D.

The days passed quickly, as Lynne and I discussed my plans and chose colour schemes and, all too soon, it was time for Lynne's hospital check-up, which showed she'd made an excellent recovery. So much so, that a week later, I drove them to Limoges airport, in Dave's car, and we said a tearful goodbye.

Dave had thought it best to fly back, so left his car for my use, as they'd have Lynne's car when they got home. He was even wondering whether to keep his car permanently in France, to use when they visited me, which Lynne said would be often.

Knowing how much I was going to miss them, I stopped off to buy decorating materials and a stepladder on the way back from the airport. I had to keep myself busy, or I could get maudlin in my beautiful, but big, house, which now felt very empty.

Early next morning I put newspaper on the floor of the snug, covered the furniture with dust-sheets, then painted the ceiling cream. By the time I finished, I ached all over, so I stood under a hot shower then put my pj's on and fell asleep in a chair. The following day I gave the ceiling a second coat, and had just finished, when I had a visitor.

It was the member of the Clouseau pantomime cast I'd named Smelly (and he still was!) He reminded me he was Jean-Claude, in case I'd forgotten (which I had), and wanted to know if I'd like him to carry on tending the garden.

I couldn't tell weeds from plants so, I was delighted to agree to 4 hours each Wednesday, with payment in cash; we shook hands and he left.

Over the next few days i painted one wall of the snug burnt orange, and the other three warm cream, and was really pleased with the outcome. It'd all been done with Stèphane in mind, burnt orange being his favourite colour, although I couldn't think for the life of me how I knew this

I added matching cushions to my shopping list, making a mental note to paint a large picture to hang on the snug wall, which would also contain some burnt orange colour and I began preliminary sketches that night.

My next target was to decorate the huge kitchen, and turn the small kitchen into a utility and laundry room, as I may really do b&b in the future.

One of the kitchen walls would be in earthy tones and on it I'd paint a full-size lemon tree, covered in fruit. Once again, I was sure Stèphane would love it.

He was never far from my thoughts and, occasionally, I looked at his website, but I'd been shocked to see how much it had changed. There were no longer any pieces being offered for sale in the way we'd agreed, and there was a new email address for contact.

Sadly, a few days later, I discovered the reason, and it was to spoil my Christmas. I'd been trying to watch a little French television each evening, and the news seemed to be the best choice, as the newsreaders spoke clearly and at a reasonable speed. This particular evening, I settled down with my supper and a glass of wine and turned on the news channel.

The main feature seemed to be coverage of a film premiere. The commentator was talking to people on the red carpet, who were posing for photographs before they entered the building.

It wasn't my sort of thing but, just as I was about to switch channels, the camera zoomed in to feature an ornate silver buckle, being worn by one of the main players, and at the same time, a cameo picture of Stèphane, clean shaven and looking extremely handsome, appeared in the bottom right hand corner of my screen.

I gasped. O.M.G! He must've made this buckle, and it was on a Balenciaga outfit, wow. How amazing was that! I could see now why he was no longer offering the limited-edition pieces on his website, if he was getting commissions like this. How exciting!

I was so thrilled and happy for him, that I wanted to 'phone and share his excitement, for surely he must be ecstatic. However, there was now no telephone number on his website, and I didn't want to call the chateau number in case his mother answered. With Stèphane's new-found success she'd probably be more determined than ever to keep me away from him.

I tried his mobile, but all I got was an announcement saying the line was discontinued. His email address message said the same. So, he'd changed his all his contact details, or they'd been changed for him!

Suddenly I felt cut off from Stèphane - my Stèphane. Until now I'd believed I could contact him easily and would do so when the time was right, but I now knew this wasn't the case and, although, still delighted at his success, I went to bed feeling very pretty low. I wasn't feeling much happier when I left for the UK a few days later.

It was mid-December and I'd decided, with Dave's agreement, to drive the car back, so I could also go and visit Rosie and Jules. The trailer would remain in France, which I was relieved about, because I hadn't fully mastered the art of reversing it. Just the thought of having to do this on board a ferry terrified me so much that I'd even dreamt that, while boarding, I'd reversed the trailer straight through the side and the ferry was sinking!

My journey to St Malo, the crossing, and my drive to Lynne and Dave's, was uneventful, but it felt strange to be back there again, in the house where I now knew I should've grown up. It was also a very new experience to spend Christmas with a house full of people.

The days before Christmas whizzed by and, under orders, I kept Lynne company. She'd sorted out photographs of their lives through the 'missing years' and we chatted about where and when each was taken. Then, at last, I had the chance to be alone with her, and I told her about Stèphane, the shock of his tv appearance, and his high-flying success.

To my surprise Lynne already knew. She'd seen a picture of him in a glossy magazine at her hairdresser's, where he'd been described as, "A new young talent on the fashion scene, specialising in commissions from the top couturiers."

I told her how I'd tried, unsuccessfully, to contact him, and how it seemed as though he'd grown away from me, but Lynne was adamant that she'd got to know him well enough at the chateau to believe that success wouldn't change him.

'He's too grounded for that', she reassured me. I just hoped she was right, but I still felt sad.

The main Christmas meal was held at Dave and Lynne's, otherwise much of the time, from Christmas to New Year, was spent socialising with their many friends. They were obviously a very popular couple. A popular family even, as the boys and their partners/families were also invited and I was now automatically included too, and made to feel very welcome.

If it hadn't been for "the Stèphane situation", I could've been deliriously happy.

As New Year approached, I thought back over the past year. My 'mother's' death, my escape to France, meeting Stèphane and staying at the chateau. My accident, seeing Christophe again, and all that had brought about. Finding the 'hidden treasures' after more than 200 years, which led to the chateau being saved, buying my Maison-de-Maitre, discovering that Lynne and Dave were both my natural parents, learning the truth about George Barker and the woman who had been my darling

Nana Molly, but whom I now despised, and then Lynne's subsequent collapse and operation.

Added to that, Madame Richarde turning on me, Stèphane deserting me and, finally, in the past few days, with all the paperwork complete, I'd assumed my new name and Lynne had taken me to see the grave where the baby they'd always believed to be theirs, was buried.

They'd replaced her gravestone and it now read 'Ferelith Margaret Elizabeth Barker', which made me shiver, as I'd carried that name for 26 years. We left some flowers and Lynne and I shed a few tears. It was a fitting end to the tumultuous year.

Back at the house, Lynne broke into my thoughts. 'You look as though you're miles away?'

I smiled, 'I was just going over the year's events. It's been quite extraordinary, amazing even.'

'It certainly has,' Dave bent down and kissed the top of my head, as he went to sit next to Lynne.

That was another strange thing; because I'd been immersed in family for the past two and a half weeks, without realising it, I now often called Lynne and Dave, mum and dad, because the boys did I suppose. It seemed so natural, and everyone just accepted it.

New Year came, but, when the celebrations were over, I couldn't believe how hard it had become to leave everyone, in order to visit Rosie and Jules. I felt sure that, if I hadn't already bought the Maison de Maitre, I'd have been happy now to get a job and a flat and live close to Lynne and Dave. As it was, I must return to France. Despite everything, I was still on a mission to win Stèphane's heart, although how I was going to do this now I'd no idea.

The night before I left, Dave, Lynne and I spent a quiet evening together, discussing my plans for my house, then, not unnaturally, Dave asked 'What about Stèphane?'

'I absolutely don't know', I replied, adding 'She's got a tight rein on her boys again, the future of the chateau is secured and they've sold the paintings and have spare money in the bank. She's even added fame to her achievements, because I don't believe for a minute that all of this stuff with the world's leading fashion houses came by accident. She's probably hoping Stèphane and Christophe will marry a couple of the world's top models, or film stars.'

Lynne snorted! 'I doubt it. Stèphane might agree to being photographed with them, and all the other pretty little things, but is smacks of a publicity stunt to me, not of Stèphane's doing.'

I smiled wryly. I'd have loved to believe she was right.

'Well, it's probably all academic. I'd just have loved to beat his mother at something, but now she's got everything. I expect she's even found the rest of the treasure as well.'

'I doubt it' Dave said quietly and my senses were instantly alert! Then he added, you've won more than you know.'

'Why do you say that?' I asked him.

Lynne's eyebrows were in her hairline and her face said, 'I thought this was a secret!'

'No more secrets,' Dave sighed, and he poured us all another glass of wine and then began.

'I'm not sure what you're going to think of what I'm about to say Fay, but I've scored a couple of victories for you and I hope you won't mind.'

I frowned, whatever could he mean.

'Firstly, I was cross that the Richardes thought the 5,000 euros they gave you was an acceptable reward, for you finding paintings worth millions, he held up his hand. 'I know you're going to say you didn't expect anything, and I believe you, but I was cross and insulted on your behalf, so I got some more for you.'

'Really?' I exclaimed, 'How?'

'Well, when she was a bitch to me, the day you and Lynne were house hunting, I decided to prepare a bill for them, saying it was for my services. Actually, it was my way of claiming the reward I believe should have received, for locating the treasure. It's in the bank whenever you wish to have it – 350,000 euros!'

'What?' I exclaimed adding, 'I'm amazed they agreed to pay it'

'Well, I took legal advice first, to be sure, on the day we saw your Notaire? If you remember you all left the office, and I stayed behind. I told the Notaire of my intention to charge the Richardes for my services, and he thought it perfectly acceptable.

He confirmed what I thought, i.e. whether they'd originally asked me to help or not, they'd subsequently taken advantage of my advice, even ordering me to carry out work on their behalf. He also thought that, like Christophe, they'd not welcome any adverse publicity if they refused to pay up.'

'Wow!' was all I could say, then I thanked him, but said I thought we ought to at least share it. He just smiled, said that wasn't necessary, so to avoid an argument, I decided to leave it like that for now.

However, I was still curious as to why Dave thought it unlikely that the Richardes would've found any more treasure.

He studied me for a moment. 'I get the impression you're hoping they don't?

'Absolutely' I agreed emphatically.

He nodded, took a deep breath then said, 'Well, the reason why I don't believe they''ll ever find it is because it's now buried in concrete.

I nearly fell off my chair. Open mouthed with astonishment, I asked what he meant, so he began:- 'Well, as you know, Madame Richarde had become quite obnoxious, ordering people about, as though they were servants. "Dig here, dig there, get on with it," certain there must be more boxes to be found but, in her haste, she'd overlooked properly examining what we'd first unearthed.

I hadn't, and among the pieces of what was left of the "coffin box" containing the treasure, I'd found a carefully concealed sliver of stone, possibly scrap from the making of the small marker headstone. On it were the words 'sous la tourelle est.'

'Under the east turret,' I breathed. 'The damaged one?'

'Quite so. Anyway, I took this fragment down to the turret and looked more closely at the base This had only become visible when we'd excavated, ready to pour the concrete, and upon closer inspection, I could see the foundations of the tower had been tampered with. Several stones had been removed, probably in haste, to hide the treasures, and not been replaced properly.

In that moment I also realised that, ironically, it was actually this tampering, not the altering of the watercourse, which had caused the subsidence of the tower!

I removed the stones, in order to re-site them properly, and using a strong beam, I could see, in the void under the tower, the rest of the silverware, a lot of glassware and porcelain, and several neatly stacked parcels of rolled up pictures.'

My jaw had dropped.

'That's what I went to tell her, and I tried to, several times, but when she told me to "shut up and go away and just get on with pouring the concrete," I went back, replaced the stones properly, then did as she'd demanded.

Two whole lorry loads of concrete went into the base of the tower and, because it was pumped under pressure, it was forced under the wall and up into the void, ruining all the treasure, but stabilising the tower. Then we got on and finished the job.

'So she's probably going to waste the rest of her life fruitlessly searching,' I grinned?

'Oh I do hope so,' Dave replied and we all laughed.

'So you see' Lynne smiled, I think you've beaten her on all fronts but one, so you'll just have to make that one happen, then you'll have total victory.'

'I can hardly believe any of it,' I breathed.

I left next morning, glad that Dave and Lynne were planning to come over to France, to stay with me for Easter. 'Perhaps you'll have some news by then?' Lynne whispered in my ear. 'You'll find a way to make it happen, I just know it,' and she hugged me tightly.

'Don't count on it', I smiled wryly, as I got into the car, then, as I drove off, I wound down my window and called 'You're the most wonderful parents and I love you both!'

CHAPTER 22

As I drove to my flat, I thought back over this recent conversation and smiled happily, then when I arrived, I rang Rosie and Jules. After this I began unloading my food supplies, plus towels and bedding I'd remembered to bring from France, however, the one thing I had forgotten, was how bare I'd left the place. Stripped and, ready to rent out, it felt quite impersonal.

The girls arrived whilst I was still emptying the car and mucked in. They were great. Why had I let Christophe poison me against them? I was just so glad they'd never realised.

Jules put the kettle on, 'Wine later,' she said, noting my surprise. 'New Year's res. We're like cutting down on the booze babe.'

I nodded. Tea made, we all sat down, and they waited expectantly, so I brought them up to date on all that had happened, since I went back to France, but none of what Dave had told me last night.

'Tell us about this house you've like bought then babe,' Jules said, so I got out my camera and showed them the pictures I'd taken.

'Bloody hell, it's f . . . .ing enormous. Whatever made you buy something like that?' Jules asked incredulously.

'I think it's wonderful,' Rosie sighed dreamily. 'I'd buy it tomorrow if I had the money.'

'Don't be ridiculous', Jules chided her 'It's like the size of a bloody hotel!'

'Well, that's the fall-back plan', I admitted half-heartedly. 'If I can't get Stèphane back, I'll run it as a Chambres d'hotes'.

'A what?' they chorused.

'It's like a b&b' I explained 'and I bought this house because it needs to be something special to tempt Stèphane away from the chateau.'

While Rosie drooled over the pictures, Jules asked how I planned to get Stèphane back and I admitted I'd drawn a blank at trying to contact him, and daren't turn up at the chateau. Anyway, I still had to finish the alterations and decorating first.

'I think you should start to run it as a b&b anyway, instead of waiting for something that might never happen', Jules remarked candidly.

I knew she didn't mean to be insensitive, but it still hurt, because it was all too possible.

'Do you know what' she continued? 'I reckon it's going to be too much for you. I get that you'll have workmen in for like the major stuff, but you need like mega help with the rest.'

Rosie stopped looking at the photos, 'Why don't we come and help!' she shrieked.

'That's what I was trying to suggest,' Jules said, petulant that Rosie had hijacked her idea.

They looked totally serious, so I reminded them they both had jobs, but I then learned that their employer had just dropped the bombshell that he was retiring and, unable to find a buyer was simply going to close down, early in the new year.

He'd assured Rosie and Jules they'd get redundancy money, but it still left them without jobs.

'So you see we can come back with you, no probs,' Jules said matter-of-factly, adding,'You can design, like a b&b website, get the place sorted, then you can find Stèphane. If things work out, the two of you can like fill the house with babies and we'll come home, and if it doesn't work out, we'll stay and help you run the "chamber dotty" thing.

I didn't know what to say. If I were honest with myself, I didn't want to go back to the Maison-de-Maitre to be on my own. They were right, it is enormous and, after Dave and Lynne had left, I'd felt lonelier than I'd ever done in my life before.

'Ok then that's decided,' Jules said decisively.

Rosie clapped her hands together, looking for all the world like a sea lion, and we all started to laugh, then I rang the ferry company and added two passengers to my booking.

'Come on Rosie Bud, time to pack,' and Jules pulled Rosie to her feet, then she hesitated; 'Just one thing, so's you know, the Rose Bud and me are an item. You O.K. with that?'

My eyes widened in astonishment, 'You mean?'

'Yeah, I mean we're gay, just so there's no misunderstanding. Can you hack that?'

How had I never guessed, I wondered. Oh, how my original parents would've reacted. My dad would've thrown a fit.

At this point I realised that, even if I never got together with Stèphane, I'd still have my wonderful natural parents, my brothers and their families, and Rosie and Jules for friends, which was a lot more than most people had.

Suddenly I was determined to enjoy the moment, and the excitement of Jules and Rosie coming to France. Worrying about Stèphane was for another day, and who knows, they may come up with a brilliant idea as to how I can get him back.

Next morning, I put my flat on the market, got rid of my furniture and booked into a b&b for a couple of nights. Meanwhile Rosie and Jules stripped their own flat, which they'd decided to rent out for a few months, to give them an income.

We loaded Dave's car, which even though it is a large estate model, was still stuffed to the gunnels by the time we'd got everything in, then we set off to catch the ferry.

The crossing was calm, so we ate well and, having stocked up on bottled water and snacks for the journey, we drove straight down to the Maison D, stopping only for the occasional pee.

It was very late evening when I turned in through the electric gates, and, just as I'd hoped, Rosie and Jules were both knocked out by the Maison D, illuminated in my headlights.

Unloading only what was necessary, I made up a room for them, said goodnight and fell into my own bed, exhausted, but loving there being someone else in the house with me.

The following morning Smelly turned up, so I knew it must be Wednesday. 'Bon jour Jean-Claude "ca va?" I called.

He asked if I'd had 'bonne vacances', I replied "oui merci". Our conversation was never much livelier than that.

In the afternoon, his brother, "Smartie Clouseau", turned up, welcoming me back and explaining that he'd called because Jacques, the estate agent who'd shown me the house, was a friend of his and had suggested I might want some work doing.

This was interesting, but it but wasn't clear to me why he was asking. He didn't look as though he was about to don a pair of overalls and get his hands dirty, any time soon.

Sensing my confusion, he explained that he had a small building company, employing various members of his family. We can do everything,' he declared emphatically.' Knock down, build up, electrics, plumbing, heating, woodwork,' the list seemed never ending, so I held up my hand to stop him.

'Je vous dit qu'est que je veux que vous faire.' I hoped I'd just said I'll tell you what I want you to do.
Until then, I'm sure he thought I didn't speak French, but I wanted him to be aware that, if he worked for me, I'd understand anything I overheard, well that's the theory.
The effect was that it brought a new respect, as he told me that many British people arrogantly don't bother to learn French; but because I had, he'd happily speak to me in either', then he added, with a laugh, 'and probably swear about you in both!'

Blunt, but it got the point across. Obviously builder-client relationships were much the same in France as at home, so I laughed too and said I reserved the right to do the same. Then we shook hands, to cement our new friendship, (apt word for a builder I thought).

I then took Smartie outside, to explain that I wanted the ground floor outhouses turned into a workshop, gallery and studio. These were intended for Stèphane, so might now be pointless, but an estimate would still be useful and I said I wanted a flat created, on the floor above.

'Perhaps to let out, or to live in myself, if use the main house for chambres d'hotes', I explained.

We went indoors and upstairs, where I told him I wanted a small bathroom constructed in each bedroom; the existing huge bathroom to be converted into a bedroom with en-suite shower room.

My plans clearly appealed to him. Before this I believe that he also thought I was mad to buy such a huge property, but to put it to use as a b&b made good sense to him.

I left the blue sitting room, and the enormous open area on the top floor, out of my request for quotes. These were earmarked for Stèphane and myself to plan together, (fingers crossed), but I was not about to share this information.

Smartie left; Jules and Rosie had emptied the car, so I made coffee and told them my plans, as I'd relayed them to Smartie, suggesting they might like to live in what had been the housekeeper's flat, above the stone arched former carriage store. It was obvious Rosie would've preferred to live in 'the big house' but she accepted that was to be for the b&b guests

At this point I realised that my thoughts were in danger of becoming more "chambres d'hotes" and less and less Stèphane living here.

I sighed inwardly.

As we ate lunch, I longed for the warm days when we could swim in the pool and eat on the terrace, but for the moment, Jules and Rosie wanted to talk about Stèphane, to see if between us, we could come up with a plan.

We couldn't, but Jules said, 'Don't worry babe, we'll get him back for you if we have to drag him here – and I do believe they would, so I smiled.

Smartie drew up plans and quotes for the work I'd specified and Rosie, Jules and I decorated the former housekeeper's flat, I bought some furniture, and they moved into it.

Having approved his quotes, Smartie's men began on the upstairs bathrooms, whilst I finally painted the full-size lemon tree, on the kitchen wall. and was delighted how well it turned out.

Then, we moved the snug furniture into the kitchen, and my bedroom furniture down to the snug, so Smartie could get on with the bedrooms.

After that, Rosie, Jules and I, spent most evenings together in the huge kitchen, lounging on the sofas, watching satellite tv, and in early March, Rosie and Jules, finally left their jobs and Rosie took up making jewellery from beads and wire. This proved surprisingly popular, on the stall they'd taken on once a week in the indoor market, in the nearby small town.

Meanwhile, using some of her redundancy money, Jules had bought a bright red Renault car, to transport them to market and she'd taken up baking. She now sold bakewell tarts, treacle tarts and other goodies, on the half of the stall which Rosie couldn't make enough jewellery to fill.

They were even learning French, both from Smartie and from some of the other stand-holders. I thought of it as "market French," because it mainly involved sizes, weights, costs and ingredients, but it was great to see them so happy. They seemed really settled here in France. I wished I could say the same.

The weeks went by, and as each of the bedrooms was finished, I decorated and furnished, and at Easter I moved into my new flat, so we had the snug back, and Lynne and Dave came to stay.

The weather was warmer, so Smartie's workforce began creating Stèphane's studio and workshop. He assured me all the work would be completed by the end of May, in readiness for my chambres d'hotes venture. He even made me a 'rooms to let' sign, to hang on the front wall, but I put it in a cupboard for now.

Easter, and I picked up Dave and Lynne from Limoges airport; It felt like forever since they were last here, and, immediately we got home, they wanted a tour, to see what had been done.

'You can give me your opinion on everything' I laughingly told them. 'Pretend you're paying guests and make a note of anything that's not right', but all the while I was desperate to get Lynne on her own, and guessing this, she sent Dave out on an errand.

It was market day, so Jules and Rosie were missing too and, as soon as we were alone I took her into the snug and turned on the television, and recorder.

Following on from the original tv appearance of Stèphane's buckle, and the cameo picture of him on the screen, it had all gone downhill for me, as he began to appear, actually in person, at such events, treading the red carpet, and often described as one of France's most eligible bachelors!

I felt as though the final curtain had fallen on any future I might have hoped for.

One after another, I showed her clips I'd saved, awards ceremonies, film premiers, and other important functions. It seemed as though he was invited everywhere, and he was always accompanied by a beautiful – and I mean stunningly beautiful – young woman!

We sat in silence as we watched, one after another, these women and this handsome, perfectly dressed, immaculately coiffed young man, who seemed no longer to be Stèphane.

When they finished Lynne asked, 'How often do you torture yourself by watching those?'

'Not often, but when I do, I feel sick to the stomach at the playboy he's become. I couldn't begin to compete with those fabulous creatures, nor would I ever want a lifestyle even remotely like that. I've lost him Lynne, he's not the same person.'

She put her arm around me and rested my head on her shoulder.

'You haven't lost him,' she said wisely. 'You're assuming that, because his outward appearance has changed, the innermost Stèphane has too, but I think that's unlikely and, if you notice they're different girls each time, so none of them have turned into anything more serious.'

I hadn't realised that, and I supposed she was right.

'However, I think it'll need careful planning Fay,' she continued, 'because now it's not just a case of turning up at the chateau, or waiting for him to appear so that you can waylay him. He may not even be at the chateau much. Perhaps you should try and get an idea where, and how, he's spending his time, and who he's spending it with?'

'I've tried that, trawling "the web", but there's very little on there I didn't already know.

'Well I still have this absolute conviction it will all come right Fay. My mother had sixth sense and sometimes I think I have it too'.

I so hoped she was right.

She and Dave went back home in early May, and I was even more glad of Rosie and Jules' company. By the middle of May, Smartie had nearly finished the workshop and studio, so I asked him to put up the b&b sign.

We had our first guests almost at once, a charming French couple, who were touring the area, and just happened to drive through the hamlet and saw the notice.

Two days later, in response to my new website, we had more people and, from then on, we got a steady trickle, until, by early June we were fully forward booked until the end of July.

****

Rosie, Jules and I had got into a routine of cleaning, washing, ironing and shopping. It worked well, and I paid the girls out of the b&b money, mostly cash, which was what they wanted. I laughed at how French they were becoming.

Unfortunately, while the chambres d'hotes was working well, my dream of future life with Stèphane had receded further and further into the realms of the unlikely.

Jules and Rosie were present almost every time he appeared on the t.v. and shared my pain, but, like Lynne, they were both convinced that if he knew where I was, I'd be the young woman on his arm, strutting my stuff along the red carpet.

However, as I explained to them, more than once, it was this very success that had killed our future, not whether he knew where I was. He now had a lifestyle I'd hate, and I had a lifestyle that I was certain he wouldn't want, and that was that. Because we were now very different people, leading totally diverse lifestyles, I'd have to finally accept it was over.

It was the one thing "La hag Richarde" had won after all, but I kept this thought to myself!

June was with us, the weather was beautiful, the heated pool was fabulous and as soon as the guests had left each morning, we changed beds and cleaned rooms. I then had until 3pm to swim, sunbathe, snooze, or anything else I cared to do.

The only thing missing was someone special to share it with, but my life wasn't empty by any means and the Tour de France was about to hit town!

We'd known for some time that the nearby small town had been chosen as the starting point for one of the stages of this world acclaimed cycle race. It was the same town where Rosie and Jules had their market stall, on Wednesdays. The stall which had been procured for them by a sceptical Smartie, (who seemed to be the go-to-person for everything), but had, nevertheless been delighted by their success.

He'd helped us locate good local eating places, even accompanying us on a couple of occasions and, come mid-June, an excited Rosie rushed in to tell me that the nearby town was buzzing with excitement, because the arrival of 'Le Tour' was imminent. Apparently Smartie would be picking all of us up, the day after tomorrow, to take us to watch it set off on its next stage.

'He says that there'll be nowhere to park because the town will be full of press and tv types, plus hundreds of bikers,' she gabbled breathlessly. It made me wonder where Smartie would park, but this turned out to be no problem as, apparently, he lived close to the square where all the excitement would be, so would use his own drive.

I'd been watching le Tour every day, mainly to see the fabulous French scenery, and learned that the cyclists would arrive the next evening and depart early the following afternoon.

Then Smartie called in and told us with a grin, that "Monsieur le Maire will make a long, and very boring, speech to welcome them and send them on their way, so It will be surprising if any of them are still awake enough to pedal by then."

I looked at him. I'd discovered he was a man of many parts and I'd been right about him not donning overalls, but he wasn't above helping the workforce unload lorries, and muck in when an extra pair of hands was needed.

I'd also found him to be very well read, and well-travelled, unusual in rural France. However, I never really learned anything about his personal life, but then I deliberately side stepped telling him anything about mine, so I couldn't complain.

He arranged to collect us at 11.30. the next morning, for aperitifs and a light lunch at his home, so, it appeared we were now about to enter a new chapter, going to dine 'chez Smartie'. It would be interesting to see where he lived. Would there be a partner perhaps?

He'd told me he wasn't married, but that didn't mean that he was unattached, and Jules and Rosie had heard that he was known locally as having a woman in every village. I'd laughed but there might be truth in the rumours.

On the dot at 11.30 he came into the courtyard and tooted his horn, checked we had sunhats, sunglasses and cameras and drove us to his home.

It was a very nice house, what they called a raised bungalow, with a basement underneath and steps at the front up to the living area, which was all on one level.

Aperitifs and nibbles were served on the terrace dead on 12 noon, followed by a ham and cheese salad, with wine, after which there was a selection of fruit, and a bowl of locally made ice cream for dessert. Then it was time to go.

As we walked down to the square and saw the enormous and densely packed crowds, I wondered how on earth we'd see anything. We even had to hold tightly onto each other, so as not to get separated, but, somehow we found a way through, right to the very front. The Maire saw us, or rather he saw Smartie, and beckoned us over to the dais where he was standing.

It became clear that we'd been expected, as the two men embraced and shook hands. Wow! we were now in prime position, right at the front, and next to the Maire. Smartie had put his arm around my shoulders, to draw us all close, and he left it there. It felt comforting, if a bit proprietorial, but the man had just given us lunch, and brought us here, so I said nothing.

The Maire made his speech, with Smartie making yawning faces to me behind his back. He did go on a bit I must agree, but then the cheers and the band became deafening, and they were off. Down the narrow streets went hundreds of cyclists plus dozens of press, motorcycles and team cars. It looked like total chaos, because the crowds rushed after them too.

'Come on,' Smartie said, and grabbed my hand, and I grabbed Jules and she grabbed Rosie, but I'd no idea where we were going.

It turned out we were getting Smartie's car, to follow the Tour by the back roads, because Smartie knew the route. It was exhilarating, but by 4 pm we'd all had enough, so Smartie took us home, to our newly arrived b&b guests.

It was another day that changed my life, although I didn't know it yet.

CHAPTER 23

A few days later, it was market day, so I was alone, clearing up after breakfast, cleaning rooms and stripping beds.

I was delighted at Jules and Rosie's market stall success, but I occasionally joked I'd have to give up on the chamber d'hotes, if they became much more successful, because I couldn't manage on my own.

Thankfully I'd taught Smellie (who still was!) how to do pool maintenance, so that was one less job. However, running the b&b had become more strèssful than I'd expected, so I'd started drawing and painting the plants in my gardens, for relaxation, and Jules and Rosie display some of these pictures on their stall each week, usually selling at least one or two.

I also I display them, with discreet price labels, in the guests' breakfast room, where they've also proven popular, which is a nice feeling.

I put the first lot of washing into the industrial size machine, made a cup of coffee and went into the snug where I turned on the tv. I told myself it was to check on the latest stage of the Tour de France which was coming to an end in a couple of days' time, but in truth, I'd turned on in the hope of seeing Stèphane featured somewhere, although heaven knows why I watch, because it only makes me miserable.

I'm continually shocked at just how successful he's become, and yes, there he is, escorting yet another beauty along another red carpet.

He's clean shaven and dresses with casual elegance, looking at ease in the plush surroundings. Oddly, I'm still happy at his success, but so very sad, because, with every increase in his status, he grows still further away from me.

I turned off the tv and went back to the laundry and by late morning, it's all done and my back aches from the ironing.

The beds still to make, I poured myself a cold drink, intending to sit in the garden, when Jules and Rosie suddenly appeared.

'Goodness, you can't have sold out already?'

'We have, and we've sold three of your pictures,' they exchanged glances and giggled.

'And the joke is,' I enquired irritably?

'Oh nothing, just a rather dishy young man bought them. He spoke a bit of English and asked who the artist was.'

'I hope you didn't tell him,' I said, alarmed. I didn't want uninvited visitors turning up when my privacy time was little enough already.

'Well, it was tempting to tell him you were beautiful, but lonely, but no, other than saying that you're also English, we told him nothing.'

I relaxed.

'Anyway,' Jules continued, since we finished early, we wondered if you'd mind if we went to La Rochelle. I'm hankering after a swim in the sea and to get sand stuck to my wet legs and feet.'

'O.K. but only if you'll make the beds before you go, 'I answered, and upstairs they went.

I looked in the mirror. I looked a fright. My face was bright red and my hair was stuck to my scalp with sweat.

Jules and Rosie soon made up the beds and were gone, so I went out to the pool and lowered myself into the water. It was bliss, until I noticed a car parked higher up, amidst the vineyards. I was pretty sure it was Smartie's, which wasn't a problem, but seeing he was using binoculars was!

My swim spoiled, I got out, showered and dressed, then went back indoors, to smarten up before any guests arrived. I then went upstairs, where, keeping myself hidden, I crept to a rear window and checked the vineyards again.

Smartie's car was still there, and again, I saw the glint of sun on the glass of the binoculars.

I'd never felt unhappy about being in this house on my own, before, but I did now.

"Oh come on, it's only Smartie!" I told myself," and went downstairs but, as I reached the hall the front doorbell rang. I froze. He couldn't have got down here that quickly so I turned and looked out through the kitchen window, but could see his car driving slowly down the hill, so it couldn't be him at the door.

Knowing then that it must be a guest, who'd arrived early and ignored the sign asking for no b&b callers before 4pm, I decided to ignore it. However, the bell rang again so I forced myself into 'polite mode', fixed a smile on my face and opened the door, to find, neither Smartie, nor a guest, but Stèphane!

I stood staring at him, open-mouthed.

'At least when you visited our village, I invited you in and gave you coffee and lunch,' he said, raising an eyebrow questioningly.

There was a very expensive looking sports car parked in my courtyard behind him. Shock, then horror, as shades of Christophe came to mind!

I looked from it to him, 'You look … ' I couldn't think of a flattering description, 'What are you doing here?'

'I wanted to meet the artist,' he said, and held up one of my pictures.

'It was you,' I gasped, realising that Jules and Rosie must've recognised him, hence their grins when they told me.

He stepped into the hall and shut the door behind him, then followed me through to the kitchen where I mechanically put on the coffee machine.

'I've been looking for you, ever since you disappeared – yet again,' he said.

I bridled. 'You mean ever since your mother replaced me with another web designer, sent you off to Reunion and then threw me out, telling me I wouldn't see you again.'

Whereas he'd looked as though he might be about to give me a hug, Stèphane now looked positively hostile.

'Even though Lynne was desperately ill, your mother moved Dave and I, plus my brother, who'd arrived from England, out of the chateau and into a hotel in Poitiers. The bitch never even contacted any of us, not even to find out how Lynne was.'

'How dare you tell such lies?' he responded. 'It was you who left, like you said you left your mother's funeral, and like you left the chateau after your accident. Just gone, not a word, not a note, no telephone call, nothing!'

By now we were shouting at each other. The back door burst open and Smartie appeared in the kitchen. Coming straight over, he put his arm around me.

'It's ok cherie' he said. 'You're safe now. I've been up on the hill for the past hour, keeping an eye on this man. I saw him in the market. He was watching Julie and Rosie. They must've taken a lot of cash, but surely not enough to interest someone who drives a Lamborghini?

When they left the market, he followed them, and I followed him!' he finished triumphantly.

'So that's why you were on the hillside' I relaxed against him.

'What? Did you think I was spying on you?'

'I wasn't sure.'

'I had a view down past your maison, to where he was parked, so I waited to see what he'd do. He didn't move until your friends left, then he drove in and I knew it was time to come down and make sure you were safe.'

I was looking at Stèphane, remembering a time when, by now, we'd both have been in fits of giggles, at the absurdity of this whole situation. But that was a very different Stèphane to this beautifully dressed, pompous looking recreation of Christophe, who stood before me.

'Do you know Stèphane, when she threw me out, your mother accused me of destroying her family, but looking at you, a clone of Christophe, I think she did that all by herself. You're certainly not Stèphane any more. Now please go,' I finished.

Smartie looked confused.

'You know this man?' he asked, in astonishment.

'No, I knew the man he used to be,' I answered simply. 'This is a man who ponces up and down red carpets, with a different woman every time'.

Smartie's face intimated that he couldn't see anything wrong with that, so I now wanted to slap him as well.

Stèphane stood his ground. 'I've searched and searched for you, even going to England three times. Once I found your mother's address but the house had been demolished. Then I located your apartment, but the people knew nothing, The third time I traced your solicitor, but he said you'd forbidden him to divulge your whereabouts to anyone. I never ever thought of you being in France, but now I see why,' and he looked meaningfully at Smartie.

'So, how did you find me,' I demanded.

'I was watching the La Tour de France, last week, and there you were, with this man, filling my television screen!' He scowled at Smartie. 'I checked the starting point for that stage, and today I came to the town. I'd seen you speaking with Monsieur le Maire, so I visited him, but he couldn't, or wouldn't, help me.

I was about to leave, until I saw the market, and there were your friends. I remembered them from your Skype and I couldn't believe my luck. Then I recognised your paintings from that funny little animal you paint in the corner, instead of signing them.

I figured if they had your pictures, and a stall, you must all live somewhere near, so, when they packed up, I followed them here, parked down the lane and waited until they left. Then, hoping you'd be here on your own,' he glared at Smartie again, 'I came and knocked on your door.'

'Seeing the two of you at le Tour, looking so friendly, I now realise I should've left well alone' and he turned to go, saying, as he walked across kitchen to the hall, 'You could've shared in my success Fay, but I wish you well and hope you'll be happy.'

I followed him to the hall, shouting after him, 'You think I want to look like a pampered poodle, and strut my stuff on a red carpet, I can't think of anything I'd less want to do. So cheap, so shallow. So just as well you're going!'

The door slammed behind him and, with a throaty roar of the Lamborgini's engine, he left and I slumped onto a chair and burst into tears.

'You care about him that much?' Smartie asked and I nodded and blew my nose.

'I thought I'd got over him, put it behind me and moved on. Oh why did he have to come here?'

'He came here because he loves you very much I think,' Smartie said simply. 'Has he come far?'

'No, only about 40 miles. His parents have a chateau', and I told him where.

Smartie whistled and nodded.

I made coffee, then we had salad sandwiches on the terrace, under the huge sun parasol. Smartie nodded off, but I wasn't in any mood for a siesta and, just after 3 o'clock Rosie and Jules came home.

They looked surprised to see Smartie and looked about them.

'Who are you looking for? Stèphane?' I demanded, and Smartie awoke with a start.

'O.K. I admit I did recognise him, but honestly, I said nothing', protested an offended Jules.

I was about to apologise, but before I could Rosie quickly followed up with, 'No but you did drive really slowly, when you saw him following, so he wouldn't lose us.'

'Well you can bloody well manage the guests on your own. I'm going out and I don't know when I'll be back', and I ran up the stairs, got my bag, hat and sunglasses and ran down again.

'Perhaps you'd care to join me? I asked Smartie, who looked surprised, but accepted.

'We'll go in my car, I think it'll be safer' he said.

Poor Smartie. We went back to his place, and all I did was talk about Stèphane, starting from when we were children and finishing by saying that Stèphane and I could never be an item now, because I hated his new lifestyle!

He sympathised, took me out for dinner and then took me home -

probably glad to see the back of me, and so I wasn't at all surprised not to see him for several days. Rosie and Jules gave me a wide berth too.

I forced myself to begin planning changes I was going to make. The workshop I'd paid a lot of money to create for Stèphane, could now be divided into at least 3 rooms, and used as a holiday let, and I could cut out all the work of the b&b, by abandoning it altogether and moving into the house. My flat could then be another holiday let, and if Jules and Rosie did the same, that would be three holiday lets.

Rosie, Jules and I cleaning 3 flats, once a week, sounded infinitely preferable to our current daily grind of huge amounts of washing, bed changing, ironing and cleaning, not to mention preparing all the breakfasts, doing the shopping and washing up.

But where were Rosie and Jules? Except for bed making etcetera, I'd not seen them for several days and things had been strained between us ever since Stèphane's visit.

The next day, immediately we'd done the rooms, they went to their flat and, shortly after, I heard their door shut and saw them drive off. However, weirdly, they seemed to immediately turn in next door, so I ran to the gap in the hedge, and watched, astonished, as they put their car in the barn.

This barn and all the surrounding vineyards still belonged to Smartie and his family, and he now drove into the yard, they got into his car and he drove off. I'd watched with a sinking feeling and began to panic.

I guessed that Smartie was taking them house hunting, and it was all my fault. They way I'd behaved, since Stèphane turned up, must have made them want to leave. I felt sick at this turn of events.

I dare say, if I made huge changes, I could manage 3 holiday flats on my own, but I didn't want the girls to go, either back to England, or to find a place of their own.

They were missing all day and, when they returned, I tried to be my normal self, not the grumpy bitch I'd been of late. They pretended to be fine with me but were hiding something I was sure. I had to put things right.

It was my birthday in a couple of days' time, so perhaps we could do something together to celebrate. However, next day, when I apologised for being such a pain and, without mentioning my birthday, suggested I should take them out for a meal the following day, they said they couldn't come. I felt crushed.

'Smartie's having a party, next door', Rosie said. 'They've sold the barns and the vineyards and there's going to be a big celebration. We've already agreed to go. '

Now I felt even more crushed. Firstly, because I'd not been invited, and secondly, because I was going to have new neighbours.

What if they wanted to turn the barns into gites, for the kind of people who played loud music and had barking dogs? What if they didn't run the vineyards properly and they became overgrown?

I looked forlornly out of the window, imagining how my view might change.

Needless to say, I didn't sleep well and, when I awoke, I was twenty-seven.

Our guests left mid-morning and we changed beds, washed and ironed and cleaned the rooms, then Jules and Rosie went to their apartment, got ready and left for the barbeque celebrations next door. I was devastated. Not even a 'Happy birthday," nor a card.

Come to think of it, the postman had been in his yellow van, and there'd been nothing from anyone, not even Lynne and Dave, who are my parents after all!

I went into the kitchen and looked out at the garden and the vineyards beyond. I could hear the sounds of merriment from next door, with loud music, which could soon become the norm. I shuddered.

Had I really upset them all that much that I was to be punished so harshly, and on my birthday too?

Then I heard a noise behind me, and spinning round I was shocked to see a man standing in the kitchen doorway. He was holding a massive bouquet of flowers, the biggest I'd ever seen, and it was obscuring his face,

Sure that they must be meant for the celebrations next door, I said 'Je pense vous cherchez mes voisins'.

Then he moved aside the flowers and it was Stèphane. I couldn't speak.

'Joyeux anniversaire Fifi,' he grinned, that cheeky, wonderful, happy grin, and he looked exactly like the old Stèphane, in t-shirt and jeans, unruly hair and curls tumbling over his forehead, far removed from the debonair fashion puppet on the red carpet.

As if he'd read my thoughts he said 'I'm back - the real Stèphane,' and he stepped forward and put the bouquet down on the work top.

'You remembered my birthday,' I said in awe.

'Of course,' and the Gallic shrug, to say "why wouldn't I?"

'How did you get in?' I asked and learnt that the front door hadn't been properly closed.

'I thought I was never going to see you again,' I said hesitantly.

'I know, and you may not have but Jean-Michele, (I frowned then remembered this was Smartie), Rosie and Jules came to see me, at the chateau.' I gasped. 'They told me everything. How two babies had been switched at birth and Lynne is really your mother How Lynne had collapsed when she was told, and been taken to hospital, and how my mother had treated you.

I feel so ashamed of what I said to you, and of what my mother said also.'

'Oh Stèphane, none of it was your fault, but when she told me that I might've saved the chateau but I'd destroyed her family, that really hurt.'

'I know. I've also been to see Christophe and we've talked, like never before. We agreed that Maman had pushed us up the ladder to success, but it made neither of us happy; the pressure of success was too much.

His escape had been in gambling and he feels terrible about what he did to you. Strangely, he's grateful to you now, for the threat of court action because it made him turn his life around. In fact, he's now married to the solicitor he went to for professional help, and they're expecting their first child.

'Oh Stèphane, I'm so glad,' I breathed, 'so very glad. I hope they'll be wonderfully happy.'

'Also, whilst I was in Paris, I saw my parents. I repeated what Rosie, Jules and Jean-Michele had said, and my father was shocked. My mother had told him that there'd been nothing wrong with Lynne after all, and you'd all gone back to England.

I know now why I couldn't find you anywhere, as I understand Ferelith Barker was the name of the baby who really died, and that you have a new name, but I'm glad you're still Fay.'

'Wow Rosie and Jules really did tell you everything, but why did Jean-Michele, tag along?'

Stèphane laughed, 'Oh he wanted to be sure I was told, as strongly as possible, how you felt about me, but also to make me understand that you could never live the red-carpet lifestyle, so I MUST find a solution.

He also told me how he met you when you bought this house, and he'd hoped one day you'd buy the barns and vineyards.

'I wish I had' I sighed. 'The new owners might do anything with them,' and I told Stèphane my fears for their future.

'So where do you live in this beautiful house?' he asked. The sudden change of subject surprising me.

Oh, I use the main house for the guests and I have an apartment.

'Show me,' he demanded, and then glanced at his watch, as though he had somewhere else to go - and fear gripped me because I didn't want him to leave – ever!

I took him through and up to my apartment. It didn't take long to show him round, but there was one room I hadn't shown him, and he opened the door to my bedroom and went in.

I could do nothing but follow him.

He shut the door behind us, and I caught my breath.

'Now what was it you said about me never having kissed you properly?' and he took me in his arms and kissed me, more and more passionately, until we were tearing each other's clothes off, and fell onto the bed in a frenzy of desire.

It was then that I learned the difference between 'having sex' and 'making love, as our kisses and caresses became ever more intense, and our bodies rose and fell, until l it was over, and we lay in an exhausted heap.

I'd never felt so fulfilled and so deliriously happy.

To my surprise Stèphane looked again at his watch and said we must dress. I just wanted to stay there, but I went into the bathroom to freshen up and came back into the bedroom to find Stèphane with my wardrobe doors open, looking through my clothes.

'Well you know me and women's clothes,' he laughed.

'Oh Stèphane I'm so sorry about that'.

Then he exclaimed 'Ah here it is,' and held up the dress I'd worn the night he took me to the Moulin Blanc, for my previous birthday.

'I want you to wear this because it's special.'

I got dressed quickly and then, to my surprise Stèphane asked to see the rest of the Maison.

So I took him out and showed him the workshop and studio I'd created and he loved it, then we went back indoors.

'Magnifique, superbe,' he exclaimed at the blue sitting room.

I couldn't have been more pleased, but, when I showed him the snug, he turned on the tv, sat me down, produced a memory stick, and started it playing saying, 'I recorded this earlier today.'

It was a newsflash announcing "the unexpected retirement from the fashion scene, of Stèphane Richarde, the talented etc etc", I'd stopped listening in shock, and only started listening when the announcer continued that "Monsieur Richarde was intending to marry soon and take up wine making".

I turned to him 'You're getting married?'

'I do hope so,' he smiled and from his pocket he produced a small box.

'I made this whilst you were staying at the chateau, when you first came back to France' he explained. 'Will you marry me Fifi?'.

'Of course I will', I breathed, as he slipped the ring onto my finger. It fitted perfectly. Stèphane saw my surprise and explained that one day, when I was asleep in the garden, having my siesta, he'd used a ring gauge to get the size of my finger. We both began to laugh, and his unruly locks, which I knew and loved, fell further forward over his forehead.

I ruffled his hair with my fingers, now the transition back to the old Stèphane was complete.

'But what about wanting your own vineyard Stèphane? Oh if only I'd known, you could've bought the vineyards next door'.

'Well, when Jean-Michel brought Rose and Jules to see me, I also learned that he's a very good salesman,' Stèphane grinned.

'You mean?' I hardly dared voice what I was hoping.

'Yes, I'm the new owner, and we must go next door, to the celebration,' but first, we quickly toured the rest of the house.

When we got to the top floor, I said that I had wondered if it should be a huge art studio, for the two us perhaps?

'I agree we should share this room', he smiled with his arm around me, as we stood at the window, but can you imagine waking up to this view each morning? This must be our bedroom.'

Then he took me in his arms and began kissing me again, when a voice called 'Fay, where are you? Stèphane are you here'?

Footsteps reached the bottom of the stairs and then came up and, seeing us with our arms around one another Jules said matter-of-factly, 'Thank God for that, at last you two have got it together. Took long enough. Smartie sent me to fetch you both.'

'Come on,' Stèphane said as Jules set off, but, as we left the house I said 'Why was Jules calling your name? How did she know you were here?'

'Who do you think left the front door open for me?' he chuckled, in that wonderful happy way that I loved, and hand in hand, we went through the gap in the hedge, to the barn next door.

I kept looking at my ring, a stunning creation of white gold, diamonds and rubies, and I could feel it had been made with Stèphane's love.

The music had stopped. 'It's very quiet,' I whispered, perhaps they've all gone home, but the number of cars in the yard belied that thought. Also, there was a very strange mix of caravans and camper vans and I wondered if these were what Smarties' family lived in, but, if so, why would they bring them here?

Jules went into the barn, and we followed, then a huge cheer went up. I assumed it was for the 'purchaser' - Stèphane.

 It was very dark, but I could just make out Smartie's clan and I said 'bon jour'. Then a voice said 'Happy birthday my baby girl' and the lights went up. I swung round to find Lynne and Dave, and all my brothers, their partners and families were there.

 I clung to Stèphane as I recovered from the shock. My left hand was in full view on Stèphane's arm and Lynne exclaimed 'Aha, I smell a wedding', and Stèphane hugged me and grinned.

After hugs and kisses all round from my family, a chorus of 'Happy Birthday,' started up, mainly from the English contingent and during it I pulled my twin brother, Tom, to my side, to make sure he felt included, since it was his birthday as well.

There was more cheering, and lots of smiling faces, then Stèphane announced that we were now officially engaged to be married.

Then there was even more cheering and my wonderful father proposed a toast.

After that I learned all the camper vans and caravans had all been borrowed, by Smartie, from people he knew, so all guests could stay overnight and enjoy themselves.

'Guests!' I exclaimed, 'we've forgotten all about the b&b guests, I'd better go back', but Stèphane caught hold of my arm, as Jules said, gesturing at my family, 'These are our b&b guests, complimentary of course. I booked them in under false names weeks ago.'

'You mean you never forgot my birthday?'

'Of course not, you dingbat' and she hugged me. 'The Rosebud and I had it all planned, but it was an added bonus when Stèphane appeared on the scene a couple of weeks back, but we had to knock some sense into him to make sure he turned up today.' I hugged her gratefully.

I then opened all my presents, including the one from Christophe and Maria. It was a shock to find he was here, but he took the opportunity to apologise, in person, for his behaviour.

I thanked him and said we could now forget all about it, then Stèphane's older brother, Romain brought his wife and family to meet me. Thankfully the senior Richardes were not present, nor even mentioned.

'When you start planning your wedding, maybe you'd care to consider the chateau?' Romain said, and Stèphane, who was standing beside me, explained that Romain and his family were moving into the chateau, planning to run it as an up market chambres d'hotes and functions venue.

'What a clever idea, it should work really well', I replied, but then I explained that Stèphane and I had already had a little talk and decided to be married, in September, at the little church, near Dave and Lynne, in England. Dave would give me away and my nieces could be two of my bridesmaids, with Rosie and Jules the other two and in charge of them.

My parents had been thrilled by these plans and it was agreed that we'd have a small reception, in an hotel, after the service, then a huge reception back in France. It would be held here, at our home, because this was where our future was.

The huge blue reception room would be perfect, with a marquee on the lawn for catering and dancing. Pierre, from the Moulin Blanc who'd arrived, with his staff, to cater for the evening's festivities, had already agreed to look after all the arrangements for us.

Romain thought it sounded perfect and wished us luck, then he asked how we were going to run both the vineyard business and a chamber d'hotes.

I told him that the b&b was now history, as the vineyard would be enough work on its own, even though Smartie and his family had agreed to help with the autumn grape picking for the next five years, as part of the deal.

'So what about your friends?' Romain asked, gesturing toward Rosie and Jules, and I suddenly felt guilty because it would leave them without jobs.

'In that case', Romain said, 'Would you have any objection to them coming to work at the chateau, in our new venture? Perhaps they'd agree to be our 'Hotel Managers'. We could convert an outbuilding into a comfortable apartment for them, as we are doing for my parents?'

'So how do you come to be in the chateau' asked Dave, who'd just joined us.

'Long story, but basically Corelle and I fancied a change of lifestyle and, although they'd made some money from the treasure you found for them, by the time my parents had paid for the chateau repairs, and also settled the outstanding debts, there was nothing left.

Maman, desperate not to have to sell, because she's convinced there are more treasures, agreed to us taking over ownership of the chateau, but our terms were that they promised to move into one of the outbuildings, when we'd converted it.'

'I guess that didn't give her much choice,' Dave remarked.

'It's the only way to deal with Romain's mother,' Corelle said firmly and her husband nodded.

The Dave suggested 'Perhaps, since Stephane will have no further use for them, you could convert his workshops, and showroom, into an apartment for Monsieur and Madame Richarde,' adding audaciously, 'I believe it has a lovely view of the east tower.'

I struggled to hide my astonishment, and didn't dare look at him, so I was hugely glad when Jules and Rosie and Jules joined us at that point. I quickly changed the subject and suggest Romain put his job offer to them.

'Sounds good to me,' Jules decided for them both, but how come you're at the chateau. I understood that you thought this coffin tree thing, brought bad luck?'

'Ah the coffin tree', he sighed. It no longer exists.

I was alarmed, if he really believed the coffin tree could bring bad luck, surely if he'd felled it this could make things worse??

Stèphane then explained, 'There was a terrific storm and It was struck by lightning, the night I went to Reunion. If that had happened sooner, we'd never have located the lost treasures and saved the chateau, so perhaps the tree wasn't unlucky, after all.'

I wasn't so sure about that, but was shocked that the coffin tree had been struck down the very night I told it I hoped it would die.

I felt a pang of guilt at this turn of events, because 'The Coffin Tree' had drawn me back to the chateau, which brought about my parting company with Christophe, and made me realise how much I loved Stèphane.

Then because it had played such a large part in my life over the past few months, I called for silence and proposed we drank another toast, Pierre's staff filled everyone's glasses and, when we were ready, I raised my glass and said 'A toast to "l'arbre de cercueil - The Coffin Tree"'

There was a clinking of glasses and a huge roar of -

'The Coffin Tree!'